THE MARK OF OLDRA BOOK 2

THE HEART OF OLDRA

GEORGINA MAKALANI

Georgina Makalani

Cover Design by Deranged Doctor Designs (www.derangeddoctordesign.com/)

ISBN: 978-0-9945131-2-0

OTHER STORIES
BY GEORGINA MAKALANI

The Magics of Rei-Een:
The Hidden Princess
Hidden Promises
The Hidden Phoenix

The Raven Crown Series:
Raven's Dawn
The Caged Raven
Raven's Edge

The Legend of Iski Flare (Novella series):
The Legend Begins
Red Wolves
The Riddle of Daralis
The Last Child
The Tree Maiden
Reflections
The Beast

Mark of Oldra Series:
The Mark of Oldra
The Heart of Oldra

Short Stories:
Stuffed Frogs and Spinning Teacups
Searcher
The Silence (in Glimpses)

To all the girls looking to make their own mark on the world

1

The warm rock against her palm was almost smooth, small dimples on its surface keeping it in her loose hold. The flashing blue light lit up the world. Panic closed in around her, making it hard to breathe. Although she could hear her heart pounding fast in her ears, it was as though it had stopped in her chest.

As she focused on the man in dark green clothing by the porch, the egg dropped from her fingers. Its shell broke on the gravel with a quiet crack. Yolk oozed slowly out between the sharp edges of what had once kept it safe.

The whole world closed in around her.

Cora sat up, dragging in deep breaths. Each time she had the dream, the strange world she found herself in made more sense. The odd metal machine was a car, the rock was an egg, and that the man with his hat held too tight in his hands, didn't want to be there.

Cora slid into the bench seat at the low table before the fire. Her mother remained silent, standing between her and the flames. The last time Cora had dreamt of the blue lights, she had woken to find her mother standing in the same place, but she had moved back to the sleeping area without a word when Cora had sat at the table.

Other than her father's gentle snores, the rest of the cavern was silent. She looked away from her mother's rigid back and glanced across the dark space. No one else moved, although she could feel Deen's gaze on her.

Her mother turned slowly from the flames and sat opposite her. Cora looked down at the table, running her fingers over the wood's grain.

Her mother cleared her throat.

'We don't have to talk about it,' Cora offered quickly.

'How often do you dream this?' her mother asked.

'You know.'

'I do,' Cora's mother admitted, reaching forward to take her daughter's hands.

Cora pulled her hands away. She didn't want to feel her mother anymore that night.

'That was the day I left,' her mother said in a sad voice.

'It felt as though the world was ending,' Cora said, reliving the pain her mother had felt that day.

'It was also the day your father found me in the snow, disappointed that I wasn't what he wanted me to be.'

Cora looked up then, surprised at her mother's words. She knew the story. The entire cavern knew the story of how the great Oldra, Gerry, had come to them from a land so far away. But it was always accompanied by the story of how much Pira loved her, how they were linked from the beginning. How this was where she was meant to be.

'I can't imagine that,' Cora said softly.

'Essawood was so different from the world I knew. I had lost so much, and I was so lost myself. They needed a man. They needed a warrior.'

'They got one. You are amazing with a bow.' Cora watched the woman opposite her carefully. 'I thought you were meant to be together.'

'We were,' her mother said, the smile forming easily on her lips as she looked back at the sleeping area. 'But I didn't know that, and he fought it for so long.'

'When did you know?' Cora asked.

'That I loved him?'

Cora nodded once.

'When I lost him.' Her mother sighed. Cora reached across the table then and took her hands. 'You have heard the stories of the battle when he fell from dragonback and we feared him lost forever.'

'You and Ariandi found him, and saved him.'

Her mother shook her head. 'I found Sarn that night. Looking for one man, I found another.'

'But that helped end the war.'

Her mother pulled her hands away. 'They were both so broken, so close to death.'

'You saved him,' Cora said again. 'You saved them both.'

'I remember wondering how I would live if Pira died. How easily the world would go on without him. I was so scared,' she added in a whisper.

'You are never scared.'

She gave a little huff of a laugh. 'I am scared more often than not. I am scared that babies will not survive, that the darkness would take us over, that Pira could slip from dragonback on any hunting trip.'

'I didn't know,' Cora whispered.

'I knew that I loved him, but I didn't know what we had until he showed me.'

Cora raised her eyebrows. She wanted to know… And yet, this was not something she wanted to learn about her parents.

'When two Oldra come together, they are bound in dragonlight.'

She expected comment from the dragons then, but there was nothing. She could feel them close by, and yet they were out of the cavern hunting. Usually they returned by the time she woke.

'Why could I not choose my own dragon as the others did?' Cora asked instead, drawing the conversation away from her parents' union.

'Ariandi chose me after a long time with no rider. Dra chose you, because you are the greatest Oldra of them all.'

Cora looked down at the table again. 'I don't think I can live up to that.' She put her hand over her chest, where the mark lay cool against her skin, directly over her heart.

'You will understand some day.'

'And if I don't want to understand?' Cora asked, sounding far more like a child than she wished.

Her mother smiled indulgently, like she had when Cora was small. 'This is your fate. This is who you are.'

'My healing skills are limited at best, and I'm not the warrior you were, nor am I needed to be.'

'You are the greatest Oldra,' her mother insisted.

'How do you know that? Why are you so sure I can be so strong?' she asked more loudly than she'd intended, the frustration evident in her voice.

Her mother stood slowly from the table. 'Because you have already saved us all from the darkness, and there will come a time when you will find the shadows again.'

Cora stared after her mother as she made her way back to the sleeping area and curled in beside Pira, Cora's father. He groaned as she elbowed him, and they rolled together as one before his snoring ceased. One of Cora's brothers muttered in his sleep. She looked back over her hands, despite being taught by both her mother and the Ancient Arminel, her healing skills were not what they thought they should be.

Arminel would place a surprisingly steady, weathered finger on her chest, knowing where her mark was, and smile. 'One day soon,' he would say. 'One day soon you will burn.' But it had been years since she had started her training, and she wasn't getting any better.

Cora would shake her head at his words. She was marked—she was destined for greatness, like the leader her father was, the healer her mother was. Yet Cora knew she was something very different, despite her mother's assurances that she was something stronger. Now she claimed that Cora had already saved them from the darkness, but she hadn't been there in the time of the shadows, and many of the men who had been had left this world already and gone to Essara.

She looked again around the cavern. It was still dark, and she knew it was the middle of the night, but she wanted to see Re-Mah. She was one of the few people who might be able to help Cora understand her mother's words.

The dragons hadn't returned, and it was too far to walk. She shivered at the idea. The Keetar settlement was far enough away that they lived independently, but close enough that they could visit regularly with each other.

Cora had grown up hearing stories of the constant fight between the clans, and there were times when the older members of the cavern struggled a little with their visits. The world had changed when Cora's mother arrived. Sometimes she wondered just what her mother had given up by coming to Essawood, and yet her dreams told her there was nothing left for her.

Maybe her own destiny lay in the land her mother had come from. She wondered if it was a place she could visit. She had only ever suggested it once, and her mother had shaken her head. When Cora pressed her, she said it wouldn't be the same—or that it might be just the same, and she couldn't face that. Their life was with the Penna.

Cora tried unsuccessfully to stifle a yawn, but it didn't matter where she was. Either at the table or lying in her blankets, the same thoughts would keep her awake. Or worse, she might sleep and dream something else.

She jumped as Deen slipped onto the seat beside her and wrapped his strong arm around her shoulders. For a man his size, she was always surprised he could move as silently as he did. He kissed her temple, and she tried not to sigh. He was always watching out for her, and he clearly cared for her. She felt safe with him, and at the same time a little trapped by his embrace.

'You should be sleeping,' she whispered, trying to smile for him.

He shrugged and pulled her closer. 'As should you. More dreams?'

She nodded, but she hadn't told him what she dreamed of. There was some expectation from people—not all the people, but most—that she had the same skills as her mother and her dreams would foretell what was to come. 'I only dream of what has been,' she murmured, answering the question before he had a chance to ask it.

'Do you dream of me?' he asked, leaning in close, his warm fingers working their way under the hem of her singlet. His rough hands tingled across her skin.

She pushed him away, looking back towards her parents. Their relationship was not frowned on, yet her father always gave the idea that it would not last. Not that it was wrong, but that it wasn't quite right. Temma,

Deen's mother, was a cuddly, friendly woman always keen to pull Cora into conversation when she visited their hearth. She didn't get the same feeling from his family that there could be anything in their future but each other.

Cora kissed Deen on the cheek and nodded back across the cavern. As he walked away, she climbed back into her sleeping mat. Her father had started to snore again, and her little brother continued to mumble. There was always noise of some sort in the cavern, whether it was conversation, children playing, pots against fire grates, or dragons murmuring at the back of her mind. And as she focused on the quiet noises of the people, she drifted back to sleep.

The world Cora found herself in was different and yet the same. It was dark, and thankfully there were no blue lights. She crept through hearths, even though it violated so many customs. She needed to see people. But the people sleeping around the fires were not people she knew, nor were the hearths like those of the Penna.

She heard someone behind her and froze, wondering how she could explain herself. Turning slowly, she came face to chest with a tall, broad man. She looked up into his brilliant eyes. Reflecting the firelight, they looked lighter than those of the average Penna. In fact, they were similar to the amber eyes she had inherited from her mother. She was momentarily distracted thinking of Darring's blue eyes, and how surprised her mother was that Deen had inherited them.

The man smiled down at Cora. Her heart stopped, as though nothing else in the world mattered. Then movement caught her attention, and they turned together as an older man appeared from the shadows. He was a similar age as her father, perhaps a little older, but he too was not someone she knew. When his serious face split into an odd smile, her chest hurt as though someone had pierced her heart with a blade.

Cora sat up, the pain still sharp in her chest. She glanced across at her mother and wondered if the woman saw every dream Cora had or only those connected to her own history.

She shook her head and curled back under the blanket, trying to remember the face of the man who had stood before her. The man with light eyes and a smile that stopped the world. She couldn't quite remember anything other than his eyes as she rubbed at the burning sensation across her mark. Was this what her mother meant, or was it something else?

2

Arminel was standing at the workbench when Cora entered the Ancient's cavern the next morning. He was focused on a pot over the small fire before him. She paused for a moment to take in his bright red robes, the silver hair flowing around his shoulders, and his familiar crinkled face before she sat without a word amongst the cushions that surrounded the central fire.

'What has happened?' he asked. When she looked back at him, he was still focused on the pot.

'Why do you assume something has happened?' she returned.

'There is something different about you.'

'No. Still the same not very useful Oldra, despite my mother's assurances that I am something more than I thought I could be.'

He chuckled quietly. 'She was always clever. And she is not wrong.'

'She said that I had already saved the people from the darkness, and that I would again see the shadows.'

He looked up then, concern further crinkling the corners of his old eyes. Arminel had been an old man her entire life. Although he had moved quicker than he'd appeared able when she was younger, he creaked when he moved now. It was as though his bones had aged to match his face.

'Do you have anything to add to that, great Ancient?'

'Don't get too clever, little one.' Arminel shuffled across the small cavern and lowered himself into the cushions beside her. He sighed and reached out for her hand. For the first time in her life, Cora didn't hesitate to put her hand in his. Closing his eyes, he placed another hand over hers. Cora watched him for too long before she closed her eyes and allowed him into her mind.

The cavern she had seen in her dream, with the different arrangement of hearths and people with different clothing, became vivid in her mind. She could see it more clearly with her hand in Arminel's than she had in her dream. The clothing wasn't woven like their own, but made from the hides of animals. The people looked like the Penna. Cora wondered for a moment how long it had been since she had visited with the Keetar.

'Not Keetar,' Arminel murmured.

The small cavern was still dimly lit. Shadows filled not only the edges of the cavern, but the small spaces between the hearths as well. Cora searched the shadows for the man she had seen in her dream. But she couldn't make him out amongst the shapes of people within the cavern.

'Oh, my little Oldra,' Arminel sighed. As he released his hold on her hand, the world around her disappeared and she refocused in the light of the Ancient's cavern.

'What did Mama mean about me chasing away the darkness?'

He sighed, looking at the flames. 'Before you were born, you helped her defeat the shadows. Your strength as Oldra burned away the darkness and allowed her to channel the dragonlight.'

'Channel it?' Cora asked, wondering why she had never experienced the memory herself.

'It was the only way,' he whispered, still focused on the flames, and Cora could feel the sadness around him like it was solid.

'Ariandi pushed her light through her?'

'They all did.' He sounded distant as he stared into the flames, as though he was there watching it happen.

As the magnitude of what her mother had done settled on her, Cora felt a new respect for her. A cold shiver covered her skin. 'She could have died. We both could have died.'

'She did not know of you at the time, and the people had to come first. It was a sacrifice. Of which there were so many that day.' He sighed again and turned to her, his cheeks wet.

'I'm sorry,' she said quickly, reaching for him.

'For the loss, or that you will leave us?'

Cora sat back, surprised by his words. 'I'm not leaving.'

'There is something greater out there for you.'

She shook her head. 'I thought you told me that my greatness was here. That I am a healer and like my mother.'

'You are alike, and yet very different.' He took her hand and pulled her closer, surprising her with the strength of his hold and the power to pull her into his arms. 'You will seek out your own destiny.'

Cora walked along the familiar tunnel and out into the main cavern of the Penna. She stopped and looked around as though seeing the people for the first time, like she had in the unknown cavern of her dreams. The balls of fire that hung from the ceiling were bright, indicating that it was still the middle of the day, and yet she felt drained.

Larek sat by the fire at his hearth. Cora smiled and nodded, but he barely looked up. Her parents had told so many stories about him being a great Draga, one of the strongest warriors, but he spoke little now. His son spent much of his time out hunting or with other men his age, yet little with his father. Larek's mate had died when Cora was young, and she didn't remember the woman.

She sometimes found him playing a game with Arminel in the Ancient's cavern. It involved a wooden board with hollows carved in it, and small rounded rocks they moved between the hollows. It wasn't a game she had ever worked out how to play, and she was never sure who won the games she did watch.

She looked ahead for Deen and instead saw the carver, Tarn, waving her across to his hearth. Smiling, she walked towards him. She had somehow managed to lose her bow on a hunting trip, and her father had chided her over it ever since. She still wasn't sure how it had happened. It was so well worn and familiar, and yet it had simply slipped from her hand. Dra had questioned if she was herself at the time. She had started to wonder if the repeated dreams of blue lights were impacting her days.

'Hello?' Tarn asked, and she blinked into his concerned face.

'Sorry?'

'Did we talk about another bow, or did I dream it?'

'Funny,' she murmured to the man as he sat on the large mat by the fire and indicated that she join him. She remembered doing the same thing as a child, and then again when she was old enough and tall enough to carry a larger bow like her parents. Both had dragon-scale patterning, except Tarn's father had made the first one. Tarn had worked with him for as long as Cora could remember. As his father aged, Tarn had done more and more until he became the carver. His own sons now sat with him on the mat, carving strips from chunks of wood.

Cora reached out and lifted a handful of wooden curls to her nose. Her mother would often drop them in the fire, a playful glance across at Larek when she did, and Tarn would scold her like a child. They smelled sweet and, as much as Cora enjoyed the smell of them burning, she loved Tarn's mother's meat smoked with the wood better.

'You have the replacement bow?' she asked.

'I would hope that you think of it more fondly than just a replacement,' he murmured, reaching across the mat to collect a bow. 'It isn't finished yet. I wanted you to feel it.'

'You are certainly taking some time with it,' she said. 'Father will send me with my first bow next time we hunt if it isn't ready.'

He laughed. 'I imagine Pira thinks only of the needs of the cavern.'

'There won't be too much provided if I take that little thing out with me.'

'I am surprised you still have it.'

Cora shrugged. 'We formed an attachment,' she said. 'Although my youngest brother teases me for it.'

'He must be ready to ride out himself soon,' Tarn said, looking in the direction of their hearth. 'I am sure I saw some growth,' he added, patting his chest.

Cora shook her head. 'He does not need the encouragement,' she muttered.

Tarn nodded once and then held out the bow. It wasn't strung and appeared longer than it would once it was pulled back against itself. But the overall shape and length were similar to her last bow. She stood slowly, using the bow to support her, and then lifted it easily in one hand.

'Is it too light?' she asked, unsure whether it was just different from her last weapon.

'It is a different wood,' he said, climbing to his feet. His brows pulled together as he looked it over. 'It could be that you have grown of late and are stronger than I remember.'

Cora sighed. 'I have not grown in some time. But perhaps I am stronger.' She took the bow in her other hand and tested its weight. It was very smooth and felt comfortable in her hand. 'Have you thought of a design?' she asked, handing it back.

'I thought I would wait for the wood to tell me. I'll bring it to you when it is ready.'

'Thank you,' Cora said, bowing her head in farewell. Then she headed back to her family's hearth. She wasn't as focused on those around her, and she knew her mother would be preparing the midday meal soon. She tried to help when she could and keep watch over her brothers. Dra was at the hearth when she returned, and she greeted him first.

'I thought you had disappeared,' she whispered as she rubbed her face against his. The large silver dragon pressed forward to meet her.

We explored a little further, he purred inside her head. I found a place where the turvie grow large.

'As large as a dragon?'

'And you didn't bring us any?' her mother asked, her back to them as she stirred the contents of a pot over the flames.

Cora tried not to sigh. Both of her parents, as Oldra, could hear all the dragons. Even though she fought against her mother's ideas of everything else, Cora loved the constant conversation with the dragons, but it was never private. Arminel had the same skill, and yet it appeared he chose not to listen.

Do you have your new bow yet? I am keen to show you what I have found.

Cora shook her head and leaned into the great dragon. As the eldest, he was the leader of the dragons, although he had only stayed by Cora growing up while Ariandi had been more of a leader. Unlike her father, where little trails of grey gave away his experience and age, Dra was older than she could ever know.

It was because she was Oldra that Dra had connected to her at such a young age. Unlike other children of the Penna, she had slept against him most nights and learnt to climb up on his tall shoulders and fly out into the wind. Her mother always smiled when she did. Others looked more nervous, and yet it was as though that was where she was meant to be. Dra had chosen her, and that was all there was to it.

The Draga warriors were the only other members of the clan able to select dragons, or at least go out into the world and hope to find them, when they were deemed ready to fight. Although it had been some time since the Penna had needed to fight, it had been their way for so long that the traditions had continued.

Despite her longing to be like the others, Cora's connection to Dra was strong and she never wanted to be parted from him. Nestling down against him, she watched her mother work over the fire. Cora tried to imagine the woman taking on the dragonlight directly and wondered if her mother would ever tell her how she had managed to survive.

3

The next morning, Cora woke to the frantic calls of her mother echoing through the cavern. Cora jumped up and ran after her just as the woman's white tunic disappeared through the main doors. The cavern was still quiet, other than the slow waking of others at the noise her mother had made, and Cora realised the dragons hadn't returned.

Her mother held the large hide back at the mouth of the cavern, looking out into the dark and then back to the dimly lit crystal trees of the front cavern that marked the burial places of the Ancients. Cora had heard many stories of Wyndha, the last female Draga and Ancient who had died before the battle with the darkness. She also knew that her mother still missed her, as much as her own mother, only she had no mark of where she was.

'What has happened?' Cora asked, reaching out. Her mother jumped. 'You should transition,' Cora suggested as she changed her own skin to the hard, icy shell that protected her from the cold.

Her mother shook her head and looked out again into the dark.

'Mama,' Cora said loudly, drawing her attention.

'Your brother has run off.'

'He wouldn't go too far. He is probably hiding with his friends somewhere. Did you try the warm room?'

'I know he isn't in the cavern,' her mother answered softly.

· 'The birthing chamber? There are many who sneak off to hide in there of a night. I…' Cora wasn't quite sure what she was about to tell her mother, but her look of surprise made Cora gulp back whatever it was she was going to say.

'Deen?' her mother asked.

Cora shook her head. She had hidden there at times with Deen when

11

they were children, and perhaps once or twice since they'd grown. But it wasn't as her mother imagined.

'Why would he run off?' she asked instead.

'He thinks he is ready to be a Draga, and he wanted to prove to your father just how grown he is.'

'This is something a child would do,' Cora murmured. 'Did the dragons go with him, or he with them?'

Her mother shook her head. Cora closed her eyes. She knew the answer to that herself. They would have shared the knowledge, and all the dragons had riders.

'Is anyone else missing?' she asked.

Her mother let the curtain drop and turned back to Cora. 'I don't think so.'

'Let's check first and if needed, I will go and find him.'

'Thank you,' her mother said softly, throwing her arms around Cora's shoulders. 'I just knew he was gone, and I wasn't sure what I could do.'

'We'll find him. Where is Father?' Cora asked as she led her mother back into the warmth of the cavern.

'Searching.'

Cora nodded. She wondered if her mother had seen this coming. She might have tried to stop him if she had. Yet, her mother had never tried to influence them based on what she might have seen.

'What do you see?' Cora asked, unable to keep her curiosity to herself.

'Not Wyn,' her mother said sadly.

They stopped at the first hearth to ask if everyone was well and if anyone had seen Wyn. The responses were the same at each hearth they visited. Cora left her mother and tried hearths on the other side of the cavern, including Deen's. Darring was sitting at the table while Temma leant over a pot on the fire. Deen's younger sister, Junah, was still curled in her sleeping mat. Cora couldn't see Deen.

'He has gone out early,' Temma said without turning.

'Wyn has run away,' Cora said quickly. 'I was wondering if you had seen him.'

Temma turned then, her brows creased. 'I don't think so.'

'Might he have gone with Deen?' Cora asked.

Darring looked up from his bowl. 'Why would he do that?'

'Mama is desperate,' Cora said. 'He thinks he should be training as a Draga. She fears he has gone to prove himself.'

'Did he take his bow?'

Cora nodded.

'I think Deen would have sought Pira's permission before taking his youngest into the woods. Although there are times that boy is still trying to prove something.'

Temma rested her hand on her mate's shoulder. Cora wasn't sure what he might mean, but it wasn't the time to be trying to work it out. Wyn was very much like Cora had been as a child, yet she had been given more freedoms because she was Oldra. The dragons could keep a close eye on her, so she had often headed out and hunted with them without either of her parents when she'd been younger than Wyn was now.

She sighed. Theirs was a difficult family to grow up in. Despite the openness, and despite their considerate and accepting parents, they were the clan's chiefs. Her mother was also a healer and seer. She would likely take Arminel's place as Ancient when the old man eventually went to Essara. And they'd been encouraged growing up to do all they could to be of use to the rest of the people.

Cora had only some of her mother's gifts, but she trained with the Ancient. Her brother Ayden had their father's skill with the sword and bow, and he had easily become one of the best hunters the clan had seen. He had found a dragon in the woods when he'd been sent to become a man. The beast had joined the rest of the clan and dragons with ease.

Cora looked around the cavern. The dragons had still not returned, and it made her a little nervous. With four dragons at their hearth, she felt the space they left when they were out. She wasn't sure how they could cope with a fifth, but Wyn was desperate to be like his brother and father.

'Anything?' her mother asked, finding Cora standing in the middle of the cavern.

Cora shook her head. 'Can I borrow your bow?' she asked. 'Mine isn't ready, and I would rather be out looking in the snow.'

Her mother nodded and then shook her head.

'What is it?' she asked, trying to read her mother's expression.

'Go to Tarn.'

Cora looked towards the carver's hearth at the far end of the cavern and felt a pull like she did when Dra needed her. She headed off at a fast walk. Only when she was nearly there did she wonder if her mother had called by this hearth and asked about Wyn.

Tarn stood staring into the fire when she arrived. He turned sleepy eyes towards her, then held the bow in his hand out to her without ceremony.

'Did mother wake you?' she asked.

He shook his head. 'I dreamt of your bow and was up early finishing the carving.'

Cora took it and again wondered at the weight of it. The wood was soft to the touch, and it felt different from her previous weapon. She turned it slightly and then lifted her arm. It wasn't the time to argue that this might not be to his usual standard. She caught sight of the carving, which was also different from her previous bow's.

A vine appeared to grow along the edge of the bow. It disappeared on the hand hold, and Cora realised Tarn had tied soft, thin leather around the space. That was why it felt so soft to the touch. But the stem and leaves of the vine twisted up and along the rest of the bow as though growing from where she held it.

'I don't recognise the plant,' she whispered.

He shook his head. 'Neither do I, but it is what it is.'

In some ways, the leaves reminded her of the crystal tree that grew from Wyndha's grave, yet it was something very different. Cora had a brother to find, and she didn't have the time to be debating artwork with a carver. She bowed towards him in thanks, and he grinned.

'Go and find the boy,' he said, rubbing at his eye with the heel of his hand as he tried to stifle a yawn.

She ran towards her own hearth. There were less people around, even for the early morning, and she wondered if they were all out searching for the wayward boy. Her mother stood stock still before the fire at their hearth, her eyes closed.

'I'm going to find him,' Cora said, reaching for her sheath of arrows. 'And I'll find the dragons on the way.'

Her mother nodded and then turned to her, reaching out for the bow. She sucked in a breath before closing her eyes again. Cora waited, but she simply released her hold and turned back to the fire without opening her eyes.

'Go,' her mother whispered.

Cora turned and raced to the doors, which already stood open to the cold. Out in the snow, the wind pulled tendrils from her plait before she transitioned. The hard ice shell protected her from the cold, and she closed her hand tighter around her bow. It felt warm in her hand. She put the other hand to the strap of her sheath, just to reassure herself that it was still there. She reached out for the dragons. Although she could sense them, they were far away.

The hunting is good, Dra hummed in her mind. *The boy will not be far. Perhaps he has found a dragon of his own after all.*

Cora wondered what he could mean. They would surely know if another dragon had found its way to a Draga. But was Wyn ready to be a Draga yet? She struggled to remember when Ayden had found his dragon. He might have been a similar age, yet it seemed as though his dragon had lived at their hearth forever. What was it that prevented Wyn from being the man he was so desperate to be? Had Cora's mother seen something she wasn't willing to share that had prevented her from letting him go?

Her mother's reaction to the bow had been unexpected. What had she seen that had made her react so? But she had still sent Cora out into the world, so it wasn't death or danger, or she might have protected her from that too.

When Cora was younger, she had asked her mother what she saw for her, but her mother would only smile. 'You will be what you will be,' she would say. 'Knowing it will make no difference to either of us.'

There were times Cora had wondered if her mother might have seen something she didn't want for Cora, or something that might make her worry. But either way, she would not share it. There were times when she had woken tearstained before the birth of a child, and Cora had known the birth would not go as the mother hoped. But it was not something their people talked about, and Cora could only offer silent comfort to her mother.

She sucked in a deep breath. No matter what she thought her mother might want for her or what she might see, it wouldn't help her find her youngest brother. Wyn had always wanted more than he could have. Even when he was little, he would take balls and the like from other children and their father would march him across the cavern to return what he had taken. When Cora had her first bow, Wyn had spent the first hour of her return to the hearth trying to take it from her hands, although he was only just walking on his own.

Yet, he had been much older than she had been when he received his first bow. For Ayden, their father had insisted on a bow from the moment he was old enough to close his hand around it. Perhaps if her brothers had been treated the same, Wyn might not have wanted for as much, but then her parents always had a good reason for everything they did.

Cora looked up in the sky then, longing for Dra to appear and carry her away, but he didn't. She knew the dragons were still some distance away. The snow was thick, but it had been trampled down by the entrance to the cavern. Footprints disappeared too quickly in the snow as others searched for her brother.

It didn't take long for Cora to get into the thick of the forest, the trees closing in around her and blocking out the early morning light. It was the first time she had come out alone, she realised as she stepped up onto the tall root structure of a tree. There had always been someone or a dragon with her, and the silence now was momentarily overwhelming.

She closed her eyes, remembering a story her mother had once told her of the snow. But the snow didn't talk to Cora, nor did it appear to give her any hints as to where her brother might be.

Unable to feel anything around her, she wondered what other skills she might have. Her mother was so determined that Cora would be something great, and yet she had nothing. Only the dreams, but they were always of the past, even if it wasn't her own. For a moment she could see blue light amongst the trees, and she shook her head. She hoped the dreams weren't preparing her for her own loss.

She jumped down from the tree and made her way forward. All of the trees around her looked the same. She squeezed her hand around the soft handle of the bow. *Where would they have found a different type of wood?*

'Wyn,' she called into the empty world around her. The noise startled a distant animal, and she heard the movement across the snow. But she couldn't see anything. The snowy ground was more protected from the wind amongst the trees, so there would be footprints if he had come this way. 'You have made Mama worry,' she called out. 'She only worries with reason,' she added quietly, more for herself. Cora worried that her mother had seen something she hadn't been able to tell them.

She shook her head and carried on. After a while she was sure she saw something ahead and picked up her pace. How long before she found her brother? Or had he disappeared? How long had he been out here alone?

A small clearing opened up amongst the trees with no sign of her brother. There were some indentations in the snow, but she knew they were not his footprints, more likely a turvie. She started to worry. She had thought he had just wandered away, but the longer she looked, the more she feared he had run. Except she wasn't sure where to. He could have been taken—but again, who would do such a thing?

The ground beneath her feet had become harder and she moved higher amongst the trees. Then she was standing in an open area, on a hill looking over the world around her. She took a step and then stopped as the snow at her feet slipped into a crevice. She carefully leaned over and looked into the open tunnel beneath her.

It twisted through the rock beneath her feet. She moved along the edge, wondering where the tunnel led. She wasn't sure how far she was from the cavern, and she hadn't been here before. She looked across the hilltop and saw the twisted, crossing paths of exposed tunnels cover the entire surface. As though a labyrinth of tunnels had been woven beneath her and their tops had caved in long ago.

She made her way carefully across the surface to where she thought it finished and found a single round hole in the snow. She lay down and peered in. It was a perfectly round cavern, and a small opening indicated that the tunnel appeared to lead to it. The light behind her allowed her to see it fully, and for just a moment she thought she could drop down into it. But she wasn't sure how she would find her way through the maze of tunnels.

Cora sighed, the sound echoing in the space. Then she sat back. There was no sign of her brother, and he would likely be calling for help if he had become lost in the pathways. She leaned forward again and cupped her hands around her mouth. 'Wyn!' she called, then sat back as the sound bounced back at her. She sat in the snow and waited, but there was no response.

She was too far from the cavern now, and she considered heading back before night. She looked up at the sky again. She didn't think they had ever flown this way, for she would remember the pattern of the tunnels if they had. Or did she not look as closely at her world as she should? It was different on foot.

Dra landed softly beside her. She patted his side before climbing easily onto his shoulders.

He is found, his deep voice rumbled through her.

'Where?' she asked.

Deen had taken him hunting.

'Without telling anyone?' she snapped. 'What was he thinking?'

The boy is safe and more of a man than you would allow.

Cora wanted to laugh at the idea. She'd had that very same thought not so long ago. What he could be doing at his age, and yet her parents would not allow it. So they all had treated him as a boy. Perhaps it came with being the youngest.

Perhaps it does.

'Do we have to go back?' Cora asked. 'I haven't seen this part of the world, and I would like a chance to explore some more.'

Dra lifted from the ground, and she looked over the patchwork of pathways beneath her. It was as she had imagined, and she was certain they had not flown this way before.

Many have been this way. It was a Draga training ground for generations. Gerry was the last.

'The last Draga?'

The last to be trained. You are all Draga.

Cora sighed. She wasn't quite ready to try to fit back into what her mother wanted her to be. Dra obliged, flying out across the world, further and further from the cavern. Just as he entered flicker flight, where the world appeared to stop around Cora and every ice crystal showed itself to her, she asked, 'Can you show me the new hunting ground?'

It is far the other way.

Cora nodded silently. She just wanted to fly. She allowed the transition to slip so she would experience the ice. Dra indulged her, and they flickered for longer than they usually did. Then Dra banked suddenly. Cora shivered at the lack of snowflakes surrounding them.

'How far did you bring us?' she asked, looking out at green trees.

And then she was falling.

4

Cora was sure she was standing in the driveway again. The blue lights flashed. Her heart ached at the news of her mother. Only it wasn't her mother's loss she was feeling. The world shifted sideways. She was falling, and then she was standing in the snow. It moved around her slowly, as though she was flickering on dragonback, but she stood still, unsure what surrounded her. The house she had walked towards in her dreams appeared before her and the snow disappeared, the sun warm on her skin. She looked around, knowing she was somewhere she had never been before, and yet she knew this place.

It was the world beyond what she dreamt over and over, when her mother had learnt of her own mother's death. It was her mother's world. A large tree grew at the far end of a sea of green grass, and Cora walked towards it. This was the place where her father had come for her mother, but it had been cold, and the snow had been thick on the ground. She heard an odd squeal behind her, and she knew it was the door.

When she turned, her mother stood on the porch, her hand reaching out. 'Wake up!' she cried.

Cora blinked into the sunlight. Her whole body hurt as though she had been trampled by a dragon. She couldn't quite focus on the world around her. The earth was hard, and she missed the cold snow. A shadow covered the sun. She closed her eyes again to the pain that wanted to overwhelm her.

When she opened her eyes slowly, she was inside the cavern, her bed soft beneath her and the world dark around her. She sighed with relief and then clutched at her side as a sharp pain tore through her. She cried out. A

18

tight bandage was wound around her chest, and she wondered what damage she had done. She wiped at a tear, waiting for her mother's reassurance, but none came.

She struggled to sit up, crying out again at the pain. Where was her mother? She tried to push up out of the bed and stopped. It wasn't her bed. The soft, white, woven blankets she usually slept between had been replaced with furs. They were just as soft, but darker in colour and not hers. She glanced around but couldn't see anyone. A fire burned low against the cavern wall, but she couldn't reach it. Her leg burned with a pain more intense than the sharp pain in her ribs. It had also been tightly bandaged, with something long and hard strapped against it. She tried to move, but quickly realised it was too difficult, and a dark mark spread across the white cloth at her thigh.

Where was her mother? She shivered, looking at the hard-packed earth around her. She was in a small cavern, like the hunting cavern by the lake or even the birthing chamber. Her mind was still foggy as she ran a hand up each arm. She wasn't wearing her tunic, just her singlet. Gooseflesh rose quickly over her exposed skin. Her leggings had been cut short on both legs, exposing the bandaging on one and the scratched and bruised skin on the other. She started to shiver more uncontrollably.

Her transition wouldn't take, and the more she tried, the harder it seemed to be. She knew she wasn't with the Penna, for her mother would be at her side if she was. She couldn't run, and she couldn't protect herself. She sucked in a breath only to cry out again as the pain sliced through her chest. She heard movement then and shuffled back against a wall, trying to get out of the dim light of the fire. But with her injuries, she couldn't move beyond the furs.

The sharp pain continued in her chest and side as a dark shadow moved into the small space. She pressed a hand over her mouth to stifle the scream that was trying to escape. A strange sobbing noise started before she could hide. The shadow of a man dropped more wood into the fire. Before he turned, and as she pressed herself into the wall to try and escape him, she again cried out.

'What are you doing?' he asked, his voice gentler and more soothing than she would have imagined. All she could was cry again. 'You will hurt yourself further,' he said, squatting down before her.

She tried desperately to scuttle away, but she wasn't getting anywhere.

'Let me help.'

She shook her head. He nodded once and stepped back. Another form entered the cavern, with an arm raised in the air. The light increased, and Cora could see it was a woman. She rushed forward. Cora tried to push herself deeper into the wall, but she only succeeded in hurting herself further and cried out again, grabbing at her ribs.

'You need to rest. You are hurt very badly.'

'What happened?' Cora managed.

'You fell,' the man said. Cora looked at him and then shook her head to try and remove some of the fogginess. He was the man she had dreamt of. The only dream that was not of her mother's past. She wondered if her mother had seen him.

Cora rubbed her hand against her temple. She was lost in a dream. She had to be. 'Where is my mother?' she asked.

They looked at each other, and then the girl crept closer. 'I think you are far from home.'

'Who treated my wounds?'

'I did,' the girl said.

Cora nodded once to show she understood. 'Dra,' she murmured, gritting her teeth against the burning pain in her leg. 'How far did I fall?'

The stories of her father's fall returned in a flash, and for a moment she saw her mother's desperate attempts to stop his bleeding. She could taste the same bitter panic at the back of her throat and wondered what else these people had done for her. 'What happened?' she asked again.

'You need to stop trying to move,' the woman said, edging closer. 'You have some nasty breaks. You are lucky it is not worse, but if you continue to move about you might do more damage with those broken ribs.'

Cora put her hand to her side, cringing at the pain. 'Heal them,' she demanded.

They looked at each other again, and then the woman took another step closer. 'I can't,' she said softly. 'I can only hold them in place until they heal themselves.'

Cora was confused. 'Don't you have a healer?'

'Who is Dra?' the man asked instead of answering her. 'Was he travelling with you?'

She nodded. Her head was getting harder to hold up, and the sharp pain in her chest wasn't easing.

'Why didn't he help you?' he asked.

'Maybe he couldn't find me, or he was hurt. I don't know what happened. We flickered, the world was different, and then I was here.'

'Different?' the girl asked.

'No snow,' Cora breathed as she gave up her struggle and eased herself back into the furs. 'I need Dra. He will bring my mother,' she thought aloud. 'She is the best healer…' The world blurred again, and Cora was lost to darkness.

The world continued to swirl around her. Her mother's young and distressed face came into view. Blood smeared across it and large tears ran unchecked, desperation in her eyes as she looked at someone else. 'Pira, please,' she begged.

'Don't leave me,' Cora called into the darkness as she sat up. Then she groaned and held her side again.

'I'm not going anywhere,' a man's voice murmured.

'Pira?' Cora asked carefully into the dark. Had she lost her way completely?

'Dra and Pira. How many did you travel with?'

The woman appeared again and raised her arm, and the light increased. She had some skill, if not as a healer. Cora wondered just who these people were and what they might want.

'Have you given her water?' the woman asked the man, as though Cora couldn't answer for herself, and they both shook their heads at the same time.

'I need to get up,' Cora said.

'You need to rest,' the man said.

'Please?'

The girl handed her a cup of warm water. Cora hadn't realised just how dry she was until she put it to her lips.

'This will make my need to get up more urgent,' she said softly, looking into the cup.

The man lifted her up into his arms quickly, and Cora's heart raced.

'Watch the leg,' the woman said, and then they were outside in the dark. The air was cool but not cold. She wondered if there was any snow in this world.

Cora was worrying about just what the man might do when he set her down carefully and disappeared back inside. She stumbled a little, but the woman supported her and then helped her remove enough clothes to relieve herself. Who knew broken bones could be so debilitating? As soon as Cora could get to her mother, she would be fine. Assuming they didn't need to reset anything.

'Teven,' the woman called. The man reappeared, scooped her up and took her back inside.

Cora sighed with relief when she was placed back on the bedding. Teven carefully covered her back up.

'Where is my tunic?' she asked.

'Damaged,' the woman said. 'We had to cut it away.'

Cora put her hand over the mark on her chest and willed it to warm her.

'Where did you get that?' Teven asked, his eyes on her hand.

'I was born with it,' she said. 'I am so cold.'

The woman nodded to the man, and then the lights dimmed. 'I will return in the morning. Teven will keep you warm.'

'No,' Cora murmured as the large man lay down beside her. Despite her uncertainty, she rolled into the warmth he radiated. She ached. She closed her eyes to it, but her leg continued to throb. Arminel would have something for that too, she thought, lying beside the rigid man. It was almost as though he was too scared to touch her. But she hurt, and she didn't want him to. She just needed his warmth.

Cora woke warm and comfortable. She sighed at the relief. It must have been a dream, although it was unlike any dream she'd had before. The only thing close was when she had dreamed of the man in different clothes. She looked at the wall before her and then the furs she was curled in and realised with bitter disappointment that it wasn't a dream.

Her ribs were still tightly bound, but they didn't hurt like before, and a heavy hand rested on her side. She rolled carefully and groaned as her leg caught on something and the hand moved around her back to pull her closer. When she looked up into his face, there was something familiar about it. Not just that she had dreamed it, but as though she already knew it. His eyelids fluttered open, and he stared at her for a moment with brilliant amber eyes before releasing his hold and moving back.

'Good morning,' she said, pulling the warm furs back around her. 'Where is your mate?'

'My what?' he asked, shuffling further away from her.

'The woman—you are bonded?'

He shook his head.

'Why is there only two of you here?'

'There isn't,' he said.

Cora groaned a little as she sat up. The ribs were better, but they would be sore for some time. 'Where?'

'You are the stranger here,' he said. 'We are to learn what we can in case you are a risk to the clan.'

'Makes sense.' Cora tested her ribs a little by moving her arms and then groaned again. 'We would do the same.'

'Who are you?' he asked too loudly. Cora turned as he brushed himself down and stood by the fire. His clothes were very different from her own, but his features were similar. Cora had not travelled to the world her mother had come from, and she wasn't sure if she was disappointed or relieved.

'Who are you?' she asked, reflecting his tone.

He glared at her for a moment and then cleared his throat. 'I am Teven.'

She waited, but he said no more. She reached out then, but she couldn't sense Dra or any of the other dragons. She wondered if Dra had been lost or if they knew where to search for her. She might very well be stuck here, she thought as she wiped away the tear that surprised her.

'I am Cora of the Penna,' she said quickly when he stepped forward, holding up a hand. A shiver crossed her skin. She wanted nothing more than to transition, but it wouldn't come.

'Cora,' he repeated, and she nodded.

'Who is Dra? And Pira?'

'Pira is here?' she asked, the excitement taking over.

'You spoke of him in your sleep.'

'I called him Pira?'

He nodded once.

'Mama's dreams,' she murmured. 'He is my father.'

'What do you mean by Mama's dreams?' the woman asked, coming back in. 'Here.' She packed the space behind Cora with soft cushions, and Cora leaned back with a nod of thanks. She closed her eyes and blew out a much more comfortable breath.

'Hello?' the woman asked, poking her shoulder sharply. 'Dreams?'

Cora sighed before she opened her eyes. 'What is your name?'

'Rhali,' the woman said.

'Cora of the Penna,' Teven said slowly.

'What do you dream?' Rhali asked her.

Cora wasn't quite sure how she could explain herself. These people might be too different from the Penna, and as yet she didn't even know who they were. 'I dream of my mother's past. When she first came to the Penna, my father fell and she saved him. Last night I dreamt of her memories from that time.'

'You sounded very panicked,' Teven said.

'She thought he would die. He fell a long way.' She took a breath and looked over the two beside her. There was a closeness there. It may be that they were bonded, although it was strange that he had stayed with Cora in the night. 'Where is Dra?' she asked. She could hear the wobble in her voice, fearing the worst. She closed her eyes and again stretched out for him, but she still felt nothing.

'We have found no one else,' Teven said.

Cora felt the tears welling. Despite her best efforts, she couldn't keep them in. The overwhelming loss of Dra pulled at her more than she would have thought possible.

The woman, Rhali, put her arm around Cora to comfort her and rested her cheek on Cora's shoulder, then pulled back. 'I'm sorry,' she said. 'Is he your mate?'

'Who?' Cora asked.

'Dra,' Rhali said.

Cora shook her head slowly. 'He is my dragon.'

The girl instantly let her go, and the man moved a step closer. Cora wished she could stand and run.

'You have a dragon?' he asked.

'Where do you think I fell from?'

He shook his head.

'Your father fell from a dragon?'

'Elleric,' she said softly, 'during a battle with the Keetar.'

'Keetar?'

'We are friends with the Keetar now. The war ended before I was born.'

'When you defeated the shadows,' an older man said softly as he entered the cavern.

There was something familiar about him as well, but Cora couldn't place it. She nodded once.

'You are very strong,' he said. 'Very strong.'

'My mother tells me the same,' Cora said, trying not to wince at the pain in her leg as she struggled to sit up. How long would it be until she could try to return home?

'You do not believe her.' It wasn't a question.

Cora remained unmoving. As she watched him walk towards her, she recognised him for the man who had appeared in the dream she'd had of Teven.

'You will stay with us. The birthing chamber may be needed for another. Teven will carry you to their hearth, and we shall keep you there.'

'As a prisoner,' she said softly.

'As a guest,' he said, the smile somewhat unnerving, and then he was gone.

Cora looked after him, then at the two who stood looking at each other. Teven sighed as though resigned to do as he was told. He scooped Cora up again, and she shivered as he carefully manoeuvred her out of the entrance.

The world before her was very different from the one she knew. The tall trees were covered in leaves, some bright green and some dull. It was like the warming cavern, only outside. She stopped shivering; the sun was warm on her skin. She looked back at the cavern they had been in and smiled. The hillside around it was green with grass. When she looked up, Teven smiled too, but then his smile slipped.

'We need to go in,' he said, turning away from the trees and following the hillside around to another opening.

She could feel the pull of the trees, or something in the trees. She wanted desperately to get out of his arms, but he held her tight. 'Wait,' she said. 'There is something out there.'

'And that is why we must hurry.'

'It means no harm,' she said.

But he didn't stop. He carried her through a large leather hanging, much like the entrance to the Penna cavern, and they were underground again.

'Why is it so warm outside?' she asked.

'It is always warm,' he said without looking at her. He walked fast through the people who had stopped to watch them and deeper into the cavern she knew from her dream.

5

Teven placed her carefully down on a bed while Rhali piled up the cushions behind her. She was near the wall of the cavern, and there was nothing between her and the next hearth. People openly stared at her. She closed her eyes, ready to sleep again, although she had so many questions. The people of the cavern murmured amongst themselves. She tried to ignore it as she shuffled about to find a comfortable position. Her ribs were much better, but her leg still burned. Perhaps it was more than a break. Maybe she was bleeding like Sarn had.

She shook her head and thought about the man she had known almost as well as her own parents. He came to mind in a fitful sleep, sweat beading on his brow and his exposed purple chest. Cold hands moved across his skin. Cora sucked in a breath as the man who had requested her moved appeared standing over Sarn.

She looked up into Teven's worried face and pushed his hand from her brow.

'If you die,' he murmured, 'your people might fight us.'

'They don't know where I am,' she said, aware that it was even darker in the cavern. 'No one knows where I am.' The sob caught her unawares. 'Why am I here?' She tried to sit up and look about, but her leg burned even more, so she grabbed at it. If only she could clear her mind enough, she might be able to channel some of her average healing skills and look into it herself. 'Can you take the bandage off?' she asked.

'No,' Teven growled. A little distance away, Rhali murmured in her sleep and rolled over.

'I just need to look. It is burning and I can't see.'

'What do you think you will see? Are you a healer?'

'Not a very good one,' Cora murmured. She tried not to cry, but the pain kept increasing and she wasn't sure what she could do to make it any better. Again, she wished her mother were here. Or at least that she had an idea of where Cora was. She had been panicked about Wyn—would she feel the same if Cora didn't return? Or had she already known this was going to happen?

'You said your mother is a healer.'

Cora nodded and rubbed at her face.

'Rhali knows how to bind broken bones.'

Cora sighed.

'I can help you,' Teven whispered, 'but I won't unwind what is holding you together.'

She nodded again, and he pulled the furs back. She sat forward and placed her hands on her thigh, closing her eyes. She could only feel the bandages as she pushed her hands down her leg slowly. She couldn't see anything. She couldn't even see within her own skin, let alone to the bone. She sighed in frustration and pushed harder, sucking in a breath at the pain. She had to be able to do this.

Re-Mah, Ancient of the Keetar, had been unable to heal herself. Arminel had assured Cora that it had nothing to do with her abilities, but the darkness that had infected her.

An overwhelming helplessness pushed down on Cora as she tried to hold in her fears and sobs. She pushed again on her leg and groaned. The sharp pain travelled down to her foot, followed by the same burning sensation. Then it began to cool, and the pain eased. She opened her eyes to see Teven's hands on hers and a concentrated look on his face.

'You are the healer,' she whispered.

He lifted his hands and shook his head. 'I just didn't want to see you cry again,' he said.

She took his hands and placed them back on her leg. 'Please,' she begged.

He shook his head and tried to pull from her hold. The comforting coolness she had felt before did not return, and she released him. She pulled the furs back up over her legs and closed her eyes.

'I'm not a healer, I know nothing of herbs or wrappings.'

Cora remained still. Maybe this world saw things very differently. Maybe they didn't have the same skills. The world her mother had come from was different, and no one there had the skills she did. Arminel would know. Cora just had to get back to him to be able to ask the question.

'Are you the chief?' she asked. In the following silence, she opened her eyes and looked at him.

He shook his head.

'Why am I at your hearth?'

'I found you,' he said, looking towards the fire. 'I saw you fall and I wanted to help. The chief,' he said, indicating beyond the fire by raising his chin, 'said you were something special and that we should help you.'

'I'm not,' Cora said. 'I can't even keep hold of a bow.'

'I have that,' Teven said, jumping up and moving out of her view. When he returned holding out her bow, she put a hand to her face as more tears fell. She had never been so happy to see an object in her life. She held out her hand and he laid it across her lap. Cora ran her hand over the pattern, wondering just what Tarn had seen to create it. The Penna felt more distant, despite her holding the bow in her hands.

She looked up at the man watching her too closely.

'You are still crying,' he said.

'I want to go home,' she sniffed.

He shook his head. 'Not until the chief wills it, and he has seen something in you.'

'What has he seen?' she asked.

Teven shook his head and turned back to the fire. He said nothing more.

Cora remained watching him, too sore to sleep and too scared of what the chief might want from her. As the cavern started to lighten—though not as much as her own cavern did of a morning—the older man appeared before her, grinning. Again, she felt an uneasiness. She shuffled back against the cushions and called out when the movement twisted her leg enough that it pinched. He sighed, then sat down on the woven mat by the fire. That too was similar to the Penna cavern, but there was no table.

Rhali appeared with a cup of something and handed it directly to him, and Cora realised how thirsty she was. How long had it been since she had fallen?

'I thought you might have healed yourself by now,' the chief murmured.

Cora shook her head. Her stomach pinched. She realised that they may have looked after her injuries, to a degree, but they hadn't fed her. She could smell porridge cooking over fires in the cavern. Teven stood at the fire with a bowl in his hands, but the chief shook his head as she looked up at him.

She wouldn't be getting anything until this man got whatever it was he wanted.

'I am Cora of the Penna.' She bowed her head and waited, but he didn't reply. She chewed on her lip and sucked in a deep breath. She didn't think she had any more tears to shed, but she was too angry now to find out. She stared the man down, and he nodded once after handing the finished cup back to Rhali.

'You are Chief,' he said.

She shook her head. 'My parents are the chiefs of the Penna.'

'Two?' Teven asked. But as the older man looked up at him, he hung his head.

'My father, Pira was Chief before my mother came to this world. My mother, Gerry, is Healer and…' She wasn't sure they would understand the rest. They might not have the same skills, and it might cause fear if she used words like seer.

'Geraldine,' the chief said, nodding.

Cora stared at him. Did he know her? Had he met her somewhere? He certainly didn't look like her; he had the same features as the Penna and Keetar.

He gave a small cough of a laugh. 'Little Oldra, I know exactly what you are and what you have done.'

'Oldra?' Teven asked. 'What is an Oldra?'

'You don't know me,' Cora said. 'What is your name?' she asked.

'I am Chief, and that is all you need to know.'

Cora sighed. 'Will you tell me more of your people, how you live, your connection to the dragons?' She looked about the cavern then, but there was no room for the large beasts.

'You will find out soon enough, for now you must take the time to heal. It may take you longer than you expect.'

She watched as he stood and walked away. Teven still held the bowl in his hands. When Cora reached for it, he shook his head. 'How can I heal if I can't eat?'

'We must wait,' he said softly.

After what seemed like an age, he squatted down beside her and handed her the bowl. The contents were no longer hot, but she took the wooden spoon and lifted it to her mouth. There was very little flavour to it, and she stopped after shovelling in a couple more spoonfuls. Her stomach threatened to reject what she had given it as she handed the bowl back to Teven.

He smiled at her and took the bowl away. Rhali handed her a cup of water. She took a sip and then held on to it, in fear they may not give her another.

'He is testing you,' Rhali said.

'He knows far more than he has asked about.' Cora looked beyond the fire, but she could only see the outlines of others at the neighbouring hearths.

6

The days blurred into each other as Cora sat by the fire waiting to heal. She had tried several times to see inside her own leg, but she couldn't do it no matter how she tried. She wanted to tell Arminel he had been wrong, that she had no special skills. That other than her dreams of her mother's history, she had nothing. The chief had stayed away, but she knew he would return. No one else came anywhere near them.

'I need to get up,' she said. Her body ached from lying still too long.

'You can't walk,' Teven offered.

'I can hobble,' she murmured, 'and I can't lie here any longer.'

He looked around before he nodded once, then squatted down beside her and lifted her carefully into his arms.

'This is not what I meant,' she said. 'But now you have me, maybe we could go outside.'

He sighed and then carried her out through the cavern. No one seemed to be watching her this time. Cora wondered where the chief was and whether he would object to her leaving the hearth he had confined her to. The fresh air tingled across her skin as they pushed through the hide and into the sunshine.

She put a hand up to shield her eyes. 'It is so bright,' she murmured.

'You have been inside for some time.'

'There are no clouds,' she said. 'The sun is rarely out from behind the clouds. But here…'

He carefully lowered her to the ground and maintained a strong hold around her, which she was grateful for. It was hard trying to support her weight, even on her good leg. She had spent far too long lying down and had very little to eat over her time with these people. And she still had no idea of who they were or what they wanted from her.

There was no one outside the cavern where they had remained close to the opening. Cora took a tentative step forward and turned her face up to the sun. A cool breeze wrapped around her. She tried to transition, but she still couldn't make that work either. It was as though any skill she'd possessed had disappeared when she fell from Dra. She looked towards the trees then, hoping he had survived whatever had knocked them from the sky.

She took another step forward as something pulled at her from between the trees. She was sure that whatever it was, it wanted to help her. She took another step before Teven's hand closed around her arm and held her still.

'It is not safe in the trees,' he said.

'What is out there?' she asked, looking up at him.

He shook his head and turned her back towards the cavern. 'The chief knows that it is not safe. There are many who have seen terrible things. You need to go back inside.'

'I can't,' she said, but a shiver crossed her skin. Teven looked at her with disappointment. 'Could I have some clothes?' she asked, leaning into him more than she wanted to.

'Not until the chief says you can.'

Cora sighed and rubbed absently at her leg. She had never in her life known of someone being injured for so long. Even with the damage that had been done when Sarn hit the ground, he'd been walking around the cavern sooner than Cora had been allowed out of the sleeping mat.

She looked up at the green hill that surrounded the cavern. It looked soft, with a few trees growing along its edges and none on the top. 'Can we look from the top?' she asked.

Teven glared at her.

'Are we not allowed to climb it?'

'You have a broken leg, and your ribs…'

'My ribs are much better,' she said, watching him closely. He had stayed close to her that first night, his hand on her side. She wondered if there was more to him. When he had touched her leg, she was sure he had healing powers, and yet he denied it.

He surprised her by leading her past the doorway and around the hill, where there was a less steep incline. 'I can't carry you,' he said.

'What about on your back?' she asked. She had played dragons with her little brothers often enough.

He nodded, turning his back on her.

She put her arms around his neck and leaned against him. He was a solid man. She tried to focus on her surroundings as he stood up and carefully placed his hands beneath her thighs. Her broken leg was uncomfortable as it jutted forward, but she appreciated the higher view.

They started up the side of the hill, which quickly became steeper. He took his time and didn't complain once about her weight or the difficulty in carrying her. When the hill had levelled out, he lowered her to the grass. She could only see trees, a thick forest all around them. Unlike the trees she knew, these were covered in leaves. 'Mama would love this,' she said, turning slowly. When she lost her balance, he was quick to hold her closer to him.

'Where did you get the mark on your chest?' he asked again.

'I was born with it,' she repeated.

'What does it mean?'

'It is the mark of Oldra. It marks me as Oldra.'

'Does it hurt?'

She shook her head, then pulled down at the edge of her singlet. 'It is part of me—part of the skin,' she said. But as he reached out to touch it, she took a small step back and stumbled.

Again, he pulled her close to stop her falling. And he took the opportunity to run a fingertip over the mark. 'What does it mean?' he asked. 'How did it choose you?'

'Essara chose me,' Cora said. 'I need to sit down.'

Teven nodded once and lowered her carefully to the grass. It was soft beneath her. She smiled as she ran her hand over the short, slender leaves.

'My parents are both Oldra,' she said, looking out to the trees that surrounded them rather than Teven's intense stare. 'And…' She looked up then. Her mother had told her she had been conceived in fire. That was partly why she was thought to be so strong, but she wasn't sure she could explain it to this man.

'Are there others?'

'The Ancient is Oldra, but otherwise not within the Penna.'

'Your brother?'

She shook her head. Her brothers had their own skills, but they were not Oldra. 'It marks me as the next chief, or it would have.' She closed her eyes. It was not something she had wanted, and yet it was who she was. She was starting to understand that better now, only she was far from her own people and may never be what she was meant to be.

Again, something in the trees called to her, and she noticed as she turned that Teven was looking in the same direction. 'Do you hear them?' she asked.

'Do all chiefs carry such a mark?' he asked.

'Sarn doesn't,' she said. 'Perhaps it is just a Penna tradition. My father is sure that I will follow him.'

'Is it something you want?'

Cora laughed. 'I didn't, but we get very little choice in this world. I will be what I am meant to be—destined to be, according to my mother. I must learn to embrace it, but it is not easy. I don't have the skill she does; I don't have the strength he has. And I will not be able to choose much in my future.'

'What else would you choose?'

She wanted to say Deen, but as much as she cared for him, she was more certain than ever that he wasn't the right man for her. Her father had been right. There was something else for her—someone else—and she would know that herself with certainty. She looked at the man watching her. 'Do you have a mark?'

He shook his head quickly.

'Do you have a mark of your clan?' she asked, bringing her finger to the scar at the base of her throat.

He shook his head again, then leaned forward to study her more closely. 'Did someone do that to you?'

'The Ancient on my naming day. It marks me as Penna, belonging to my people.'

Teven reached forward and brushed a finger over the small raised mark. 'How old were you?'

'Three or four days,' Cora said, and he stared at her with wide eyes. 'I don't remember it.' She gave him a reassuring smile. 'My mother does. She said it was the scariest moment of her life, with the old man and a knife to my throat. But he has a steady hand and has marked generations of us.' She shrugged.

'Your mother would have known this from her own mark.'

Cora shook her head. 'My mother came to this world. She was not born Penna and so doesn't wear the mark of one.'

'But she has the mark of Oldra,' he said. When she turned, he was studying her features.

'The mark is partly what called her here. She is Penna now, no matter what she was before.'

'She doesn't look like the rest of your clan,' he said.

Cora nodded.

'You are just different enough to notice.'

She raised her eyebrows as he continued to study her.

'Almost all have brown eyes,' she said. 'Your eyes are different.'

He nodded without a word and continued to study her. 'You are tanned for someone who sees little sun,' he said eventually.

She looked back at the trees. The sense of urgency increased, and she struggled to her feet. She was needed, but they needed to help her.

'He will look for us if we don't return soon.' Teven turned suddenly to look behind them.

Cora turned to follow his gaze and was sure she saw a dark shape amongst the trees. They weren't her dragons, but she knew dragons were out there.

'Why are you smiling?' Teven asked. 'There is nothing but darkness and horror amongst the trees.'

'Have you never ventured out there?'

'There are monsters.'

'Dragons don't take people,' she snapped. *Did these people know nothing?*

'If not dragons, what would it be?'

'Other people.' Cora sucked in a deep breath to try and calm the agitation she was feeling. 'I want to meet more of your people.'

'Not until the chief says you can.'

'No clothes, no food, no people. What is the chief's name?'

'Not until he is willing for you to know.'

'I wonder that you didn't leave me out there to die,' she murmured, hobbling towards the path that led back down the hillside. She stopped suddenly and spun around to face him, pinching her leg in the process and stumbling. He rushed to her side but hesitated as he reached a hand towards her. 'What were you doing out there?'

He shook his head.

'You said it wasn't safe. You won't go into the trees, and you certainly won't let me go. What were you doing out there?'

'Yes, Teven,' a low voice asked. 'Tell us what you were doing in the trees.'

'I was looking for wood. It is my task.'

The chief nodded as he continued towards Cora, and Teven took a step away from her. 'Did you learn what you wanted from the dragon child?'

Teven shook his head, and Cora tried not to look between the two men.

'It did not search for you,' the chief said.

Cora waited, wondering what he might want with the dragon.

'Or is it waiting in the woods?'

Cora shook her head once. There was something about this man that unsettled her, yet also something very familiar.

'Have you other dreams?' he asked, leaning over her.

'Only my mother's.' She looked at him closely for a moment and then asked, 'What do you dream of?'

He smiled then, a smile that further unsettled Cora.

'Come inside now. I may ask Rhali to find you something more suitable to wear.'

Cora bowed her head in thanks.

'You are a girl, after all. We must have you look like one.' He marched off ahead, and Cora let out a sigh of relief. Then she jumped as a hand rested on her arm.

Teven helped her up onto his back for the journey down the hill. She squeezed her arms tight around his neck as she stared past his ear at the steep drop before them.

'I won't drop you,' he said.

She pressed her eyes closed. When the ground appeared to level out, he continued towards the cavern opening, and Cora took the chance to look back into the trees.

'Don't let go,' he warned as she loosened her hold for a better look, sure that a pair of golden eyes sparkled in the dark shadows between the trees.

She struggled down from his hold then and turned back to the trees, leaning on the opening of the cavern for support. 'Could you send help?' she called into the trees. 'Could you call Dra?'

There was no response, but again she was sure she could see something. Then it was gone, and she looked at Teven. His eyes closed as he gave a slight shake of his head.

7

Cora sat by the fire and tried not to stare at Teven. There was more to him than he was willing to tell her and, try as she might, she couldn't work it out. He appeared to hear the dragons—and she was certain it was dragons in the woods beyond the cavern. Yet no one would talk of them. No one ventured into the trees except Teven.

'Where do you get wood from?' she asked, trying to appear as though she were looking into the flames.

'We are surrounded by trees. Where do you think we collect wood from?' he asked.

'You said people don't go into the trees.'

'There is plenty of wood to be found without disappearing into the woods.'

Cora sighed. She wasn't sure why she thought he might allow her any insight into what he knew, but she held on to the little hope she had. 'I'm not scared of the woods. Maybe I could explore a little.'

He sat back and looked at her seriously. 'You can't even walk.'

She looked down at her leg then. She didn't need two good legs to fly a dragon. She just needed a dragon. Preferably Dra, but she would take anything at this stage. They knew that she came from a family with dragons, yet they'd seemed surprised that she would travel with one. She began to wonder about her family again, whether Wyn had gotten into trouble for frightening their mother. And whether Deen had thought through taking him hunting.

Cora's father would not look kindly on him taking the boy out without permission, and Deen would have known that. Why would he risk Pira's anger for Wyn's favour? She might never find out, for she might never see them again. She looked beyond the fire through to the other hearths and wondered if she would ever learn who these people were and what they wanted.

She sighed again. She was used to knowing everything. Matters of the people were discussed openly with the Penna, and her parents had never excluded her from conversations. In many ways, she was sure this was her father's way of preparing her for what was to come, for the life she would have. Only it wasn't the life it appeared she would have now. She was trapped at the hearth of a man with no station, amongst a nameless people she didn't know and a chief who would not talk with her.

'What does he want?'

'Who?' Teven asked, looking away from the flames. His face almost looked as worried as she felt.

'Your chief. I still know nothing of who you are, what you do, what you want. And yet you will not let me go.'

He shook his head and turned back to the flames.

'Teven,' she said softly as she shuffled closer, trying not to drag her leg across the mat. 'You have to tell me something.'

'I can't,' he whispered. 'You should rest. When he wants you to know, he will tell you.' He stood abruptly and disappeared into the dim light beyond the fire.

Cora tried not to sigh again. She glanced around and realised she was alone at the hearth. There was no sign of Rhali, and she couldn't make out anyone else beyond the fire. If not for the glow of other fires, she might have thought they were alone. She shuffled back across the mat and onto the furs, thankful that the cushions were still piled as she eased back into them. It was a little harder to move the furs around her legs, and she wondered just how long it would take before she was well enough to run away.

She placed a hand across her ribs, grateful that they at least didn't hurt as much as they had, and that breathing was no longer so painful. As she closed her eyes, she remembered Teven's cool hand over hers, but she shook the thought away. She couldn't spend the rest of her life trying to guess what and who these people were.

Her mother's hands came into view again, and she could feel the cold in the air as though they were her own hands over the hot body beneath them. She sighed at the sight of the bruising, the blood pooling where it shouldn't within his abdomen. She looked back over her shoulder at the other man sleeping fitfully, Pira. Behind him in the shadows stood an older man. At first, Cora thought it was Arminel, watching over the healing of the two men, but it wasn't. This man was shorter, stockier, not Penna. It was the chief who would not let her go.

Then her father cried out, and her mother's panic filled her chest. She was sure he wouldn't survive. The man stood over them all the while, watching everything she did.

Cora woke with a start, groaning at the pain in her side when she sat up. She felt desperate to get to her feet, but she couldn't. Why did she never have any of her mother's good memories during her dreams? Always darkness and pain and fear.

She wiped a hand over her sweaty brow and longed for a brush to rake through her hair. She might ask Rhali in the morning. Although she wondered if that was another thing the chief would have to allow before she could be given it. Her stomach growled and then quietened. She was getting used to eating less, but even if she could use her legs, she doubted she would have the energy to get very far.

If he was hoping she could heal something, he was in for a surprise. Her limited skills were even more diminished given her current state. There wasn't even anything she could help herself with. She did have her bow, she thought as she reached out for it. Yet her arrows had disappeared, and she wasn't sure if that was from her fall or if they had been taken.

She lay back, her hand still closed tightly around the bow and her eyes searching the dark void above her. In the low firelight, she couldn't make out the ceiling of the cavern. She had dreamt of Teven, of standing before him at the hearth, the old man watching their every move. Would she still be here, helpless and trapped, until she was able to stand on her own?

She might be able to use the bow to stand, but she might also snap it in two trying to get there, and then she would be lost. Not that she thought Tarn would create a bow so easily broken, but she had started to lose faith in herself. She had always known that she could not be what her parents had hoped she would be. Particularly what her mother had hoped she would be. Now she was proving them right, all of them, and she would never be able to let them know how sorry she was to have let them down.

She squeezed her eyes closed, willing some tears at her predicament, but she couldn't even find them. Arminel came to mind, looking worried, his eyes closed and brow creased. For a moment, it was as though they sat holding hands amongst the cushions of his cavern. She sighed at the feeling of comfort. Then he opened his eyes and stared straight into her soul.

'Where are you?' he asked.

'Here,' she whispered.

'Where are you?' he asked desperately.

'Far away,' she breathed, and then he was gone, replaced with the scowling face of the chief.

'What are you trying to do?' the man asked, too loudly. She blinked into the dim firelight again.

'Sleep,' she murmured. 'Yet you continue to interrupt every dream.'

He growled something she couldn't make out, and he moved over to shake Rhali awake. She mumbled something, then sat up quickly as she focused on the man over her.

'What has happened?' she asked.

'The girl is ready to deliver.'

Rhali threw the covers back and glanced at Cora. 'She might be able to help me,' she said, chewing on her lip.

'You are a healer of sorts,' the man said, looking her over. 'Have you helped at births?'

'Many,' Cora said.

The chief sighed. 'Teven,' he said, and Teven rolled over in his furs. 'Take the girl with your sister to the birthing chamber.'

Before Teven could even agree, the chief stalked off across the cavern. The relationship between the two of them suddenly made more sense to Cora, yet she wasn't quite sure what use she could be. She couldn't bend her leg, and although her ribs were better, she was still sore in the chest.

She barely had time to consider her options before Teven had her up in his arms as he carried her through the cavern. Rhali rushed ahead of them. The cool air wrapped around Cora as they exited the cavern. Although she was relieved by the cold, she shivered. Would she ever be able to transition again?

A scream met them as they entered the smaller cavern where she had first stayed, and in shock Teven bumped her against the wall. She groaned. The scared woman, alone in the space, blinked at her.

'Why did he send her to me?' she asked.

'She is a healer,' Teven said. 'She might make this easier for you.'

'I can try,' Cora said. 'Put me down beside her.'

He nodded and did as she said. Sitting beside the young woman, who appeared very young, Cora faced in the opposite direction with her leg jutting out towards the wall. The sooner it was healed, the better.

The girl began to sob. Cora wrapped her arms around her and pulled the girl against her chest.

'Take a deep breath,' she instructed, and the girl did as she was told. 'Good. Now another.'

Cora could feel the tension in her body, but she was starting to calm down. She held the girl tight and moved her hands slowly over her back. She continued this way until the girl stiffened in her hold and moaned.

'This is good,' Cora whispered. 'This is how it is supposed to be.'

She held the girl back and looked at her. She still appeared quite scared, but she wasn't as panicked as she had been when Cora had entered.

Cora smiled calmly, trying to imagine just what her mother would do. It was easier assisting with the Penna women in birth, as she knew them all so well. And despite her lack of skills, she was the daughter of the chiefs and next in line, so they listened to what she said.

'I am going to have a feel around your belly to see what this child does,' she said softly, moving her hands down the woman's arms and towards her midsection. Cora doubted she would see anything like her mother, for whom whole lives unfolded. She paused. She would have seen such things for every child who had survived to their naming day, and those who hadn't. What else might she know that she hadn't told?

'Can you heal the child if he is sick?' the young woman asked.

Cora shook her head and closed her eyes. She could sense the child. There was movement, and she looked beyond the skin. She wanted momentarily to pull back, but she thought the movement might scare the girl even more. She sucked in a deep breath and focused. 'A girl,' she whispered.

'He said I would have a son,' the young woman said, sounding scared again. Cora looked at her and smiled.

'Maybe the next will be a boy,' Cora whispered. When the girl slowly lowered her head, Cora closed her eyes again.

She focused on the baby she could see as well as feel, and the child's bright eyes took her in as though she was the most important person in the world. Then the child was alone and cold. Cora wanted desperately to pull away from the image, but then the child tottered along by the fire, arms outstretched and with a wide smile.

Cora sighed with relief and looked up at Rhali, who appeared almost as panicked as the young girl.

'Why is there no one else here?' Cora asked.

'Who would come?'

'Her mother, other women of the clan.'

'Not for this,' Teven said, and Cora wondered why he would have stayed where he was.

She was about to ask what he meant when the girl cried out again and clutched at Cora, her fingers digging into Cora's skin as she gritted her teeth. Cora tried to look about the space then. The fire was still low and there was no water, nothing to indicate they awaited a child.

'What is the expectation here?' she asked carefully. 'What does he want from me?'

Teven shook his head. Rhali started to cry.

Cora could feel the anger burning inside her. 'Boil water,' she snapped at Teven, 'and find some blankets. You,' she continued sharply to Rhali, 'help this woman forward.'

'What do you mean to do?' Teven asked, looking over his shoulder.

'Deliver this baby. She is coming whether we are ready or not.' She tried not to groan as she hit her leg against the wall, nestling into the cushions behind the girl's back. The girl leaned back into Cora. She took her hands, clenched her teeth and nodded towards Rhali.

Together, they tried to help the young mother deliver the child. Cora thought light had started to shine through the doorway as the girl finally began to push the child free. She was exhausted, and she had barely anything left when Rhali cried that she could see the head.

Cora sighed with relief before Rhali slowly shook her head. She felt the life slip from the woman in her arms with the child. She waited desperately for the cry, but it didn't come. Rhali looked away as Cora pushed the lifeless woman from her body and reached for the child.

He was blue, the cord too tight around his neck. She wondered what she had seen. This girl was far too young for a child, let alone two. She saw the similarities between the child of her vision and the woman before her. Had this young mother been the smiling child of her vision, and not the baby?

'Who told her it was a boy?' Cora asked, staring at the child.

The two looked at each other and then back to the child.

'You knew this would happen,' she said, trying desperately to get herself out from beneath the girl and failing. Then Teven was pulling her free, and although she wanted to cry for the girl she didn't know and the child she hadn't sensed, she simply rested her head on Teven's chest.

He didn't move, allowing her to lean against him. She had been no help for this girl, and she would be no use to her own people. She couldn't see as her mother could, nor could she heal as her mother could heal. She might be useful with a bow, but she would never be the warrior her parents were. Perhaps it was best that she was lost to them now, and her brothers could step up and be what she could not.

Exhaustion washed over her as she stepped back. She staggered on her leg and reached out to put her hands on Teven's chest. The mark of Oldra burned hot and bright in her mind, as well as against her right hand.

'You have the mark,' she murmured, looking up into his face.

He shook his head violently, clutching at her arms to hold her up and away from him.

'I can feel it,' she said.

He pushed her down to the fur, beside the girl. 'You couldn't even tell it was a boy.'

Cora looked from the girl to him and back again. 'I can feel it,' she said again.

Anger twisted his features and he pulled at his top, surprising her with a well-muscled chest that reminded her of her father when her mother had tried to save him. He stood before her, scowling. Instead of the mark of Oldra over his heart, he was heavily scarred as though someone long ago had taken a knife to his chest and carved back and forth.

She struggled to her feet and almost fell forward into him. But as she reached for the scarred skin, he grabbed her hand.

'There is no mark,' he said with an anger that terrified her.

8

Rhali helped Cora out into the cool air. As they made it outside, she pushed out of Rhali's arms and leaned against the smooth, soft grass of the outer wall. She had only been pulled from her sleeping mat to watch the girl die. Not one of them had expected her to live, and no healing powers had surfaced, despite Arminel and her mother being so sure she had them. Nor had Cora's skills as a seer. If what she had were such skills.

Dreams of the past, and mostly her mother's, were not enough. Again, she wondered just what her mother had seen, what she already knew of the people around her. Cora had always been so busy fighting against her, and now she wanted nothing more than to sit and talk with her. She looked out into the dim morning light and the dark trees. She couldn't feel anything there now, no sense of dragons, no golden eyes in the darkness.

She squeezed her hand closed. She could still feel the heat of the mark in her hand, and a sadness swept over her. Whether Teven was Oldra or not, this was not the place for her. She stepped out across the dry ground, still missing the snow. Rhali didn't try to stop her as she hobbled painfully towards the trees. When she reached the first one, she leaned into it.

It felt just like any other tree, maybe less damp due to the lack of snow, but otherwise it was just a tree. And for the moment, Cora was just a girl. She closed her eyes and reached out for Dra. The emptiness took her breath away. Would she spend the rest of her life searching? The chief's serious face appeared in the darkness behind her lids, and she sighed.

The rest of her life might not be very long. She didn't know what he wanted, what any of them wanted. Her father would have a sensible plan, but her mother would know what was behind this, why she was here and why they hadn't returned her.

She glanced around at Rhali watching her and wondered whether they could return her even if they wanted to. Teven had expressed concern for what her people might do. But if Cora explained that they had tried to help her and treated her injuries, it might be enough. The Penna didn't know these people or where they were, and they had been willing to take in Sarn knowing he was an enemy.

As she stepped away from the tree, she noticed a sturdy branch had fallen nearby. She stooped awkwardly to pick it up. It was rough but strong when she leaned on it, and she moved a little more easily towards the cavern.

She wanted to look over her shoulder and disappear into the trees. But she needed to learn what the chief was and how he could get so easily inside her head. Despite Cora's fears, she knew that if it were her mother in this situation, she would try to learn all she could. Teven hadn't reappeared from the birthing chamber, and she wondered why they'd been called on as they had.

Cora followed Rhali into the cavern and tried to count the number of hearths. The edges of the cavern were still dark, despite the soft light starting to fill the space. She could hear crying, and the rest of the cavern was silent as she looked towards the soft noise. It was as though everyone had held their breath.

She blinked quickly and shook her head as the chief came into view, unsure whether he was a vision in the dark or actually there. But he wasn't focused on her. He stood by the fire of a hearth, staring at a woman who sat crying on the mat at his feet.

Cora started to walk towards him, but Rhali slipped a hand under her arm and guided her towards their own hearth. She wanted desperately to ask questions, but she bit her lip. In the silence of the cavern, anything she said would be shared with everyone. It wouldn't be this way with the Penna.

As Rhali helped her to sit on her furs, a young man appeared in the hearth light. He could have been her brother, young and ragged, although he was pale and his eyes appeared sunken. Rhali gave him a quick shake of her head as she looked past him back to the chief, but the boy dropped to his knees.

'You can't be here,' Rhali whispered.

'Tell me,' he breathed, the strength behind the words surprising Cora.

Rhali looked at Cora and then back to the boy. 'You don't need me to tell you,' she said softly, kneeling down in front of him. He nodded once and swallowed loudly. 'He would not let them live.'

He climbed slowly to his feet and disappeared. As he did, Rhali slumped forward. Cora cursed her leg again. If only they had a real healer, she could be of some use—or at least she could run. As she looked across to where she thought the chief was, she decided that was why he didn't want her healed.

'Where is Teven?' Cora asked.

'He will take them into the woods,' she murmured.

'On his own?'

'It is his task.'

'He seems to have many. I thought the woods weren't safe.'

Rhali glanced around at her then, although Cora couldn't read her expression in the dim light. 'He is what he is, and he does as he does. As do we all.'

'Will there be a ceremony for them?' Cora asked.

Rhali shook her head slowly. 'There will be nothing, and they will not be spoken of again.'

'But the girl was named. She was part of the clan. Would she not be remembered?'

'Not for what she did.' Rhali climbed slowly to her feet and then shuffled towards her sleeping mat.

Cora watched her for a little while longer, waiting for some explanation, some expression of her grief or reaction to what had happened, but there was nothing. What could this man do that they would allow a girl to die?

In the silence of the cavern, Cora waited. There was not a sound, not a whisper nor a cry for the girl or her child. There was also very little movement. Despite the rising sun, no one prepared a meal or got on with their tasks. Cora gritted her teeth and pulled herself up on the rough walking stick.

She was the next chief of her people, and she wasn't going to sit around any longer. She leaned heavily into the stick and slowly made her way to the pathway between the hearths. They were all quite small and close together. The tension increased to a palpable level, but the silence remained.

She looked around at the faces pointed in her direction and then forced herself forward, deeper into the cavern. As the light increased a little, she could see that it was very similar to the cavern she had grown up in, although much smaller and with no space between hearths for dragons. She looked openly into the spaces she passed, and the people held her gaze, but they were not as great in number as she had first thought.

At some hearths, there were only a couple of people; at others there were four or five. But she didn't know whether they all lived there or were visiting. Looking at the simple rock markings between the hearths, she doubted anyone visited much. She smiled, thinking of the path between their hearth and Nira's beside it. At one place there was an indent—nothing significant, but when sitting at the table, it was clearly seen as the point at which they crossed. They crossed often, all of them. If Cora had taken the time to look around her own people, she was sure there would be such an indentation in the ground between every neighbouring hearth. There were no such markings here.

Despite the increasing light, it still felt dark within the cavern. Cora looked ahead along the path and continued until she reached a doorway within the earth. There was no covering over it, and she paused only momentarily before she stepped through. It was dark beyond. She maintained a straight forward path, the sound of murmuring increasing behind her. Then her stick hit wall. She turned, noting the small glow of flames ahead of her and a man crouching by the fire.

'You have come then,' he said without looking up. 'You hope to learn from me.'

'What could I learn from you?' Cora asked too quickly. He looked up. The shadows around him and the light from the flames changed his features, and she wondered for a moment if this was someone she hadn't met.

'I know what you are,' he said, standing. 'And I know what you can be.'

Cora shook her head. 'I'm not very much of anything.'

'Geraldine knows different.'

Cora took another step forward. 'My mother hopes that I will be something, but I have no skill.'

'You can see.'

'Can I?' she asked. 'I dream of stories. Everyone knows the story of Gerry and Pira, and how she saved him.'

'They do not know the fear like you do. They do not know of the world beyond.'

She remembered the blue lights and the pain in her chest at the knowledge that her mother was gone. And yet, it was not her mother.

'I don't have the healing abilities she has.'

'Your ribs were broken, as well as your leg, and you no longer appear to be suffering.'

'That was…' She stopped, unsure if it had been Teven who had healed her, but there was something about that man that she was sure no one else knew. 'I cannot see as my mother does,' she continued, hoping he wouldn't guess at what she might have meant. But he appeared to know far more than he should.

'You will,' he said, with a confidence that surprised her. 'Sit,' he instructed rather than invited. She moved forward slowly and lowered herself to the mat by the fire. 'Ask me what you will, and I will consider whether I will answer.'

She looked into the flames and then back to him. 'You mean to keep me here.'

He shrugged.

'Will you allow me to eat?'

'If you are willing to work with me.'

'I don't know what you think I can do to help you.'

'You will work it out.' He stood then, and she leaned back from him. He moved over to the side of the cavern and returned with a small piece of bread. It was similar to what she had grown up with. The grain was rough, but the bread itself was warm as she snatched it from his fingers.

'What do you want from these people?' she asked before taking a large bite.

'They are my people. I only want for them to survive.'

'Just survive, or thrive?'

'They do not know what is best for them. I do.'

Cora took her time chewing the next bite of bread. 'Why do you send Teven out?'

'I know he will return.'

'That is an odd response. Do you not think others will?'

'His place is here. He knows what he is.'

'What is that?'

'Not important,' he said.

Cora took a moment trying to determine what he meant. If he thought Teven was not important, why was it so important that he do as directed and stay? 'What does he do in the woods?'

'Whatever is asked of him.'

'Can I go with him?'

The man shook his head. 'There is more for you here.'

'But no one talks to me. I am of no use.' Cora tapped her leg, then looked back towards the opening into the main cavern. The light was brighter, yet it was still dark within the space she sat. 'What did she do that she deserved to die?'

He sighed and looked at her. 'You haven't asked anything of use yet.'

Cora waited. When he didn't answer the question, she asked, 'Was your father chief before you?'

He looked at her and grinned. 'Yes, he was. I knew I was to be a stronger chief than he could ever be. I am from a long line of chiefs.'

'And will your son be Chief?'

The grin slipped, and his focus returned to the fire. 'He may not be worthy,' he murmured, then waved her towards the door. She waited, but he didn't move. After a moment longer, she climbed slowly to her feet and pushed the remainder of the bread into her mouth, then hobbled towards the door. 'Don't try to go too far,' he warned. When she looked back, he was still looking into the flames. 'I know you are strong, and you will give me that strength,' he whispered. A shiver covered her skin as she moved out into the cavern.

9

Cora sat up in bed, the bowl of hot stew in her hands. She breathed in the smell of it.

'It works best if you eat it,' Rhali said softly. 'He may not allow it often.'

Cora took a small sip. It was hot against her lips, and although there wasn't much substance to it, it was the best stew she had ever tasted. She licked her lips and lowered the bowl back to her lap. Rhali looked at her with some disappointment, then turned back to her own bowl. Cora waited for it to reach her stomach. Although she had eaten very little in the time she had been with these people, she worried that too much too soon would only bring it all back up.

She took another deep breath and then raised the bowl again. As she lowered it, Teven appeared before her. He looked her over and nodded. He was covered in dirt. It clung to his clothing, marked his face, and it was even in his hair. He squatted down before her, and she held the bowl out to him.

He smiled, but shook his head.

Rhali put her bowl down and moved back to the fire.

'What did you do to get food?' he asked.

'I asked for it,' she said, carefully lifting it back to her lips. It was sitting well in her stomach so far. As hungry as she was, she was doing her best not to gulp it down.

'What else did you ask for?' he asked, standing again as dust fell about him.

She opened her mouth and then stopped, looking beyond him at an older woman approaching the hearth. She moved slowly, struggling to carry a basket. Teven turned to see where Cora was looking. He reached out to take the basket from the woman, but she shook her head.

As she entered the hearth, Cora recognised her for the woman who had been crying when they'd returned from the birthing chamber. Teven stepped back, and she placed the basket down on the mat before the fire. Cora heard water move about within it. It was tightly woven, similar to what the Penna would have used for water. For the first time, Cora wondered where the water came from. They didn't have snow to melt. She wondered if there was something like the lake, and if it was as cold.

'Thank you,' the woman whispered, bowing low, but Teven caught her by the arms to halt the movement. She sighed and nodded once. 'Please,' she said, indicating the water. 'It is hot.'

He wiped at the dirt across his cheek, and for a moment Cora thought he might have been wiping away a tear. He nodded once to the woman before releasing his hold of her arms. She turned without another word and disappeared into the dim light beyond the hearth.

'Take the time to wash,' Rhali said, 'before you eat.'

As Teven nodded slowly, Cora could see just how tired he was. She wanted to ask so many questions—where he had gone, how hard it had been, why no one had helped. Her whole cavern worked together when someone died, but not here. It was hard to believe they were a clan at all.

'How long have you lived here?' she asked. Rhali glanced at her, but Teven, kneeling by the water, continued as though he hadn't heard her. He removed his tunic and sighed as he pushed his hands into the water.

Rhali stood and moved past Cora, then returned with a piece of cloth. She handed it to Teven and he took it without a word, smiling for her and then pushing it into the water.

Cora slowly sipped at her stew, waiting for something—a response from Teven, or for the chief to reappear. In the silence of the cavern, there was only the sound of water as he slowly washed the dirt from his skin. She tried not to watch him, but there were few places she could look in the small space, and he was set up almost at the end of her sleeping mat. In many ways, he reminded her of Deen, and yet he was so different.

When she blinked, she could see her father's body, broken and bruised, and for a moment her mother's panic rose in the back of her throat. Something about Teven drew her forward, and yet she worried what it meant when she connected him so closely to her father. His broad shoulders were smooth and muscled, but her eyes tracked back to the scar over his chest. Her own hand moved to her mark, and he glanced up at her with weary eyes.

'You should eat,' she said, holding out her bowl again. But he shook his head and held up a hand.

Rhali stood behind him then with a brush, very much like Lalina had used on Cora's hair when she was a child. She remembered the pulling, but the braid was always smooth and neat and tight when her father's sister did her hair. Rhali bushed quickly through Teven's hair, the dust filling the air and then settling on his shoulders. He wiped them with the cloth before pushing his head over the water, and Rhali helped him wash it from his hair.

As he ran his fingers through it, the water trailed down over his shoulders and chest. Cora wanted to help him wipe it away, but he wrung the cloth out and wiped himself. He was still damp, the water glistening in his hair and across his body as Rhali held out a fresh tunic for him.

As he stood slowly, Cora realised how dirty his trousers were. She stared into her bowl. She had worried that it wouldn't sit well, but she was starting to feel better, and she realised the bowl was empty when Rhali reached for it.

She filled it again from the pot, but waited instead of handing it back to Cora. Teven sat on the mat in fresh clothes, his hair still wet, and took the bowl his sister held out to him. A young girl appeared, bowing her head, and then took the dirty water away without a word. Teven sighed, ran a hand through his hair and sipped from the bowl. Rhali gave him a sad smile. He nodded once, and she moved back to her sleeping mat.

'What did he say?' Teven asked quietly.

Cora took a moment to realise that he was talking to her, and she looked away when he turned to look at her. 'Not very much,' she murmured. 'I was hoping he would tell me why I'm here, or why I can't go home.'

'Did you ask directly?'

'He thinks that I am more than I am,' she said. 'Everyone thinks I am more than I am.'

'I am sure you are very important, being the daughter of the chief.'

'Where is your family?' she asked.

He looked back to the bowl, but didn't answer.

'I am sorry. It has been a long day.'

He nodded once. 'My mother died when I was young,' he said.

'Did you have to look after yourself and Rhali alone?'

He looked over to his sister. 'When her mother died, there was nowhere for her but with me.'

Cora opened her mouth to ask another question, but he looked up across the fire. She thought she saw the outline of a man on the other side. Teven shook his head, and the figure disappeared.

'Who is the boy?' she asked.

He shook his head again. 'If the chief wants you to know, he will tell you.'

Cora sighed, snuggling down into the furs. 'Then I will spend the rest of my life with the two of you, knowing nothing.'

'Maybe you will,' he said, turning then and surprising her with a smile.

'Would that be so bad?'

'Not if I get to eat more often.'

He laughed, and Cora tried not to smile as he ran his fingers through his still-wet hair.

For the first time since she had fallen, Cora dreamt of Teven. At least she thought it was a dream as she stood directly before him, studying the mark on his chest. It looked as it had that night when he'd changed before the fire, an unevenness of the skin more than a scar. But she knew it had been caused by someone. When he had first shown her, she could see the anger in it, the ferocity of the attack. But that may have been because of his own anger. She couldn't see the individual knife marks now.

She was tempted to run her fingers over it, but she held her hand away from it. She could sense the heat beneath it even though she couldn't see it. There was something inside this man that connected him to her. They were standing in the trees then, the sun warm on her skin, and he still smiled at her.

She wanted to smile back, but she looked around for the chief instead. She was certain he would be penetrating this dream as he did all the others. He had seen her before she had found them, she realised, remembering his face in the shadows of even her mother's memories. Had he been there too? Was he part of the darkness she had spoken of? And if that was the case, could she defeat him again as she had then?

Or was he something else? Cora looked back at Teven to find he was saying something, only she couldn't understand what it was. She looked closely at his face. It was as though she couldn't hear him. He was becoming more animated, but she still couldn't hear what he was saying. Then he froze, as though he saw something beyond her in the trees.

She didn't turn and look. She felt the presence and thought she knew what it was. Two bright golden eyes shone in the shadows over his shoulder, and then a face became clear. It was a dragon. Only it didn't look anything like the dragons she knew. It was smaller, leathery rather than scaly, and it looked at her with a little nervousness.

She reached out a hand towards the dragon, and it opened its mouth. Cora was hit with dragonlight. Before she could react, it pushed through her chest, and she felt the same burning sensation she had felt when she'd reached for Teven's chest. Only it was very hot—too hot—and she was sure she was burning.

When she reached out for Teven, he was gone. Another man stood where he had, another man she didn't know. A man with green-flecked eyes.

She sat up quickly, groaning at the movement and blinking into the dim light of the cavern. She glanced around, but no one else seemed to be awake or moving. There was no sign of the chief amongst the shadows. He seemed to see it all, so would he have seen this dream too? Would he know what it meant?

Someone snored, and she realised Teven was sleeping directly beside her. He had pushed the covers back, exposing his bare chest. She wondered if he might have had the same dream, experienced the same heat of dragonlight she had felt. As though sensing her eyes on him, he shivered and rolled onto his back. She reached forward but hesitated. She didn't know whether there was something beneath the scar or not. Had someone tried hard to destroy a mark?

She sat up quickly then. Without pausing, she held her hand above his chest. It wasn't as hot as it had been before, yet she knew with certainty that there was something calling to her beneath the skin. She closed her eyes and breathed deeply, and the feeling grew. Just as she placed her hand on the scar, a hot, sharp pain shot through and up her arm. Then a warm hand closed around her wrist and lifted her hand. She opened her eyes to find Teven staring at her.

'Do you think you can heal it?' he asked.

She shook her head. She wasn't quite sure what she'd been thinking when she put her hand on him; she just knew she had to. 'I can feel something beneath it.'

'There is nothing there. It is a scar from a burn.'

She opened her mouth and then closed it. She knew that wasn't true, and she could still feel the heat burning into her palm before he released her arm and pushed her away.

'There was an accident, not long after I was born,' he said softly, sitting up and leaning in closer to her. 'It was a long time ago, and no one has been able to heal it.'

'Have you tried?' she asked.

He smiled at her as he shook his head. 'I am no healer,' he said.

Cora looked at the scar on his chest. 'I want to go into the trees,' she whispered.

He looked around, glancing through the flames before he gave the slightest nod. If she hadn't been looking at him so closely, she would have missed it.

10

The sun was starting to light the sky as Cora leaned into the stick at the opening of the cavern. She had been inside for so many days. But as keen as she was to get far away, she knew that if she left them now, she would never learn any more. She glanced over her shoulder; no one else was moving around the cavern. If they were awake, she wasn't aware of it.

She had yet to learn who these people were, and, she knew very few of those she had met. The chief may never tell her exactly who he was or how he had come to be here. There must still be Keetar somewhere in the world who hadn't travelled with Sarn all those years ago, when he had come looking for her mother and a way to stop the shadows very few had believed existed.

So many had died, and yet she didn't know if those Keetar had simply stayed away or fought the others. There was still so much of her own history she didn't fully understand. Her part in helping her mother destroy the shadows was one of them. She shivered at the idea of the dragonlight. It had burned right through her in her dream, and she could still feel the pain at the point where it had hit her skin. Cora wondered how her mother had survived when all the dragons had focused their dragonlight on her.

Teven stood out in the open, but he looked around nervously as he waved his hand to indicate that she step out into the cool air. Leaning heavily on the stick, she stepped forward as he turned his back and walked towards the trees. He was lost to her in only a few steps, and she wondered if this was a good idea.

She tried to move faster. How long would it take the chief to notice that she was gone and work out where she was, and with whom? What would this cost Teven?

As she hit the shadows of the tree line, she could see him standing further inside the dim light of the trees. He waited until she reached him, and then they walked together into the woods.

'You aren't scared,' she said after a little while, pausing by a tree. Her leg ached, and her hand hurt from the rough edge of the stick.

'Neither are you,' he noted as she rubbed her hand. 'I could shape that for you,' he offered.

She looked at the stick and nodded. 'You carve as well?'

'I do what I can.'

She couldn't read his face in the dim light beneath the canopy, and she wasn't sure what he meant.

'You wanted to go into the trees. Now we are there.'

She looked around her at the trees stretching on into the distance. There was no hint of movement, no golden eyes.

'Can you call them?'

'The chief?'

'The dragons,' she said.

'There are no dragons.' He turned and continued further into the trees, not waiting for her.

'Then why does no one but you come into the trees?'

He continued at the same quick pace as she fell behind. She longed for her bow, sure that she would feel better with it in her hand. But without arrows, it was no use. She closed her eyes and drew in a deep breath. She couldn't feel any dragons around her, so she reached out. Mostly to Dra, but also to any dragon who might hear her.

No one answered. Teven continued to walk away from her, working his way between the large trees. They didn't have the high roots of her trees, ones she had climbed on as a child and sat on as an adult. The world was no longer her own, and she wondered if she would ever be able to return to what she knew.

When she felt she couldn't walk any further, a small clearing opened up and the trees gave way to the sun. She staggered out onto the patch of grass and, looking to the sky with her eyes closed, she savoured the warmth. Then she looked down at her hands. Perhaps the warm sun was the reason she could not transition. She looked around her and noticed that Teven remained in the shade of the trees.

'Are you going to leave me out here? Give me a chance to find my way home?' He shook his head as she moved back into the shade. 'Why did you bring me?'

'You asked me to.'

'I have been asking since you found me.'

He looked away then, and a cool breeze covered her skin. She breathed a sigh of relief as it washed over her, then focused on Teven standing open mouthed and staring at her.

'Are you going to tell me that I didn't ask loud enough?'

He shook his head slowly and stepped towards her. 'What are you?' he breathed.

She looked down, relieved that finally something was as it should be and her transition skill had returned. Teven reached out to touch her, and she tried not to focus on his fingers working over her hand and arm, then her face and neck. As they trailed towards her mark, the transition melted and his fingers felt like fire across her skin.

She took a shaky step backwards and promptly fell down. If he had been able to grab her, he might have saved her. If she had been transitioned, the fall would only have hurt her pride. As it was her leg burned, her butt ached and her elbow stung.

She took a deep breath and closed her eyes as the transition moved over her skin. She smiled. It had been so long since she'd been herself, and it had been even longer since she'd felt the transition take place. She let it slip before pulling it immediately back around her.

'What is that?' he asked, squatting down in front of her.

'It is my transition. My armour.'

'Armour?'

'It keeps me safe.'

'It didn't when you fell.'

'No,' she sighed. 'I wasn't wearing it then.'

'You put it on?'

'It is me,' she said, holding out her hand. As he ran his fingers over the ice, she let it go. Then she took his hand in hers and transitioned again.

A noise of wonder escaped from him as he squeezed her hand. Then he tapped on it. Holding his hand, she pulled herself back to her feet. She felt stronger with the ice surrounding her, and her leg didn't seem to ache as much. She wasn't sure if that was due to the cold or the support it provided. She could move as easily as she did without the ice surrounding her, and yet she felt stronger.

'Is it cold?' he asked.

'Yes, but it keeps me warm and dry.'

'It is amazing. Why didn't you do this before?'

'I couldn't. I wasn't strong enough, or well enough.' She walked back out into the sun, which no longer felt as warm as it had before. She let it slip, enjoying the heat of the sunshine. Then she turned back to him.

'Your leg is better,' he said.

'Don't you like the sun?' she asked. 'If I don't melt, neither will you.'

'He can't find me in the trees.'

'Who can't?' she asked, stepping towards him.

'Can you teach me the ice?'

'To transition?' He nodded once. 'I don't know. My mother learnt, but then she was…'

He waited, but she just shook her head.

'Why aren't you worried that he will find me?'

'He already did,' Teven said. 'There is very little respite from the man, but he can't reach me here.'

'Who is he to you?'

'Teach me,' he said. It sounded far more like a command from the chief than a request.

'I can try,' she said slowly. Her mother had come from a different world and learnt the skill, although she was Oldra. And Cora had no idea how the teaching had taken place. 'Imagine yourself very cold,' she said, taking his hands in hers. 'That cold surrounds you, covers you.'

He squeezed his eyes closed but remained as he was. After several minutes in the same position, he sighed and pulled his hands from hers. 'I can't,' he murmured.

'Can you find the cold?'

'Not holding your hand.' He turned his back on her and started walking away.

Cora stood just where she was. She was tired. Her leg might have appreciated the cold, but the long walk through the trees had taken its toll, and she ached. She didn't want to lose Teven in the trees, but she wasn't ready to walk back to the small, dark cavern. She looked back to the sunlight and then in the direction he had gone. She was alone.

Looking into the trees around her, Cora thought of Darring. He had also come from a land like her mother's. If not the same place, it was similar. He didn't have the sight her mother had, nor the healing ability, and he too had learnt to transition. Cora pulled the ice tight around her and sighed with relief.

She tried to remember learning the skill for herself, but it had been simple. Her mother was holding her hand, and then she was ice. She closed her eyes and imagined the snowflakes moving slowly around her during flicker flight. The fine detail of each one, how she could feel each small branching ice molecule as it landed on her skin. She looked around again, but there was still no sign of Teven.

She sat slowly and leaned against a tree, her leg still stiff and awkward. She closed her eyes and transitioned, breathing slowly. Maybe she had some more skills than she had realised. She imagined her mother, young and new to the Penna. It wasn't difficult; she had dreamed of her so many times before. She sat in the Ancient's cavern, Arminel standing over her and Wyndha before her.

Cora smiled at the vision of the woman. She knew her from stories as well as if she had lived with the woman herself. The older woman smiled at her and held out a hand. Cora placed it in hers, then realised it was her mother's hand. As the Ancient transitioned, Cora felt the shift in her skin, felt the ice form as though she could see it within the skin. If she'd had decent healing ability, she expected she would see inside the body in such a way as her mother did. Now in her mother's memories, she could see how the transition worked and cause the shift in her own skin.

Cora sighed as she opened her eyes again. It was her mother's skill as healer that had allowed her to learn. Although Cora thought that Teven was a healer, they didn't appear to have the same level of skill, and it might not be that easy. She climbed back to her feet, groaning a little from the effort. Then she realised she needed to lean over to collect the stick. When she straightened, she wondered if she could search out the memory of Darring learning to transition. It might not be hers or her mothers, but he was Penna. There was a connection to each of them, if she could find it.

She leaned heavily into the stick, the rough end pushing into her hand. Perhaps her mother was right and she did have some skill after all. She just had to find a way to tap into it. She looked around her again. Teven appeared to have left her behind, so she was either free to find her own way back or stay longer.

Something moved in the shadows of the trees. She turned slowly, trying to keep her balance and pick up what it was. It seemed to disappear as she turned. She could see it in the corner of her eye, sense it at her back, yet she couldn't see anything.

Panic started to close her throat, the constant movement hurting her leg. If only she were a healer, she might actually be able to do some good for herself. She sucked in a breath, surprised at how ragged and scared she sounded, even to her own ears. And then Teven was standing before her.

'Come,' he said.

She shook her head, unsure which way was safe.

He looked around then, and she felt safer with him there. Whatever was in the trees wasn't a dragon. She could sense something dark. Her transition was still in place as she tried to see what it might be, but Teven had her quickly up in his arms.

'What is it?' she asked.

'There is nothing there,' he said as he continued quickly through the trees.

'I have lost the stick,' she said.

He stopped and turned to look back the way they had come. He sighed, but he maintained a tight hold on her. The shadows had stopped moving, but she knew there was something else out there.

'You can put me down,' she said.

He shook his head, his grip still tight, and turned back for the cavern. 'I'll find you another stick.'

'Can we come again?'

He didn't answer as he stopped at the edge of the trees. She could see the cavern ahead of them, Rhali standing by the opening, looking out for them.

'Can you take the armour off?' he asked in a hoarse whisper. 'He shouldn't know.'

'He might already. He knows that I would have had the skill.'

'But he doesn't know it has returned.'

Cora nodded and allowed the transition to slip. She felt instantly warmed against Teven's chest, and she could feel the tension in his arms. 'Should you put me down?'

Instead of answering, he marched towards the cavern. Rhali looked instantly relieved at the sight of them. When she pulled the heavy hide back to allow them entry, sticks and wood were piled inside the door. Cora wondered if that was what Teven had done when he'd left her alone, finding a reason to go into the woods.

The woman who had brought the water to him the day before stood just inside the cavern. She bowed low as they passed her, although Teven didn't appear to acknowledge her at all. He continued towards the hearth, sat Cora down on her sleeping mat and then disappeared.

Rhali appeared beside her and handed her a hot cup of water. She sipped at it slowly as the younger woman looked her over.

'You are a mess,' she muttered in the end. 'Why he would allow you into the trees is beyond me. You would be of no use in your state.'

Cora simply nodded agreement and focused on the water. The shadows didn't move strangely within the cavern, and she wondered again what might have happened in the trees. She hadn't felt quite so scared once Teven was there, but she shivered at the idea all the same.

'Where is your stick?' Rhali asked.

'I lost it,' Cora said with a sigh. 'It was hurting my hands anyway.' She held out her hand and the girl muttered something under her breath that Cora thought was about her brother's stupidity.

'I have something that might help,' she said. 'I want to check your leg and change the dressing.'

Cora nodded. She really just wanted to sleep.

She lay back into the cushions and allowed Rhali to do as she wanted. It was not going to make much difference; she would still be sitting here for some time, unable to use her leg and unable to go home.

As she ran her hand over her ribs, Rhali sighed.

'I'm sorry,' Cora muttered, sure that she was the cause of the girl's issues.

'I have not done enough for you.' Rhali hung her head as Cora looked up.

Cora reached out and took her hand. 'You have done more than I could expect,' she said, trying to smile. 'You could have left me where I fell.'

Rhali shook her head. 'He would never have allowed that,' she whispered.

Cora let her hand go. 'The chief is in control of so much.'

'Not him,' Rhali snapped, then glanced around. 'Teven. He wouldn't leave you.'

'Why?' Cora asked.

The girl sighed again. 'It is just who he is. And it will get him killed one day.'

Cora studied her for a moment. 'What else does he do that puts him at risk?'

Rhali ignored the question and pulled Cora's hand closer, running her fingers over Cora's palm. 'This is not so bad,' she murmured. 'I want to re-strap the leg, but I'm not sure I can do it alone.'

The boy who had visited with them after the death of the girl and her child appeared behind Rhali. As Rhali chewed on her lip trying to determine what she should do, Cora watched the young man. He opened and closed his mouth several times as though trying to speak, but then he clenched his fists in frustration and turned away.

Cora called out, 'He can help.'

Rhali turned with surprise. Her features became sad, but she nodded, and the young man's face lit up.

She helped Cora from the makeshift tunic and held out a sharp knife. It made Cora a little uneasy, but Rhali was quick and careful as she cut along the material. Cora took some of it and felt the texture, a finely woven cloth. She wondered where the weavers were. There didn't appear to be activity within the cavern to produce much of anything. The pale cloth was dirty from Cora's lying against trees.

Her leg was pale and still bruised. A large tear across the upper thigh indicated she had done a lot of damage as she fell. It also explained the blood seeping through the bandages early on. She ran her hand over the mark and closed her eyes. She sighed, seeing the damage to the muscle beneath the skin with more clarity than she had before.

Her hand became cooler as the muscles tried to pull themselves back together. It was exhausting, and her hand slipped away as she leaned back.

'Do you not like the sight of blood?' the boy asked.

She shook her head and looked back to her leg, not sure what he meant. It appeared just the same, but it didn't hurt as much. She was sure that although she hadn't done very much, she had made it better. If only she could do the same for the bone. But she hadn't seen that far, and it would take her some time before she had the energy to try again.

It seemed strange that her less-than-adequate healing skills were still so much better than what these people had. Rhali smeared an ointment over the cut on her leg and some of the smaller scratches, then asked the boy to hold the stick in place so she could secure them back with fresh material. She tried not to flinch as he pushed against her. But then he released his hold, and Cora looked up to see Teven physically removing the boy.

'You can't be here,' he whispered.

'She asked me to help,' the boy said, pointing at Cora. There was a similarity between the two of them as they faced each other. Although the younger man was closer to Cora's height, looking up at Teven. The taller of the two nodded once but still waved him off.

Teven took his place, lifting her foot onto his knee before taking the stake and holding it against her skin. She leaned back and closed her eyes. He was muttering something at Rhali, who murmured back in response as she wound the strips of cloth around Cora's leg. Once they had finished and Teven had lowered her leg to the ground, they waited in silence.

Cora didn't open her eyes. She wanted to be far away. In a world she knew, where people knew her and talked to her. Why would these two not let anyone close?

The hand on her ribs made her jump, and she swatted it away as she sat up.

'I will need to look at those too,' Rhali said softly.

'I am fine,' Cora said.

'You broke three ribs.'

'I am breathing easily now.'

'There were other injuries, scratches and the like across your back and arms. I want to check for infection.'

Cora looked up at Teven and then back to Rhali. 'I don't want to do this here.'

'You will need to do it somewhere.'

'I could carry you back to the other cavern,' Teven offered.

Cora shook her head. She wasn't sure she wanted to be out there either.

'Let the girl do as she must,' the chief said, appearing before her. Cora nodded once. 'Carry her out and make sure you return her. I told you not to take her out.'

Teven bowed his head. With an apologetic look, he picked her up and carried her out into the cool air. The cavern still smelt of coppery blood, and she tried not to focus on it as he sat her on a fresh mat. He left, Rhali entering as he disappeared.

Cora tried not to sigh as she tried to remove her tunic but couldn't raise her arms. Rhali helped her out of it, then looked over the woollen singlet she still wore beneath it. The girl was quick to pull that off too. The cool air of the cavern wrapped around her, and she realised the fire was not lit.

'I'll be quick,' Rhali murmured, running her hands over Cora's back.

There were some tender spots, but nothing significant. Then she felt around her ribs, and Cora cried out as she pushed against her.

Teven raced back into the cavern, turning his back immediately.

Cora sighed. Although it hurt her to do so, she reached for the singlet and pulled it back over her head. She put her hand to her side and closed her eyes, then took a deep breath and tried to look. All she could see was muscle damage and significant bruising. Again, she tried to will the muscles back to where they should be. She shivered at the cold, her eyes still closed. She was relieved that the muscles were healing, although not as well as her mother might have managed. Maybe she was getting better.

'I'm sorry,' Rhali murmured. 'It will take some time.'

'Can you help me with the tunic?' Cora asked, watching Teven's back as he stood rigid by the door. She held up the short top, the hide heavy and thicker than what she was used to wearing.

'Where does this come from?' Rhali asked, gently touching the shoulder of her singlet.

'Wool from a turvie. They are good to eat, and it is cold where I come from. The animals have developed thick covering to keep warm. Like the fur.'

She nodded and ran her fingers over it. 'It is warm, but it would not keep you dry.'

'True,' Cora murmured as Teven turned and gave her a little shake of his head. 'We have other coverings for that.'

Rhali helped Cora into the short tunic, and then Teven had her back up in his arms. 'Will you make me another stick?' she asked.

He shook his head as he carried her out and back to the other cavern. No one watched them enter, and the chief was nowhere in sight when Teven placed her carefully on the sleeping mat. As she lay back against the cushions, he pulled the furs up and over her. She ran her fingers through her hair, and they snagged on a snarl that had developed.

Without a word, Teven moved behind her and gently untied her braid. With what she assumed was the brush, he began to pull through her hair. It was similar to the sensation when Lalina brushed it, only his touch was gentler. Cora could feel the tears welling. She sucked in a deep breath, trying to allow him to finish.

She shivered at the sensation of his fingers moving against her scalp as he braided her hair. And then he was gone. She twisted to see him climb silently into his sleeping mat. With his back to her, he remained still.

Rhali stood at the end of her bed, looking sad despite the smile she tried to give Cora. 'He looked after me as a child,' she said as explanation, then turned and walked away.

The light had dimmed in the cavern, and Cora thought it might be night. The lack of movement of other clan members confused her, and her stomach growled. Teven rolled quickly up to the fire, scooping something into a bowl, but she shook her head.

'Take it,' he murmured.

'You haven't eaten,' she said, wondering just how these people survived.

He took a gulp from the bowl and then held it out to her again. She didn't want to cry, but the exhaustion was catching up with her.

'It is not so bad,' he said softly.

She nodded and held her hand out for the bowl. He squatted down beside her again, handing it over. She took a gulp and then handed it back. They passed it back and forth, and when he handed her the last part, she pushed it back to him. He sighed but took it, finished the contents and then sat the bowl down by the fire.

'Thank you,' she said.

'He sees far more than you know, and he can make sure you see what he wants you to,' Teven whispered.

'The shadows,' she murmured.

He nodded once and turned back to the fire, sitting beside her. She closed her eyes.

She thought back to the trees, to the shadows she knew were there and yet couldn't quite see. Was he able to scare her during the day in the same way he could reach into her dreams? She tried to focus on the shadows she thought she had seen, and she saw the shining yellow eyes of a dragon in the dim light of the trees. She could sense something behind her. When she turned, she saw the same green eyes she had seen when she'd dreamt of Teven. Then they were lost to the darkness that suddenly enveloped her.

11

Cora felt less stiff when she woke. She stretched her arms out and then winced. She wasn't quite as well healed as she would like. As she put her hand to her ribs, she looked up at the chief standing by the fire.

'It is time for you to show me what you have,' he said.

'I am not what you think. I am not as strong as you hope.'

'But you are stronger than you know.'

'How do you know anything of me?' she asked, sitting forward.

'I was drawn to you, and it appears you were drawn to me. You will come to my cavern.'

He stalked off, and Cora threw the furs back. Teven was already gone, and Rhali still slept—or at least pretended, unmoving. The young man, who appeared to be a younger version of Teven, appeared before her, grinning.

Cora glanced at Rhali first, then looked back to the young man. He held out a stick, and she reached forward to take it. It was a similar length to the one she had lost in the woods, but he had smoothed the end into a soft bulb shape.

'Thank you,' she said, bowing her head to him. 'Teven said I wasn't allowed another.'

'The chief wants you to go to him; this is the best way.'

'Can you tell me your name?'

'I could, but I have not been given the permission yet.' He glanced towards the far end of the cavern. 'We will meet.'

He held out his hand to help her to her feet, and she leaned into the stick. She nodded once. He bowed his head before he disappeared again. She tried not to sigh as she made her way out of the hearth and between the others towards the chief, who was seated by the fire.

She paused, unsure whether she really wanted to be here. But she knew there was no choice while she stayed in this man's cavern. She had no options regarding whom she spoke to and what she did.

'You enjoyed the trees,' the chief said matter-of-factly.

She nodded as she made her way closer. Her strange dream might have been an indication that he was in the shadows she had seen. 'It was like home,' she said.

'Really?' he asked, looking up.

'The trees are different, but the sense of the forest is the same.'

'It is different.'

'Not as cold,' she murmured as she tried to lower herself to the mat beside him. 'What do you want?'

'I want what I know you have.'

She looked at him closely. 'What do I have that I could give you?'

'You will see.'

She tried not to sigh. This man was going to give her nothing clear she could work with. He must be mistaken about who and what she was. 'I am not my mother.'

'I know that,' he said. 'You are so much more.'

Cora shook her head. It was already hard enough to live up to the legend that her mother was, the skill she had, and the help she provided to the Penna. She had saved them all from the shadows, after all.

'How do you know about my mother?' Cora asked.

'I can see much further than others.'

She looked him over closely as he stirred something in a pot. Was it like the call she thought she had heard from Arminel, searching her out? Had this man searched her out through her dreams? She looked at him again. 'What skills do you have?'

He ignored her and continued what he was doing.

'You must have some skill to understand mine,' Cora said. 'Or think that you do.'

He glanced at her and shook his head. He poured the contents of the pot into a cup, then held it out to her.

She sniffed at the bitter contents and leaned back.

'You will drink it,' he said.

'Will it help me heal?'

'It will help you see what I do.'

She was reminded of Arminel again, how he could climb inside her mind by simply holding her hand when she allowed it to happen. What might this man do once he was inside her?

'It will allow you to see what I see, not show me what you see. I have seen all you have seen; it is only the past. The future will soon unfold for you.'

'But will I see it before it does?' she asked, taking the cup and gulping it down. She shivered as the bitter liquid travelled down into her stomach. And she pressed her lips closed to prevent it coming back up.

She put the cup down and reluctantly put her hand in his outstretched one, which was strong and firm. She tried to maintain a sense of calm. He could show her anything, and she would have no idea whether she could trust what she saw.

She closed her eyes and tried to focus on the man. He too had pale eyes, and her mind wandered back to Teven for a moment, but he squeezed her hand tightly and drew her back. Then she could see herself as a child, growing up and more recently, sitting sullen at the table as her mother smiled at her. It was as though he had watched her all this time, her whole life.

She watched herself struggle to learn the healing, unable to see inside enough to do any good. Her mother never seemed as concerned as Cora had thought she should be about her not having the skill. When Arminel would try to speak, her mother would shake her head. Again, Cora wondered just what she knew. But this was the past. He wasn't showing her anything she didn't already know, other than that he had been watching.

A range of images flashed through her mind then—her with dragons, large and bright but unfamiliar to her. Dragonlight lit the world, but she couldn't see herself in that image. Her hands were covered in blood, trying to hold someone together, but other than the leather clothing she couldn't see who it might be. Her hand on a chest, the mark of Oldra clearly beneath it. She wondered if her mind had slipped back to the past and it was her mother's memory. But it was her hand, and she had no idea who had the mark.

She opened her eyes and looked at the chief. 'How can you be sure that is me? How can you be sure from any of those images that I can be anything other than what I already am?'

'You will find another Oldra.'

'As I have been destined to do. My father has told me my whole life that I will find one.'

'When you do, everything will change.'

'How that benefits you, I can't understand. And of course my life will change. To find my mate will change everything.'

'Who is the man you heal?'

'I didn't see healing,' she murmured. 'I saw desperation. I can't even heal a few scratches.'

'Finding him will help.'

'You have not seen enough to convince me I will be anything other than what I already am,' she said, climbing awkwardly to her feet. She swayed a little from the effects of whatever she had drunk, leaning into the stick.

'There is no Oldra here,' she said. 'You don't even have dragons. Why do you think bringing me here will help you?'

'When you are what you need to be, I will take that power for myself.'

Cora gulped down the bitter taste at the back of her throat. She didn't want to ask how he might do such a thing, or why he would think she would come back to him. If his idea of the future was correct, there was an Oldra out there for her, and dragons she was yet to meet. The dark faces she had seen in her dream were not the large, glistening dragons of his vision. They were snow dragons. If any of what he had shown her was to take place, she needed to return to Essawood.

'If you leave, I will find you. If you stay, the power will find you.'

'You have not seen enough to be sure.'

'But I am,' he said, his grin unnerving in the firelight.

She shook her head and made her way out of the cavern.

'You will see,' he called after her.

She moved faster, trying with everything she had to move through the cavern and out into the light. She sucked in a deep breath and allowed the air to blow around her. Running a hand over her perfect braid, she winced at the pain in raising her arm.

There was no sign of anyone around as she headed towards the trees, and the chief hadn't followed her. If she could find a way to teach Teven how to transition, he might be able to help her return home. When she reached the trees, she took several steps below their branches and then turned back to the cavern. He'd only had glimpses of something that might have been her future. Her being here would change that. It wasn't clear from what she saw that it meant what he thought it did.

Perhaps she could see his past if she tried. If she could work out how it was done, she might be able to see who these people were.

Cora stumbled through the trees, her leg aching. Although the stick was smoother than the one she had found herself, it was just too short, and it was getting more and more difficult to make her way through the trees as she became more tired and sore.

She finally came to large tree and leaned into it, using it to sit down against it. Arminel would know what to do. Her mother would know what to do. As the image of her hand across a mark of Oldra returned, Cora knew that even her father would have a better idea of what was to come than she did.

She would need to find a way to leave this place if she was to find the Oldra she had seen, and the dragons. The chief must understand that better than anyone, so she wondered why he insisted on keeping her here. She may be able to find a healer. She wasn't sure what to make of the image of her bloody hands over a wound. Or to whom the wound might belong. Yet at the rate she was going, it could be another injury of her own.

She ran her hand over her strapped leg, knowing where the gash was. Closing her eyes, she held her hand over the place. It was as it had been the day before. She could see the tear in the muscle, only it appeared to be better, and she wondered if she had managed to heal herself somewhat after all. She tried to look deeper, but she couldn't see beyond the muscle.

She would never be what her mother thought she would.

She sighed, leaving her hand on her leg, and the bone came into sharp focus. She tried not to smile as she moved her hand across her leg. It was a jagged line across the bone, but keeping it aligned had helped. She focused on the bone, imagined the line becoming finer and finer until it was no longer there. Then she lifted her hand and shivered as the cold penetrated her body.

She put her hand back and, with very little effort, she could see the world beneath her skin. It was healed. She almost pulled the bandages free, then decided it might be best to allow them to think she was still healing. She looked back at her hands and pressed one to her ribs, grimacing at the sharp pain. Then she studied the bruised muscles. There were no broken ribs at all, and she wondered if she had managed to heal those herself. Or had she been right about Teven being a healer?

It didn't take her very long to heal the muscles that connected her ribs. She looked over the scratches that still covered her arms, then looked around the trees. When she had first arrived, she had sensed dragons, only now there was no sign of them. Could it be that she'd been mistaken? Or that she'd only thought she could sense them?

She closed her eyes and tried to visualise the one she had seen over Teven's shoulder. There was something in these woods, and they might just be the way home. She stood, still awkward with her strapped leg, then transitioned and headed deeper into the trees.

After what felt like half a day of walking, and with her stomach growling, Cora stopped. There was nothing at all living amongst the trees, or nothing she could find. With no sign of small animals either, she wondered what meat these people ate. If she had arrows and her bow, she might be able to help with that. Yet she couldn't even see any tracks. It was as though nothing had ever lived here, or at least not in some time.

She sat down against a rock. It was cool against her back and reminded her of the snow. Even transitioned, she could sense it as she leaned back and closed her eyes. How could the chief have seen so much of her life? Particularly when he saw so little of the future. Was he able to move through the shadows as others had before, or had he watched her through her dreams?

In any dream she tried to remember, he was on the periphery of her vision. How had he become Chief?

Suddenly she was standing in a broad cavern, the lights bright. A younger version of the man she knew stood facing someone else. A terrified, heavily pregnant young woman stood beside him. A group of people stood behind him, looking equally uncertain.

'You would choose this?' a deep, older voice asked.

Cora turned to find a strong older man, his arms crossed over his chest. A woman of similar age was sitting at his feet, but she cried. Her tears continued to flow no matter how often she wiped at them.

The young woman nodded, although Cora didn't think she was very sure.

'It is time,' the young chief said beside her. 'We will make a stronger people.'

'You are not as strong as you think you are, Merik. And you will cause these people nothing but death.'

The girl shivered.

'I don't need your approval,' he spat at the older man. 'I know what I am and what we will become.'

The image faded, and Cora wondered what had happened to the woman. Was the child she carried the son he had referred to? What had he told those people to convince them that leaving with him was a good idea? She closed her eyes again and tried to return to the cavern, to see who else was there and if there were any dragons, but she couldn't.

She could only see shadows and darkness.

12

Cora woke with a start to find it was dark, narrow beams of moonlight pushing through the canopy above her. Again, she wished she had her bow with her. Being amongst these people, she seemed to have forgotten so much. There was a time not so long ago when she would not have left the cavern without her bow. If she had thought about it, she might have collected some smaller sticks to make her own arrows. Even sharpening the points like training arrows would be better than nothing.

She climbed to her feet and stretched her shoulders. Despite the sleep, she yawned and stepped forward. The dark shape before her moved back just a little, but the deep golden eyes remained fixed on her.

'Hello,' she whispered.

The beast moved forward just enough to reach out its long, slender face towards her. She reached out her fingers and ran them over the smooth, leathery face of the dragon. It was smaller than those that lived with the Penna. She wondered if the lack of snow created a different type of dragon.

'Do you know Dra?' she asked.

It pushed against her hand for a moment and then pulled away.

'Could you take me home?' she asked.

The dragon remained silent.

'Please,' she whispered.

It glanced around and then disappeared into the night. Cora wondered how it could disappear so completely when it was so large. She sighed as she searched the surrounding area. Maybe they weren't dragons at all, but a figment of her imagination. Maybe her desperation had created the image in her mind. Although, with her hand against the animal's face, it felt as real as any other dragon.

Cora wasn't certain of anything, and she started walking in what she guessed was the direction of the cavern. She had walked so far to get to where she was, it would take her half the night to return. And if she was headed in the wrong direction, she might walk in circles.

She transitioned and stopped. She had the feeling something or someone was watching her, and although the dragons might not be real, the lack of animals was. Again, she wished she had collected her bow. She blew out a long breath as the world remained still around her.

She looked through the trees, unsure of where she was and what she was looking for. She had managed, without trying, to finally find her healing skills. It seemed odd now that she hadn't been able to master them before. Might it have been because of the fear that she couldn't? Had she been trying too hard to see what was already there?

She couldn't wait to show Arminel what she had discovered. She staggered a little after snagging her foot on something in the dim light. She could do with more than moonlight, she thought as she squatted down and felt along the narrow branch she had tripped on. She couldn't quite close her hand around the shaft of it. As she felt along it, she realised it was quite long and straight. It lifted easily when she pulled on it, although there was some weight to it.

The Draga, when she was young, trained with long spears. They were always far too heavy for her to lift, and she would only laugh every time her father suggested her mother try. But they would swing them around despite the weight, high over their heads at times, and smash them against each other. Even Jeggie, whose spear appeared much heavier than those around him, had amazed Cora with his skill.

She stood the branch upright and leaned into it. It was strong and just taller than Cora, with a slight twist at the very top. She sighed and looked around, then headed back the few steps she had come. When she found the rock, she leaned back against it, laying the large branch across her lap. If the chief really wanted her back, he could come and find her. Otherwise, she would wait for the sun and then decide what to do.

Still transitioned, she closed her eyes. Flames danced over a cave wall— not a cave, an opening—and she huddled beside someone, feeling out of place as she gnawed on dried meat. It was chewy, but it tasted so good. The dragons sat across the opening, keeping them safe. Although she was in an unknown place and the man beside her had threatened her earlier, she knew she was safe.

Cora sighed into the dark. Her mother's memories again. She knew the place. She had stayed out herself as a young Draga. And despite her nervousness, knowing full well what would happen, her father had kept watch over her all night.

Dra had chuckled that he had gone soft. But he had put her through her paces that day and told her he knew she would survive no matter what the world threw at her. She wiped away the tear. He wouldn't want her crying about it. He had done all he could as her father, and her chief, to ensure she was the warrior she needed to be.

Cora had only ever considered that she would never be her mother, that she would never be as strong as Gerry. But she had survived a fall from dragonback, had now managed to heal herself and she wasn't dead yet. She allowed the transition to slip and tugged at the bandages, pulling them from her skin. The cool air wrapped around her leg, making the gooseflesh stand up. She tossed the material and the stake into a small pile away from her. If she had a dragon, she could start a fire. She cursed that she had never learnt the skill for herself. For the Penna, there was always a fire burning. If it ever went out, the dragons raised another.

She lay down with her back towards the large rock and curled up into a ball. She transitioned again, but she knew it wouldn't last. Her leg was stiff, but it was a relief to be able to bend it again.

She hugged her new spear to her chest, resting her head on it, and tried to ignore the fact that she was far from home and all alone.

Cora focused on the flames and the heat they radiated, but something was different. She sat up slowly. The flames weren't reflecting on the back of a cave wall; they were lighting the trees around them. And the man sitting beside her wasn't her father, but Teven.

'You didn't get far,' he said softly.

'I wasn't sure I was trying to run away. I was just walking.'

'For a walk, you made some distance.'

'How did you find me?'

'You leave an easy trail to follow.'

'It's the broken leg,' she said, swinging her legs around. 'It drags.'

'Yes, I could see that,' he said, looking at her naked leg pointedly.

It was hard to tell in the firelight if there were any marks left from her fall, but either way she was thankful to be back to what she was.

'You did that,' he said, turning back to the flames.

She nodded.

'How?' he asked, still looking at the fire rather than her.

'I stopped trying,' she said with a shrug.

'Sorry?'

'I stopped trying to be my mother. I stopped trying so hard to be the healer they all said I would be, and it was like I could see.'

'And the ribs?'

'I didn't heal those,' she said. 'I think you did.'

'I am nothing.'

'I don't think that is true either.' She moved closer to him and the flames. He moved across and away from her.

'Tell me about your brother.'

'I don't have a brother.'

'The boy who asked about the girl who died. He looks very much like you.'

'I am no one,' Teven said again.

'I don't believe you.'

'How can you be so sure of something you know nothing about? You haven't been here long, you haven't met with the people, you haven't talked with anyone.'

'Because your chief has not allowed it. That doesn't mean I can't see for myself just what you do for the clan, or the respect they pay you.'

'It isn't respect.'

'Maybe you need to take some time to look around, visit with your own people.'

He shook his head.

'When are you going to tell me about the dragons, then?'

'There are no dragons,' he said quickly.

Cora sighed. She nodded once and moved back to her rock. She lay back down and pulled the spear close, her back to the fire.

'You'll get cold,' he said.

She transitioned. 'I was fine before you got here,' she mumbled. But she did feel better now that he was nearby. A fur was draped over her, and he sat down beside her as she pulled it closer.

Cora sat up quickly, reaching for his chest, but he caught her arm before she could reach him.

'Some things should not be healed,' he said, his grip firm. It was only when she nodded that he released his hold on her.

'Why won't you tell me what happened?'

'It was an accident. My mother burnt me.'

'Your mother?'

He turned his back on her, but he was sitting close enough that she could reach out and touch him. 'It is all I have of her,' he said, 'and one of the reasons I no longer have her.'

Cora wanted to ask more, but he stood and made his way around the fire to sit on the other side.

Cora woke warm and cosy in the fur. Her transition had slipped again, and the fire had burned low. She searched the small clearing for Teven, but she couldn't see him. His furs were still on the ground by the fire, although far from where she had chosen to sleep. Assuming he wouldn't be far, she stood slowly and stretched.

The fire showed the remains of what had been wrapped around her leg, and any idea she'd had of hiding her healing from the chief was lost. He would already know. She looked around again for Teven, but she couldn't see or hear him. She wondered how long she should wait.

She pushed the splint closer into the dying flames, and it flared up a little. Squatting down, she held her hands out. She needed some decent clothing. She knew well enough how to weave cloth herself, but with no wool to work with and no equipment, she wasn't sure what she could do.

She looked back at the fur, but transitioned instead. She wasn't sure if this was a skill the chief knew she had. But then, he appeared to know far more than she thought he could. She still didn't understand how he had managed to learn so much. He must have the skills of an ancient, a very powerful one. But if that was the case, what did he think he could get from her?

Teven reappeared and started to gather up his things. Cora folded the fur she had slept under and raised her spear. She lifted it off the ground, thankful she still had some strength. Teven eyed it, but said nothing. He then turned and started to walk away.

Cora pushed the ashes over the flames, smothering what was left of the fire, before she followed. She wondered at the sort of reception she would get at the cavern.

Despite her healing, the walk was long, and she tired after several hours trying to keep up with Teven's long strides. She rested the spear across her shoulders.

'You aren't going to be able to take that inside,' he murmured ahead of her.

She swung it off her shoulder and leaned into it. 'I keep losing my sticks.'

He stopped then and turned back. 'You can't claim that as a stick. I would struggle to lift it.'

She smiled at him, but he continued to stare at her seriously. She held it out and, after a heavy sigh, he stepped forward and lifted it from her.

'I couldn't carry it for as long as you have.'

'My father used one, but my mother would never try. She doubted she was strong enough. I don't think I could use it, but carrying it helps.'

'He will be angry,' Teven said, handing it back and turning back towards the cavern.

'About the spear or that I left? Because he seems to know where I go. He also seems to think I need to be here to become what he needs me to be.'

'What is that?' Teven asked softly, turning back to face her.

'I don't know.'

'Then what happens?'

'I don't know that either, but he seems certain he will get from me what he wants.'

'He always gets what he wants.'

They continued in silence for some time, and Cora started to wonder if they were in fact headed closer to the cavern or if Teven might be leading her away.

'Do you have any sense of the future?' he asked.

Cora shook her head. He stopped and turned around. 'No,' she said, pushing past him and travelling along what appeared to be a path between the trees.

'That is what he seeks,' he said, his hand resting on the spear and holding her still. 'Leave it in the trees. We are near now, and it will not be far if you really need it.'

She lifted it from across her shoulders and rested it against the nearest tree. 'He can see what I do,' she said softly.

'Not always,' Teven said, standing too close behind her.

Cora tried not to tense. So far Teven was the only one she thought she could trust. But she didn't know these people or what they wanted from her. Teven might be like the chief, only not quite so open about what he wanted to take from her.

She gulped down the strange feeling in her chest and transitioned. She could feel the warmth of his skin, and although it drew her, she needed some distance. After a few more steps along the path, she could see the clearing and the cavern. Rhali stood in the cavern opening, something in her hand. As soon as she saw them, she smiled.

'Come this way,' she said, indicating the birthing chamber, but Cora baulked at the idea. She could still smell the blood. She feared she would relive the moment. 'Come,' Rhali said again, pulling her into the space. Then she held out a pile of cloth.

Cora wasn't quite sure what to do.

'It is fresh clothes,' Rhali said gently, stepping forward. Cora stepped back. Rhali sat them on the floor with a sad smile. 'I will give you some time.'

Cora looked over the space and the pile of clothes at her feet. She could hear a conversation outside the entrance, but not what was said. After too long standing still, Teven's deep voice called out, 'Do you need help?'

'No,' she called quickly. 'No, I don't.'

She shed the remains of her leggings and pulled on the soft new ones. After running her hand over them, she removed the short tunic she had on and the singlet beneath, putting on the longer one. It was as soft as the leggings, and bright green thread was sewn into the sides and hem in a pattern almost similar to the vine that grew along her bow. As she walked out into the dying light, Teven reached towards her neck, but she stepped back.

'Let me,' Rhali said, moving around him. He blushed and turned away.

There was a string tie at the neck of the tunic, and Rhali pulled the sides together gently before tying them off.

'It is beautiful,' Cora said.

'Yes,' Teven said, then disappeared inside the cavern.

13

Cora woke in the night to someone prodding her. She sat up slowly to a woman with a bundle in her arms, glancing around wildly while she pulled Cora's hand towards the bundle.

'What is it?' Cora asked, trying to keep her voice low, but the woman looked at her with fear.

'Please,' she whispered, pushing the bundle towards her.

She unwrapped the cloth to find a small child, hot and limp. Cora instantly wished for her mother. She need the snow, but that wasn't an option either. She sat up and laid the child in her lap, completely unwrapping the furs that surrounded him. There were marks across his body, and she wondered what illness would have caused them.

'Cool water and a cloth.'

The woman nodded and reluctantly climbed to her feet, disappearing into the darkness beyond the edge of the hearth. Cora tried not to sigh as she looked across at Rhali's sleeping form. She could use some decent lighting. She had raised the lights in the other cavern, but the woman may get into trouble if they lit the cavern, for bringing the child to her.

She closed her eyes and ran her hands over his body. He lay too still. She paused over his little chest. Some things could not be fixed. Not every child could be saved. She remembered her mother's own desperation at times, trying to work her skills while not being able to save everyone.

Cora had already witnessed enough death with these people. If it continued, there might not be any people left. The woman reappeared before her with a soft cloth, which was cool and damp when Cora took it from her. She lay it over the child's forehead as he remained unmoving in her lap.

She closed her eyes again and tried to breath. There was nothing she could do, she told herself, but she could look. She ran her hands over the length of the child and realised that the marks on his body were bruises. Had someone done this to such a small little being?

She pushed the idea from her mind and focused on what she could see. Everything seemed to be working, only slower than it should. Not enough to keep him going. She looked at the mother then and motioned her closer. 'Milk,' she whispered.

The woman looked down. Cora reached forward and put her hand on the woman's breast. She pulled back when she felt the pain within it. Taking a deep breath, she reached out again. The milk was not flowing as it should. Cora closed her eyes, trying to move past the pain she could feel and clear the way for it to flow.

It was a painful process. The woman groaned and then sighed.

'Water,' Cora muttered, and a cup appeared before her. As tempted as she was to take it, she indicated the woman sitting beside her. 'You must drink more, eat more, for your son,' she whispered.

She lifted the little one from her lap and handed him back to the woman, quickly putting him to the breast. Despite his weakened state, he latched on. Cora leaned back and sighed.

Cora dreamed of a child, skinny but strong, running through a large, open cavern. In the bright light, he leapt over the markers between hearths as other children followed behind. The cavern was not the one she was in now. It was larger, bright, filled with dragons and laughter. The child was strong and playful, and the others joined him with ease.

Then the same child but grown, a young man, smiled at a young woman while she cooked over a hearth and he carved wood. Cora tried, but she couldn't see what was in his hands, although she felt the texture of it and smelt the sweet shavings. She stopped and looked around. There were no shadows, no sign of the chief.

Cora opened her eyes to find the chief standing at the end of her sleeping mat. She reached for him, but he cleared his throat and she withdrew her hand. He looked angry as he motioned for her to follow. The woman she had helped the night before lay beside her, her back to the flames and the child in her arms. The child looked at Cora with bright, dark eyes.

The chief watched as she climbed to her feet, his eyes narrowed. He hadn't seen her healing work, then. She wondered at the strange mix of skills this man had. As she followed him through the narrow pathway between the hearths, several people bowed their heads, and she smiled at them. There seemed to be a different feel in the cavern. She wondered if what she had dreamed was a past they might be able to return to.

He pointed to the mat as they entered his small cavern. Cora sat down and crossed her legs. He looked her over and then huffed again.

'What do you feed your people?' she asked.

He looked at her for a long moment and then sat down himself. 'You are not to talk to those I have not allowed you to talk to.'

'Why?'

'Because I am Chief.'

'Are you frightened of the people discovering a better way of life?'

Cora leaned back at the look he gave her and gulped down the fear. These people did as he bid, no matter what it meant for them or their children. She wondered then—if he ordered Teven to take her out into the trees and kill her, would he?

'She came to me,' Cora said.

'It is not your place. Rhali has healing ability.'

'So it seems,' Cora said softly, patting her leg.

'She did not do that.'

'No, but perhaps it wasn't as bad as she thought.'

'If I did not know what you were, I would have left you in the trees.'

'Was it your choice?' she asked. 'I thought Teven found me. I thought he brought me here.'

'I sent him out,' the man huffed. 'I am the chief. I have the vision.'

'Do you? What do you see?'

'You,' he sneered. 'I see exactly what you are. The greatest Oldra of them all, and you will give me that power.'

'It is not something I can give,' Cora said, climbing to her feet.

'You healed what you thought couldn't be healed. I have skill; I have power. You can make it stronger.'

'How?'

'Like you healed the child.'

'I healed the mother,' Cora said, and he looked confused for a moment. 'You only want power. You would rather see your people die than allow them to truly live, and that doesn't show power.' She took a step back towards the door. 'It shows weakness.'

'You know nothing,' he snapped, reaching for her, but she was too far away.

'It is why you want me here, because I know these things. I know what it is to be a leader. I understand the sacrifice and loss, the pain that comes with caring for people. But you don't understand any of that. You don't understand any of the members of your clan.'

'I am Chief. I saved them.'

'From a better life? From people who cared about them and how they survived? They live in the dark, in the shadows you have created.' Cora stopped. There was a power he had. Maybe her mother had not defeated all the darkness; maybe it had crept away to another part of the world. 'I can't be what you want me to be. I am not what you need me to be. And if I were, I wouldn't give it to you.'

'Then you will die in the shadows.'

Cora shook her head and raced from the small cavern. Others bowed as she passed through the centre of the main cavern, and she tried to show the same respect on the way back through. She no longer cared what this man wanted or what power he thought he had over her. She would find a way home. And in the meantime, she would get to know these people.

A man stood nervously by their hearth as she approached. He bowed his head to her before glancing back to the woman and child now sleeping on her sleeping mat.

'Please,' she said, indicating that he enter the space.

He bowed his head again and raced forward to look over the child. Teven and Rhali were both still absent. Cora wondered where they could disappear to so often, especially as no one else seemed to leave the cavern.

There was water boiling in a pot over the flames, and she pulled it off. She wasn't quite sure where anything was kept, nor whether it was really her place to invite someone in and make them tea.

The woman stretched and then looked at the man with surprise. After glancing around, she turned to Cora. 'Thank you,' she whispered.

'You need to ensure you drink more and eat well,' Cora repeated for the woman.

'Please,' she said, standing and taking the pot. The child remained asleep in her furs.

'What is his name?'

They looked at each other and then down.

Cora waited as the woman returned to making the tea. 'I am Cora of the Penna,' she said, tapping her chest.

'I am Jath and this is Eira,' he said. 'We have not named the child yet.'

'Are there rituals for naming?'

They shook their heads in unison. 'Once there was, but not now. We feared the child would not survive and so did not take the trouble.'

'He is strong,' Cora said. She wasn't sure that was true, but she was reminded of the child she had dreamt of. Maybe he would be strong one day, with care and nourishment.

Cora scooped him up into her arms and then took the offered cup of tea. She had invited these people in, and they were caring for her. When the child nestled into her arms, she felt a strength she hadn't felt in him the night before.

'Do you hunt?' she asked Jath.

He shook his head. 'There is little around for us. Teven will bring back meat if there is any to be found. He will go into the trees.'

Cora nodded acknowledgement. Teven did a lot for these people, even though he was so sure he was not worthy of them.

'When did you come here?' she asked.

'Our parents followed the chief. We were greater in number then.'

'Could you go back?'

He shook his head.

'What do you do with your time? There are furs and leather,' she prompted.

'It is from when they first arrived.'

Cora looked over her clothes.

'It was his mother's,' Eira whispered.

Again, Cora wondered why Teven was the man he was, who his relations were and what the connection was with his sister. He had inferred that they didn't share a mother, yet he hadn't mentioned his father. Cora looked up and across at the young man who had helped her.

'Is it so different from your clan?' Eira asked.

Cora nodded. The Penna embraced each other, supported each other. These people were almost afraid of interacting.

She looked again at the child in her arms, and the idea of the young boy came to mind. Was her dream related to the child?

'Where do you get water?' she asked.

'There is a stream near here.'

'Could you show me?

The man shook his head.

'I will return,' she said to reassure him. She wouldn't want them in further trouble for allowing her to leave.

'That is not what we fear,' he said softly, looking about. 'The few who have ventured far from the cavern have never returned. Other than Teven.'

Perhaps, Cora thought, they had taken the chance to go far away and start a new life. Maybe they were simply lost, or the chief had something to do with it.

'Why does he not like you to go out?'

'It took a lot for our people to come here. If we were discovered by the enemy, it would all be in vain.'

'What enemy?'

Jath shook his head.

'Teven does a lot for this clan,' Cora said.

They both looked down. 'We have not been very good to him, but he brings wood and water and what food he can.'

'Do you not bring in your own food?'

'There is some that grows nearby,' the woman answered. 'We will go sometimes with Rhali to find it, but we fear being found.'

'Has anyone been found?'

'Maybe those who didn't return.'

'Has there been fighting? Has anyone come?'

'Only you,' she said.

Cora sighed. 'My people fought for many generations with another clan. Selfishness started it; pride continued it. But it was seen, felt, heard by the whole people.'

'Do they still fight?'

Cora shook her head. 'The clans came together. We still live separately, but we visit often.'

The couple glanced at each other.

'You cannot continue in fear of what you don't know.'

'The chief knows,' Teven said behind her. 'He does what he can to keep us safe.'

She bowed her head to him. He placed two containers of water down on the mat. Long woven handles stretched above them and then flopped down beside them as he let them go. 'Take one for the child,' he said to the couple seated at his hearth, and they bowed to him.

The man took a container and waited as the woman took the child from Cora's arms. Then they disappeared into the dark. She looked after them wondering if she would get the chance to talk with them again. Teven remained standing at the fire and staring at her.

'I could help you get more,' she offered, and he surprised her with a nod.

She followed him towards the door and found a pile of closely woven baskets piled high. What else did this man do for these people?

As he collected several of them, she did the same and followed him out into the sunshine. She longed for the trees, but instead followed him around the cavern. Then she stopped, jogged back to where she had left her spear and lifted it up over her shoulder. She paused for a moment, sure that the shadows moved around her as they had before. They were just out of sight, yet she knew they were there.

She barely contained her shiver as she rushed back to where Teven waited. The stream was only a short walk from the cavern. Of those she had met, they could have easily travelled the distance. They were in the open as they walked, but the world was silent around them. Perhaps the people had experienced the shadows as well, or something very similar. She could understand why that would keep them inside, but was it the chief doing such things to keep them there?

She stood at the edge of the narrow stream as Teven filled the containers and lined them up along the bank. He didn't appear cold. The only running water Cora had ever seen was in the lake by the hunters' cavern, which was icy cold even when she was transitioned. She had only ever put her hand in it. But she had dreamt her mother's experience with the water that made her bones ache. Her father still shook his head at that story. He said she had constantly confused him, but that she was more confused than any when she realised she was standing in the lake.

'Can I touch it?' Cora asked, watching the clear water rush over the golden rocks.

He nodded. She stepped forward, squatted down and put her hand in the water. It was almost warm. She laughed as she splashed at it. She wished her mother were here to experience this.

Moving back to her spear, she looked over the containers and realised they had filled more than they could carry.

'We will do several trips,' Teven said.

Cora lifted the staff and placed it across her shoulders. 'You can load them onto this,' she said.

Nodding slowly, he carefully placed one on the end of the spear. She had to adjust to maintain it, and he moved quickly to level out the weight. She nodded. 'More.'

'You are sure?'

'I have had to carry far more in my training alone.'

'What did you train for?'

'To be a warrior. To fight.'

'Who do you fight?' he asked, putting another basket on the spear.

'No one anymore, but we still train. Our clan is built around strong warriors. We may not have an enemy, but we train all the same.'

'Women as well?' he asked, putting the fourth basket on.

She nodded and turned slowly towards the cavern. 'My mother was the strongest female Draga the Penna had seen in some time. If I am to be chief, I must have the same skill.'

'If you return,' he said behind her.

'Yes,' she murmured. 'If I return.'

He placed the baskets down at the front of the cavern and helped unload those she had. Then they headed back to pick up the rest. She carried the spear over her shoulder, but he put out a hand to stop her before they reached the water.

'Fish,' he murmured as he crept towards the water.

Cora followed, but she couldn't see what he was looking at.

As he stood looking into the water, she stepped back. Would she get the chance to go home, or was the chief correct? That she would stay until she was what he needed her to be and then he would take that away. She put her hand over her mark and turned to stare into the trees.

She had spent so much of her life resisting her mother, yet she wanted nothing more than for her mother to walk out of the trees right now.

'Don't fear,' her mother's voice whispered in her ear.

Cora breathed out slowly.

'What has happened?' Teven said, too close behind her.

She startled and swung around with her hands up, which found his chest. The sharp, burning pain coursed through her, taking her breath away. She cried out as she pulled back from him.

He stepped forward and she stepped back again, nearly tripping. He reached out and took her by the shoulders. She clenched her fists in front of her in case she accidently touched him again.

'I'm sorry,' she murmured.

'What did you see?'

She shook her head, still trying to catch her breath. He reached for her again, and she stepped back. 'How do you live with such pain?'

He looked confused, so she pointed to his chest.

He put his hand over the point the scar sat beneath his tunic. His face clouded in anger for a moment, but it passed quickly. 'It doesn't hurt. It is ugly, but it doesn't hurt.'

She nodded once and took a deep breath. 'We should get the water,' she said, pushing past him and back towards the stream. She lifted the spear back onto her shoulders and then turned, looking back towards him. 'I can't do this alone.'

He nodded once and helped her load the baskets. They moved in silence back to the cavern, where he unloaded the baskets and she noticed the other baskets were gone. She leaned the spear against the wall by other containers and headed back to the hearth, but Teven wasn't behind her when she turned. He didn't appear to be in the cavern anymore.

Cora sat on the mat before the fire and stared into the flames. Again, she was alone at the hearth and wondering where they'd gone. Was there more to this pair than she was aware of?

When she closed her eyes and thought of Teven, the same burning sensation filled her. Although not as intensely as it had when she'd put her hand on him. If he wasn't in pain, was it another type of pain? Emotional rather than physical? It seemed strange that she would pick that up. Perhaps it was his mother's pain. Causing such an injury to a child must have been devastating.

If she could teach him to transition, she might be able to work around it, find a way to heal him without feeling his pain. She put her hand over her mark. She had been so sure that she had heard her mother's voice by the stream. And yet she knew it couldn't be. Cora had burned quite brightly herself at one point, long before she was born. If she was to meet another Oldra as her father was sure of, she would burn again. Was there a connection with Teven?

14

Cora walked out into the morning sunshine. The hearth had been empty again when she woke, and although the people of the cavern were nodding in her direction, very few of them were talking to her. Other than a few names, she knew no one and had no real idea of who these people were or what they were hiding from.

She stretched in the sunshine and pointed her face towards it, closing her eyes. She still couldn't quite get used to the warm sun on her face, but she loved it. As the days slowly passed, she missed the snow less and less, but she still often headed into the cool woods to transition.

The chief had not called her back, nor had he reappeared in her dreams since she had so forcefully denied that she was what he needed her to be. Cora continued to wonder just what she might be and how he might take that from her.

She had dreamt of Teven. The burning pain in his chest seemed to follow her around, and she found it hard to breathe when he was close, even in her dream. It wasn't a feeling either of her parents had relayed to her. And despite the clear connection between them, she knew it was not what her parents had.

It was a relief to find him gone when she woke. But if she could find a way for him to transition, she might be better able to understand him. She stopped at a tree not too far within the wood where she could still see the sunshine. The transition was easier in the cool shade. Closing her eyes, she tried to remember Darring. He looked more like her mother than any other member of the Penna, yet he was so clearly one of them.

Human was the word her mother had used. But she was Penna now, no matter where she had come from. Cora ran her hand over her own nose, lower than that of the others and a little rounder, as were her ears. She tried not to sigh. Deen had similar features.

If she ever managed to find a mate, her children might be similar. Her father's gentle smile came to mind. He loved Gerry so completely. And he would give Cora that very smile when she raised any concerns for her future. Like he knew what the future held for her better than her mother could.

She didn't feel that way when she looked at Deen. She wanted to—she wanted desperately to feel more than she did, partly to prove her father wrong. That she didn't need another Oldra to be happy. And she missed Deen now, his quiet confidence and mindless chatter.

The cavern here is far too quiet, she thought as she looked back towards it.

Cora took a step closer to the cavern, wondering what might be on the other side. She had headed out into the woods directly from the opening. She had sat on top of it and looked out across the trees on all sides, but was that all there was? What did these people fear so much that kept them locked away while two young people cared for their needs?

Cora walked quickly around the cavern and thought of Rhali. The girl disappeared all the time. No one questioned where she might go or why she would leave the cavern when no one else did. But she never returned with anything. Not with food, or wood, or water, that Cora had noticed. She wasn't helping her brother, although he had done so much to help her.

Cora rounded the hill that was the cavern and wondered for the first time whether these people had built it. Someone must have built the cavern she lived in with her family—or had it always been there? She shook the idea away and noted that the soft green grass covered the entire structure. There was no way to climb up from this side. It was too steep, with no steps or paths cut into the grass.

She looked up for a moment, wondering if Rhali simply lay in the sun all day. Looking back into the dark trees, she headed forward, then stopped briefly to check her tracks. She wasn't leaving any marks that she could see in the dirt and leaflitter, but it was different from snow. She might not have the skills she thought she did.

Walking as straight as she could through the trees, Cora hoped she could find her way back. When she saw movement in the trees, she slowed her walk.

She half expected another dragon, but there was only Rhali standing in the trees. As Cora drew closer, she realised Rhali was talking with someone else, someone with his arms around her.

Cora froze. Perhaps they weren't brother and sister after all. A disappointment washed over her, although she wasn't sure why she would be disappointed. Then the other person moved, and Cora saw it wasn't Teven. He was human, like her mother; tall and broad, like Darring.

He took Rhali's face in his hands and bent down to kiss her lips, and then he was disappearing back through the trees. How had he come to be here? She moved quickly through the trees to remain out of sight as she headed towards Rhali. Then she stopped and looked back after the man.

Cora thought to call out after Rhali when she turned and headed in another direction. Not back to the cavern. Cora wondered what else this girl might be up to. She waited a moment longer, her back to the tree. Did Teven know of the man? Or what his sister did of a day? Did he understand what this might mean?

Cora was torn between following Rhali or the man. After too long, she decided to follow him rather than Rhali. Maybe he had only just arrived; maybe he was alone in the world. As she tried to follow the direction he had gone, she considered whether he might belong to the people the clan was scared of. But if they were this close, they would attack, or at least try to do more than ignore each other's presence.

Cora walked for a long time, but she saw no further sign of the man or any people he might be with. He had been dressed in leather clothing similar to Teven's. She wondered if he had found the clothes or been given them by Rhali.

Cora was starting to think that she had imagined the whole episode when she caught sight of a man in the trees. And then, just as quickly, he was gone again.

She took a deep breath and transitioned in case there was a danger to her, hoping she was following the path he had taken. There were no signs in the dust that he had come this way, but she wasn't sure if he was able to cover his tracks or she wasn't able to read them as well outside of the snow.

She stopped intermittently to listen, but there wasn't a sound. Again, she thought she might have actually imagined the whole situation when the trees opened up before her and the sun shone brightly.

She was above the trees. Raising her hand to shield her face from the sun, she smiled into the light. She was standing on top of a ledge, a very high ledge, which reminded her of the training ground she had found. It was higher than being up on the cavern, and the trees spread out before her, bright and green. With so many different greens all blended together, she wondered if they were different types of trees. She closed her eyes and tried to remember the Essawood. There were different types of plants, but the trees were all the same.

She looked down again. She could see so far, and amongst it all was silence. Not the sound of a bird or cry of an animal. Not even the wind in the leaves. The wind always seemed to clatter branches to some degree in her own world. Cora wondered again if she had come to a new world—not just a different part of her own, but one like her mother had come from. That might explain the human.

A branch snapped behind her, and she turned to find Teven quickly closing the gap between them. 'No one comes here.' His voice was gruff, although there was a hint of something else. Fear perhaps.

Beyond him, in the shadows of the trees, Cora was sure she saw the chief. Teven continued towards her, and she could feel the heat of his pain. She stepped back, her hands up. His angry features turned to concern as he slowed his step, but she backed up once more, and then she was falling.

She'd had only long enough to realise she was falling when she stopped with a thud. Teven's worried face appeared over the edge of the cliff top. Cora climbed slowly to her feet and brushed herself off. She had jarred herself, but she hadn't fallen far enough to do any damage.

'Don't move,' Teven called.

She turned slowly and looked out over the same view. Thankfully, she had fallen onto a narrow ledge below the main one. She could have been less lucky. She leaned over a little and was surprised by the sheer drop and darkness beneath her.

'I said, don't move,' Teven growled. She looked back up at him holding a woven rope down to her.

She tried not to sigh as she tied the rope around her waist and worked with him to climb back up. He had to lean over the edge of the world to pull her up the final part, and he groaned as she landed on the firm soil.

'I'm not that heavy,' she murmured as she lay down, her feet still over the edge and her focus on the bright sky above. It wasn't just bright; it was pale blue and clear of clouds.

He sighed, and she turned to see him holding his arm.

She sat up quickly, but he waved her off. 'It is just a scratch.'

'I don't think so,' she said as the blood seeped through his fingers. 'Let me look.'

He pulled the short tunic he wore up over his head, groaning again as it lifted over his arm. The blood flowed quickly, and she leant forward to press her hand over it. He sucked in a breath, and she closed her eyes. The tear was rougher than she had expected. She could see a small part of the rock that had cut into him still in the wound.

She lifted her hand away and peered into it. 'This is going to hurt,' she said, then quickly pushed her fingers into the wound. She felt around and pulled the small stone out.

'Is this how you fixed your leg?' he asked, his face growing paler.

She shook her head and pressed her hand over the wound again. Closing her eyes, Cora willed it closed. The muscle moved back into place and the skin healed over.

'That is cold,' Teven said.

Cora nodded and removed her hand, then held it up against his skin. Was that the blood she had seen in her vision with the chief? She hadn't felt any of the desperation her mother had felt while trying to hold her father together. And there was still no mark.

Teven put his hand over his arm and looked at it closely. 'How?'

She shrugged then, tempted to lie back down. Wiping the blood from her hand across the grass, she wondered whether her mother tired so much when she healed.

'Cora?'

She looked up at him, and he tapped his chest. The mark looked less ugly today, yet without getting close she was sure she could still sense the pain.

She shook her head. 'You don't need…'

'What did you see when you touched me?'

'Nothing.'

'Yet you cried out—was it so bad?'

'I couldn't see anything. I felt the pain of the scar, I think. It was sharp and hot, and it burned right through me. I can still feel it burning.'

'You thought you could see something at the birth. You were sure the child was a girl.'

'But I was wrong,' she said, climbing to her feet and brushing at her clothes. The twigs and debris remained firmly attached, and she managed to smear some blood over her tunic. 'I saw her past. I can only see the past.'

'What of your own?'

She shook her head and turned back towards the trees. 'Where did the rope come from?'

'I keep some supplies in different places, just in case someone goes over.'

Cora turned back to look out over the view. 'There is a whole world out there that we don't know.'

Teven pulled his tunic back over his head and then looked at the slice on the sleeve. 'Why did you come this way?'

'I thought I saw someone,' she said.

He watched her for too long before he spoke. 'First dragons and now more people,' he said with a slight grin and a shake of his head.

Cora turned back for the trees. She knew there were dragons, and therefore there must be other people. But were they friendly, or were they the enemy the people believed them to be?

15

The following morning, Cora gulped her breakfast down quickly. Before she could even suggest heading out, Teven shook his head. 'No,' he said sternly.

'I haven't asked a question,' Cora moaned.

'Let me repeat it,' the chief said behind her, and she turned slowly.

'Why?' she asked.

'Did you give your father such grief?'

'You would know,' she said, looking into her empty bowl. She felt a stab of homesickness at the thought that her father would have been the first to join her in exploring the new world.

'You may go out, but only to where you have been before,' the chief said sharply before he disappeared back into the shadows. Cora wondered again how it could be so dark all the time.

'I've been there before,' she whispered, giving Teven a cheeky grin, and he almost growled. 'Where is Rhali?' She asked it mostly just to bait him, but she wondered if he really did have any idea where Rhali went of a day.

He looked towards the fire, ignoring her. She held her hand out for his bowl, but he shook his head.

'It is my turn,' she said.

'You are a guest.'

'Is that what I am?' Cora asked slowly as he glowered at her. 'Fine,' she said, handing the bowl over.

He took it, and she stood slowly as he focused on the task of cleaning. He barely glanced up, and she took a slow step backwards. There were dragons and people, and if she had any connection to them, she was going to find them. Cora might not be what her mother thought she was, but she would find a way out of this.

She took another step back and then turned. She was partway around the cavern before she heard him calling after her, and she took off at the fastest run she had. She could barely make out the trees around her. Although she looked, she couldn't see Rhali.

Her heart pounded as she made her way through the trees. Struggling to maintain her too fast pace, she could hear Teven running behind her. His heavy footfalls and his determined call.

She didn't slow as she burst out through the trees. It was further than she remembered, and her lungs were burning. The sun was almost blinding and Teven's call more desperate behind her as she raced straight for the cliff. Her foot found the edge, and she pushed off into nothing.

'Whoohoo,' she called like a madwoman on the way down. 'Anytime,' she added. And then her arms closed around a dragon's neck, and she shot straight back up into the air.

As she passed Teven standing on the edge of the cliff, his arms hanging by his sides and his mouth open, she waved. 'Over the trees,' she whispered to the dragon. It turned and glided over the trees she had looked over. They seemed to stretch on forever, and the ground was dark and unknown beneath them. 'Are there more people out here?'

You should return to Teven, a voice hummed in her mind. It was younger, not as deep as Dra. She ran her hand over the soft leathery skin. They were so alike and yet so different.

'Are you alone?' she asked.

Don't be sad, the voice hummed. *We are enough.*

'Do you have a name?'

You have so many questions, Oldra, but I think you could find it.

Find it? Where would she find the name of a dragon? They landed softly before Teven, and his surprised look had been replaced with an angry one. As Cora slipped down to the ground, she was reminded just how much smaller this dragon was than the ones she knew. Perhaps it was young.

Teven grabbed her arm and pulled her away. 'What are you doing?' he snapped, his hold tight.

She pulled her arm from his and moved back towards the dragon. 'You knew.'

He shook his head as the dragon rubbed her nose along Cora's arm.

He is lost. Be kind.

Cora turned to the dragon and ran a hand over the soft leathery skin, feeling the difference from the scales of the dragons she knew. She listened to the sounds the dragon made, checked over her fine wings and long tail as she tried to ignore the man still watching her too closely.

'Do you know her name?' she asked.

When there was no answer, she turned back to Teven. Sighing, he shook his head. The dragon sat down, curled partly around Cora and folded back its wings. Cora leaned into the dragon and sighed. She missed Dra. She missed all the dragons, and she realised it had been so silent in her head without them. She rested her face against the dragon, again noting how different it felt, but it sounded just the same. She had sat with so many dragons in her time, only they glistened with scales.

'I wish you could come out of the shadows, Serassa,' she whispered, patting across her leathery skin. She could feel the dragon's strong heart beating within her chest. The warmth and comfort radiated from her as Cora closed her eyes.

'Serassa?' Teven questioned.

She nodded and motioned him forward. 'You know them,' she said softly as he moved hesitantly. When he was close enough, she pulled him to sit beside her.

'How do you know her?'

'I know all dragons, in a way. It is part of the Oldra skill.'

There is more that you can do. You will find your way, Cora, Greatest Oldra of them all.

'Don't say that,' Cora murmured. 'Wyndha was the greatest, Mama is the strongest. I have only just worked out my healing skills and…' She stopped.

He cannot take what you will not give.

'What is he exactly?'

Not what he looks like.

She sighed and leaned back.

Let her heal you. Let her reveal who you are.

'I can't,' Teven whispered.

I will keep you safe.

Teven looked at Cora and slowly shook his head.

Cora looked him over. He might be Oldra as well, or he might simply be a warrior. All warriors could talk to their dragons, if not all dragons.

'Have you met before?' she asked.

'I have seen several dragons in the trees,' he whispered.

'Can you hear them all, or just this one?'

'I'm not what you think,' he said, looking out beyond the cliff.

Cora followed his gaze. She was still mesmerised by the differences between this world and hers, yet she was sure they were the same. Serassa nudged her, and she reached around to pat her without taking her eyes from the sky. 'You don't know what I think you are,' she said to Teven.

'You think I might be like you.'

'You might be more like the men of my clan. Each of them connects to a single dragon.'

'Everyone?' he asked.

She nodded as she leaned back into Serassa. This was the most comfortable she had felt since arriving here. She had thought it might be a way for her to leave, but she understood in meeting Serassa that she wouldn't be able to. Not until she became what she needed to be.

'Don't be afraid,' her mother's voice whispered in her ear. But for the first time, Cora wasn't afraid. She knew she was where she was meant to be, and that her mother knew it too.

'Do you know what skill I have?' Cora asked the sky.

The dragon chuckled inside her head.

'So I must find it on my own.'

'She didn't say anything,' Teven said.

'But I have heard that laugh before. Ariandi has a similar way of letting you find out for yourself what others already know.'

'Does the chief know?'

Cora nodded. 'Merik knows exactly what I am, but he also thinks he can take that for himself.'

She stood and walked towards the edge of the cliff, flinching as Teven closed his hand around her arm.

'I don't want you to fall.'

'Who is down there? Who is the man Rhali meets with?'

Teven released his grip and moved back.

'Can I get down there?' Cora asked. She heard the rustle of wings as the dragon got to her feet.

'It isn't safe. We can't leave the cavern.'

She turned back to him with frustration. 'We've already left the cavern. You leave it every day.' What else was he trying to hide from her?

He shook his head.

'Serassa, would you mind?'

The dragon bowed her head. *There is a path,* she said with a flick of her head. Then she lifted into the air and disappeared.

'How did you know her name?' Teven asked as Cora headed in the direction the dragon had indicated.

'I felt it,' she murmured. The path dropped suddenly, and she hugged the wall as it went down below the cliff line. She could see the sheer drop on one side. Although she wanted to see what was down amongst the other trees, she didn't want to fall all the way. She wasn't confident Serassa would sweep in to save her again.

'This is a bad idea,' Teven murmured behind her.

'And yet here we go.'

It took some time to reach the base of the cliff. Cora looked back up from the shadow of the trees, wondering if he was right and this wasn't a good idea. She had nothing with her, no bow, no spear, no idea what these people might think of her when she appeared amongst them. If she could find them.

She looked amongst the trees for signs of a path or track, but there was nothing. Teven took the lead, appearing to know the direction to take, but he moved slowly.

'I don't think this is a good idea,' he murmured as they made their way into the trees. They had a slightly different feel down here, a little cooler as less sun penetrated the canopy. Cora looked up as they walked and realised just how dense the foliage was above her. She wondered what her own trees would be like when she returned; they would look so bare compared to these that she wasn't sure she would want to be out amongst them.

Teven stopped and looked about. She wasn't sure if he was looking for a way through the trees or for someone. As she opened her mouth to ask a question, he held up his hand. She couldn't hear anything, and then she could. Like when she hunted with her father, she got a sense of something moving closer. She stepped towards Teven.

In some way, Cora expected the shadows to shift about her as they did at times in her mother's dreams—as they had when she had wandered from the cavern in the other direction. Cora sucked in a breath. Was that the shadow of the chief amongst the trees? She took a slow step forward and was halted by Teven's strong hold around her arm.

'You were told not to come here,' an older voice said from the shadows, but it wasn't the chief. 'And you know not to bring others.'

'She is different,' Teven said.

Cora tensed as she heard the arrow pulled back, drawing across the bow.

'Not enough,' the voice continued. Cora squeezed her eyes closed against the arrow she knew was coming, but she couldn't tell from where.

Then Teven was groaning as he pushed back against her. She couldn't hold his weight. He had stepped between her and the arrow, and he lay at her feet.

'No,' she cried as she dropped to her knees. The arrow had struck the centre of his chest, and it was only luck that it had missed his heart.

Someone swore in the dark, and then someone else was dragging her back as she tried to place her hands on him.

'I can heal him,' she said, surprising herself with how much she sounded like her mother. She wondered if she really could do for him as she had done for herself.

'No one can heal that,' a younger man beside her said, still tugging at her arm, but Teven had gripped her wrist. Despite his failing life and the other man's determination, he maintained the hold.

'Bring them both,' the older man sighed.

Teven grunted as more men appeared from the trees, bows slung over their shoulders. Cora was thankful that they hadn't all released their arrows at her, or neither of them would have survived.

The cavern they entered was unseen amongst the trees until they were through the heavy leather curtain. Then the lights showed her a different world. There was a small entrance, as there was with the cavern of the Penna, although no crystal trees. Cora wondered if it was because of the snow, or lack of it, that they were so alike yet so different.

The number of men surrounding them surprised her, and she understood her mother's fear of the shadows. She just needed to shine a light on them, she told herself.

They moved through another curtain and into a cavern much larger than the Penna one. It was bright, and she breathed in the familiarity. As they pushed her along and half carried, half dragged Teven, they continued to the centre of the cavern, where she noticed another doorway. The hearths were more similar to those of the Penna than the cavern she had been staying in, and it appeared that every member of the clan was standing and watching them enter.

The group paused at a doorway to the next space with only a look between the men before they entered. Those who had carried Teven laid him down in the centre of the space by the fire, then disappeared. The man at Cora's side and the older man were the only ones to remain with them.

The cavern they had entered was smaller, but still larger than she'd expected. It had a high ceiling, with more little suns like her own world. Cora focused on the older woman in red robes, with a long grey braid that travelled down the centre of her spine to the back of her knees.

Cora dropped down beside Teven. 'Ancient, please allow me to save him.'

'You can heal such a wound?' the woman asked.

Cora nodded as she looked back to the woman's kind face, which reminded her of Arminel. She smiled and nodded once.

'Henda, you cannot allow this woman to...'

'Can't I?' she asked.

Cora was reminded of her mother asking a question they all knew the answer to.

The man bowed and backed up.

'Would you rather he die?' Henda asked the man.

'You can save him.'

'I could not before,' she said, her voice sad. Cora looked up at Henda as the woman looked down on Teven. Then she nodded to Cora.

Cora rushed forward and, without hesitation, pulled the arrow from his chest. Blood rushed from the wound, and she pressed her hands over it. There was no movement and very little breath from Teven. She hoped it wasn't too late. She tried to calm the too-fast beating of her heart and the panic that threatened to overwhelm her.

Cora closed her eyes and breathed slowly as she looked deep inside Teven. The blood slowed and the damage to the bone repaired as she watched, the muscles around it closing over. She sat back slowly and wiped a bloody hand over her brow, willing herself not to cry and hoping she wasn't too late.

Teven remained still, his breathing slow. Cora started to chew on her lip.

'Get the girl some hot water,' the ancient snapped, and the younger of the men ran out through the hide. 'You have not finished,' she said.

Cora looked at Teven and then shook her head. 'Can you help me?'

His clothes were intact but covered in blood. She had worked over the remains of the material to heal the hole in his chest. The man reluctantly assisted in pulling his tunic away as the other man returned with hot water.

Cora took the cloth from his hand, then wet it and ran it over Teven's chest. There wasn't a mark. Not even a scratch. Only the burn over his heart. She moved her fingers over it and then clenched them into a fist.

'He doesn't want me to,' she whispered.

'It is time,' the old woman said, squatting down opposite Cora. 'I tried when I could, but there was so much fear.'

Cora nodded. The sharp pain she had felt was his mother's fear. But was it fear at what she had done, or was it the reason she had burnt him?

'It hurts,' Cora whispered. Although she realised then that the hole in his chest hadn't hurt her. She sucked in a deep breath and placed her hand over the scar. She groaned as the pain burned into her. Before she could pull away, the old woman had placed her hand over Cora's.

'So much strength,' she murmured. 'You know this is what you must do.'

Cora closed her eyes, trying desperately to ignore the pain as she looked into the skin. There was only scar tissue. He had lived with this his whole life; it may never return to what it was. She thought of Larek and the scar he carried in his heart from when his mate died.

When Cora looked up, the woman smiled at her and nodded once. Cora tried to look for the emotional scar Teven carried, although in many ways it was his mother's scar and not his. She had done this to her child. To her baby. There must have been a reason. There must have been something behind the action Cora was yet to learn.

Serassa had asked Teven to let Cora show what he was. Was he Draga or their equivalent? Or was he Oldra?

As she closed her eyes, she thought only of Teven. What he did for the cavern, the silent respect the people paid him. She could see him walking confidently through the trees, smiling at her—or was it someone else? He was a chief, a leader, and yet he allowed what he did to occur in the cavern.

Was he protecting them by staying by their side? These people knew him. They knew what he was and where he was from, and yet they didn't want him there. Was he an outcast? Was he trapped in the little dark cavern rather than there by choice?

'He can't answer your questions. Even if he wanted to.' The older woman appeared beside Cora in her mind.

'How can I heal him?'

'You have,' she whispered. Cora opened her eyes to see the old woman now sitting beside Teven.

Cora was too scared to look. But there, as in the chief's vision, was the mark of Oldra on Teven's chest where the scar had been.

The tears surprised Cora. She was stronger than she had realised. She had managed to save him, and he was far more than she had thought, although exactly what she had suspected.

'Henda,' the man said softly. Cora turned to look up at him. 'They must go.'

'When he wakes,' Cora said.

'It may take longer than either of you would like,' Henda said. 'You have an interesting skill,' she said, taking Cora's hand.

'I don't understand what I did.'

'It is not what you thought you were, or what you thought you had. But your mother is correct; you are stronger than you know.'

'So Merik believes.'

The old woman grunted. 'He wants it.'

'I don't know what he wants, but he seems to think I can give it to him.'

'Then why go back there?' the man asked.

'Because you don't want us here, and Teven would rather watch over his sister and the others.'

The man looked at the ground. 'I'll tell the chief,' he murmured, then disappeared.

Cora tensed at the idea, and the old woman gently squeezed her hand.

'Our chief is not like Merik.'

'What will happen?'

'I don't know,' she said honestly. 'But you will need to rest. Come have some tea with me, and then you can sleep.'

'The chief…'

'He will not rush to see you. He will come in his own time.'

Cora opened her mouth to ask the first of many questions, but Henda held up a hand and, although smiling, shook her head. 'There will be time to tell you what you want to know. Rest.'

16

Cora knew the woman squatting in the dark, giving birth alone, was Teven's mother. There was a similarity between them in their looks, and something in the way she held herself. There was also fear. Cora could taste it. The woman bit down on her lip, trying to be quiet, and Cora recognised the trees by the cliff top. She thought she sensed a dragon nearby, but she could see no one else.

She glanced about for a sign of Merik, but he wasn't peering at her from the shadows as he had done in so many other dreams. Maybe he knew enough of this one already.

The woman grunted, and a baby's cry echoed through the trees. More dragons watched from the shadows, their golden eyes glowing in the dim light. Cora wondered if the woman knew that they were there. She tried making her way down the cliff to the other clan, but they blocked her.

'Please save him,' she begged. The desperation was more than Cora could bear; she could feel the woman's heart breaking. She was weak and tired, and she headed back up the steep climb to the other clan and Merik. The higher she went, the more exhausted she became and the more the fear overwhelmed her. All the while, she held the baby tight in her arms. Too tight.

At the top of the cliff, she met a dragon—not leathery like the ones Cora had met here, but brilliant green and glistening as though made of the snow Cora had left behind. The beast nodded to the woman, who put the child down before it. The dragon nuzzled the child, but when she raised her eyes, the woman shook her head.

The woman sat beside the dragon. With something small in her hand, she caused a spark that jumped to the small pile of sticks beside her. They sat for a time, the baby back in her arms and the dragon watching over them, the small fire burning brightly.

Then, without expression, the woman leaned forward and picked up a branch from the fire before dropping it again. 'He can't take him,' she said, a strength Cora hadn't expected in her voice. 'He can't have what he wants from my son.'

The blade surprised her, glinting in the firelight as she carved quickly at the baby's chest. He screamed out in pain. The dragon tried to nuzzle her out of the way, but she maintained a tight hold on him. When they were both covered in blood, she reached back for the fire, sealing the wound closed with the heat of the flames. The baby screamed once more and then was silent.

'Watch over him,' the woman whispered to the dragon, and Cora wondered if she too was able to communicate with them. Then she was gone, falling over the cliff. She didn't scream, didn't call for help, and for a moment Cora waited for a dragon to save her as Serassa had done for Cora. But no such rescue came, only the sickening thud as she hit the ground so far below.

When Cora turned back, the dragon was gone and the baby lay silent by the fire. A younger man rushed forward. Merik. He seemed worried for a moment, as though looking for someone, but then he was cradling the child in his arms and rushing back to the cavern.

He was Merik's son, but Cora doubted he planned for Teven to take over as Chief when he was gone.

'It is a regret that he was not taken in, that we did not save them both,' Henda said softly as Cora blinked into the dim light of the cavern.

'Is he awake?'

Henda shook her head.

'Does he know what she did?'

'In some ways, but not really. Another woman raised him. Although Merik knew who he was, he would not accept the boy with the scar. He had thought he would be something else.'

'And so he hid what he had.'

'You knew.'

'I sensed the dragons. I knew in some way that he did too. Everyone else was too scared to leave, but not Teven. He knew they would not hurt him.'

Henda nodded. 'Although there is one dragon who will not see him.'

'She protected him, in a way.'

'But not enough. I can see the many questions on your face. Shall we start with more about the dragons, or is it someone else you wish to know of?'

'The human,' she said quickly. 'I saw a human man with Rhali. My mother is human.'

Henda smiled knowingly, and Cora wondered how the Ancients knew all that they did.

'Although she is not anymore. She is Penna. But she came from somewhere far away, as did Darring,' Cora said.

Henda nodded slowly. 'He is keen to explore, and he is not keen to give up the girl.'

'She is also Merik's daughter.'

'Our chief does not want his brother's children here. He fears they may be what their father is.'

'Brothers can be very different. But they can also work together.'

'Do your brothers work together?'

'Rarely,' Cora admitted. 'They have such a different view of the world. But my father is sure they will be what they need to be for the Penna.'

'Yet you will be Chief,' Henda said.

'If I return.'

The woman laughed. As she put a finger to her lips, Cora realised Teven was awake and watching them both.

'Why is that funny?' he asked softly.

'For a girl determined to fight her way through life, she has discovered that she has more choices than she knew.'

'Does it come from being more than I thought? I didn't think I had the skill they were so determined I had.'

Henda shook her head.

'Will he take it?' Cora asked.

'You haven't determined what it is yet, and it may not be something that he wants.'

'He is sure that it is. It is why he has looked for me all these years, why he thinks I came to him.'

'You are a healer like your mother,' Teven said, struggling to sit up. The blanket exposed his chest, and he put a hand to the spot where the arrow had hit.

'She is very different from her mother.' Henda announced.

'Am I?' Cora asked, watching Teven closely. He looked down at his chest to see what damage had been done, and then he saw the mark.

Anger flashed across his face. 'What have you done?'

Cora looked down at her hands. She wasn't really sure what she had done to make the mark appear on his chest, but the feeling she'd had when he'd dropped at her feet was similar to what her mother had felt when she'd thought Pira was going to die. Teven might not want her here, yet she had a connection with this man she could not ignore.

'It was all I had of her,' he stammered, his fingers digging into the skin.

Cora tried not to focus on the well-formed muscles beneath it.

'You have her eyes,' she murmured.

He looked at her with surprise, and she chewed her lip again as she studied her hands. 'If this is what it does,' she whispered, 'he can take it.'

'Don't say that,' Teven snapped, and she looked up.

'I don't feel well,' she said, looking at the Ancient as dizziness and nausea threatened to overwhelm her.

Henda reached out a hand and put it to Cora's head, then rested it on her chest. She murmured something under her breath, but Cora couldn't pick up what it was. She helped Cora to lie back down and covered her with the furs, running her hand over her head. 'You took on too much,' she whispered.

A sharp pain started in her chest, and she put her hand over her mark. She pulled quickly at the material to check that it was still there. It felt like she was losing herself in the pain baby Teven must have felt. And in the fear of what Merik would do to his mother. That she felt the only option was to leave her baby with a dragon and die... Cora sucked in a sob at the loss of the child, the loss of all hope.

'It is her pain,' Henda whispered, her hand still on Cora's hair. 'Poor child,' she murmured. 'This is no gift.'

'What is it?' Teven asked. She was sure he sounded closer. 'Is she sick?'

'In a way,' Henda said. 'She has taken all your pain, all your mother's pain at the damage she caused, and she is holding it in her heart so that you don't have to.'

'I didn't ask her to.'

'Essara,' Cora whispered.

'Oh child,' Henda said. 'We are far from the snow.'

17

'Arminel,' Cora called, having dreamt of him searching for her again. 'I'm right here,' she added in a whisper. But as she focused on the space around her, it took her a moment to remember where here was.

The pain in her chest had stopped, along with the throbbing in her mind. But she was stiff and uncomfortable and trapped. A strong, heavy arm was draped across her, and a heavy leg pinned down her own. She pushed back. With a groan, he rolled away from her, and she was on her feet.

He had survived the night. He didn't look any different from any other morning she had watched him sleep. When he wasn't already out and gone. Her chest ached at the thought of him. He had been angry at what she had done, but she couldn't let him die. Henda was sure that she could heal more. She put her hand to the mark again, then stepped forward at the clear call of a dragon.

She pushed the curtain back and walked into the early morning light of the cavern. 'Dragons,' she whispered, looking at the sheer number of them—at least one at every hearth. She sighed with relief. As she made her way to the centre of the cavern, they all bowed their heads to her.

'What are you doing?' a man asked, walking quickly towards her.

'I was called,' she said, clenching her hands at her sides. She was so excited she wanted to throw her arms around each and every one of them.

You must stay with the Ancient until the chief is ready for you. Then we will take the time to meet, an older female voice resonated through her body.

Cora nodded once and turned back towards the Ancient cavern.

'You look very happy,' Henda said, waving her forward. With a cup in one hand, she indicated a space by the fire with another.

'So many dragons,' Cora sighed. It was like she could breathe again.

'And are they like your dragons?' Henda asked as she handed Cora the cup.

Cora took a moment to sip at the hot tea before she nodded and then shook her head. 'They look the same, only shades of green. Our dragons are blues, whites and silver.'

'The snow,' Henda said with a nod.

'Who is Essara?' Teven asked, sitting cautiously beside her. She knew he was healed, but he moved slowly.

'Do you still hurt?' Cora stretched out a hand towards him, but she withdrew it quickly when he leaned back.

'Essara,' he said again.

'The snow,' she said, looking at Henda instead of him. 'She watches over us. And when we die, she holds us in her arms.'

'Why would you call for her?' he asked.

She shrugged and sipped at the cup.

'Last night...'

'Enough,' Henda interrupted. 'The girl was in pain. She had no idea whom she called for in the night. Did Arminel answer?' she asked, turning back to Cora.

Cora had to smile at the question. 'The question should be: did he hear me answer? He called to me all night, but still hasn't found me.'

'Is he your mate?' Henda asked. Teven looked up sharply, his face colouring a little.

'He is the Ancient of my clan,' Cora said without looking at Teven.

'I thought your mother...'

'She works with him. She will be Ancient one day, but she has too much to do first.' Cora looked back towards the main cavern. She hadn't seen the man who might have looked like her mother, but then she hadn't really focused on anyone. It was the dragons who had held her attention.

'I have not seen as well as I thought,' Henda murmured.

'What would you like to see?' Cora asked.

'You have not been willing to let others into your mind in the past.'

'I thought they expected more of me than I could give. You may be able to help me find what I couldn't before.'

'Would you want this gift?'

Cora shook her head. 'It is mine already. Essara gave it to me for a reason, and I must work with it despite the pain.'

'Did it hurt that much?' Teven voice sounded concerned, but she couldn't look at him or answer.

'You might be a great Ancient of your own one day.'

Cora shook her head. 'My place is as Chief,' she said softly.

'You weren't so sure you would return last night,' Henda said.

'Will you be Chief of your people, or do you want to be Chief of mine?' a deep voice asked behind her. She cringed before climbing slowly to her feet and bowing her head. He sounded very much like Merik, yet, he looked very different when she faced him.

He was wiry and tall. His moppy dark hair was greying around the edges, and his face was friendly despite his words. He reminded Cora of her father, and she instantly liked him.

'You have met my brother,' he said.

She nodded once.

He sighed and looked at Teven. Then he stepped forward, reached for Teven and pulled at his tunic. 'Henda, did you heal this man?'

'No, it was the girl.'

He pulled the tunic open further to reveal the mark and sighed. 'Your mother tried so hard to protect you.'

'Are you Oldra?' Cora asked.

He released his hold on Teven and turned slowly to face her.

'You are. You have already tried to introduce yourself to our dragons.'

'She called to me,' Cora said.

'You did not answer my question.'

'My father is Chief of the Penna, as is my mother,' she added. 'It is my place to be Chief when they are gone.'

'Both parents?' he asked, his voice slow and deliberate.

She nodded.

'Both Oldra?'

She nodded again.

'Do you have siblings?'

'Two younger brothers—and no, they are not Oldra.'

He smiled then. 'You will learn that not all who lead are Oldra.'

'I know another chief who is not.'

He cocked his head to the side. Her people and their allies were far away from this man, although she didn't think he was a threat to them. 'Sarn, Chief of the Keetar, is not Oldra.'

'But he is a warrior.'

'As we all are.'

He smiled again. 'Your father must be a wise man, to have taught you so well. Did you get these skills from him?'

'My mother is a healer and a seer.'

'What can she see?'

'The future, and inside my mind if I allow it.'

'You do not like such intrusions.'

'Not usually. I see enough of others.'

'Do you see your future?' he asked, indicating that she sit back down on the woven mat by the fire.

'I see the past.'

'The past?' he asked as he sat beside her.

'I grew up dreaming of my mother's life. Her adventures, her fears. Only hers. Since I have come here…' She held out her hand, searching for a name she didn't have. 'Since I have come to the land with no snow, I have discovered others.'

'Other pasts? Or others' pasts?'

She smiled at him but glanced at Henda, who nodded.

'When I first arrived, a young woman was giving birth. My mother would be able to see the child before he was born. She would know if he would survive the birth and if he would grow to be a good man. I saw a hard birth and a female child grow in love. It was not the child, but the mother's life I saw.'

He nodded for her to continue. She chewed at her lip, glancing quickly at Teven. 'Last night I dreamt of Teven's mother. Her fear and what it drove her to do.'

'It was not what her life should have been,' he said softly. 'You must return to Merik.'

Cora bowed her head to him.

'Could they not stay longer?' Henda asked.

'I fear they will visit more than they should.'

'We were not made to feel welcome,' Cora said.

'He keeps to himself and leaves us in peace,' he said, turning for the door. 'I won't risk that.'

'Thank you for your kindness,' she said to his back, and he stopped by the curtain.

'She will see you in the trees before you leave.'

'Thank you,' she said again as he disappeared into the cavern.

Cora turned to Henda and bowed her head in thanks before she climbed to her feet. They knew far more about Merik than they had told her. 'Do you know what skill Merik has?' she asked quickly.

'Not very much. Why?'

'He can see into my dreams. When I think back over my dreams, he has been in each one. I have only dreamt of my mother, except…'

Henda waited. Cora could feel the intense gaze of Teven, and she wasn't sure she wanted to share what she would with him in the room.

She sighed and looked only at Henda. 'I have dreamt of Teven.'

'My past?'

She shook her head. He stared, and she tried not to look at the floor.

'Once, the night before I came here. And then recently, I dreamt of you in the trees with the dragons.'

'Merik was in those dreams as well?' Henda asked.

'Only the first one, before I left.'

'What did you dream?'

Cora shook her head again.

'Please tell me.' He stepped closer.

'It was us at a hearth; that is all.'

'It scared you,' Henda said.

'I had never dreamed of something that had not happened before. He was different. I didn't know him, and yet I did.'

'Like I knew you,' he whispered. She looked up then, but before she could ask what he meant, the curtain was pulled back and a man stood in the doorway.

'It is time,' Henda said sadly. She took Cora by the hands. 'You will come again, and show me what you can?'

Cora nodded. If they could, she would love to get to know these people better. And they were so close to the other cavern. If someone were to take part of a tribe and run, she would have thought they would travel a lot further away. Maybe it was part of what Merik wanted, that he needed to be close, or that he would take control some day and hadn't yet been able to.

She didn't think she would be able to ask him, she realised as she followed Teven out into the main cavern. The people didn't look at them like they had before, and the dragons had gone. The man led them out through the space. Too soon, she was standing amongst the trees.

'Don't come back,' he said, then disappeared back inside the leather curtain.

Disappointment washed over Cora. It had seemed so much like home— a chief like her father, an Ancient she could talk with—and yet she was being sent away again. But then, being out on her own in a world she didn't want to be in had exposed her to skills she hadn't known she had.

Teven surprised her by taking her hand and pulling her through the trees.

'How do we explain to Merik where we have been?' she asked, and he stopped.

'You can't call him that. He likes to be called Chief. That is what we call him, and that is what you will call him.'

'Do you know who he is?' she asked as he tugged her along.

He didn't answer. Then the dragon blocked their way. Cora pulled from Teven's hold and raced forward, throwing her arms around the dragon's neck as she had wanted to do before. 'Hello,' she said, pushing her face into the pale green scales.

You are always welcome, Cora of the Penna.

'I'm not sure everyone agrees with you.'

It has been a tenuous peace. He is not what he was. The little chief wants more; he has always wanted more. He thinks that you will give it to him.

'I'm not sure what I should do.'

You will find your place.

'Can you help me get home?'

That is something for another day. Take the boy and go for now.

'The boy,' Teven murmured.

Cora smiled as she took his hand and then ran her other hand over the nose of the dragon. She bowed her head, and they walked back towards the cliff.

Beware of the shadows, Oldra.

Cora turned back, but the dragon was gone.

18

The climb back up the cliff was as hard as it had been in the dream of Teven's mother. Cora didn't know the woman's name. She wasn't sure it was something she could ask, or even something he could answer. He had been isolated because of her, paid for what she had done, and he hadn't been given the chance to know who she was.

Cora paused and looked back to see that he was finding the climb harder than she was. 'Can I help?' she asked. But he shook his head.

She moved down the path to meet him as he leaned into the stone. 'Let me support you.'

'It isn't safe. If I nudge you, we could both go over.' She raised her eyebrows, but he didn't smile. 'A dragon may not be able to save you every time.'

'I understand that,' she said. 'But you are not as well as you think you are.'

'You healed me. Maybe you aren't the healer everyone thinks.' He smiled finally, but she could see the sweat beading on his forehead.

'Sit down, let me check,' she said hurriedly. He was right. She wasn't what they thought she was; she had always said that. She had told them repeatedly that her mother wasn't right.

'Maybe you should sit down,' he said softly.

She looked at him then. He used the cliff face to lower himself to the ground, then motioned her down beside him.

'You look as though the whole world is crumbling.'

'Let me at your chest,' she said.

He sighed and pulled at the material, bloody and torn down the middle, exposing most of his chest and, with the movement of his sitting down, the mark of Oldra. She reached forward quickly. Closing her eyes, she tried to focus, but she struggled to see.

He pressed a hand over hers, and she looked up into his pale brown eyes. 'Breathe,' he said. 'You've done this before.'

She shook her head. 'Henda put her hands over mine. She might have healed you.'

'You did this,' he said.

'I can't see.' She felt the panic close her throat. 'And now you aren't well enough to make it back.'

'I'm just tired,' he murmured.

Cora touched her hand to his forehead. 'You are burning.'

'It is a steep climb. It is hard going.'

Cora felt suddenly out of control, as though things were even harder than they had been before, unsure of why she couldn't pull together what she thought she could. 'I'm too far from the snow,' she whispered.

'Cora,' he said loudly, grabbing her by the shoulders. 'You have to come back from wherever you have gone.'

She stared at him.

'I'm fine,' he continued.

She nodded but leaned into him, feeling a little more centred. Then she stretched out her hand and pressed it to his chest.

'That is so cold,' he murmured.

She closed her eyes, now able to see again as she had the day before. There was bruising, but the damage was repaired. She pulled her hand back and nodded. Then she stood and looked up the path. 'You need some rest, and some water. How far to the stream?'

'You'll get lost on your own.'

'No,' she said.

'Don't go.' He grabbed at her again. 'I just need to rest. Then we can make it to the stream together. It flows across this side of the cavern.'

Cora leaned out over the path.

He laughed, and she turned back with a frustrated groan. 'Does it flow right off the cliff?'

He shook his head. 'It disappears into the ground.'

'We don't really have water that flows where I'm from.'

'I guessed as much.'

She sat back against the hard, rough rock and looked over the trees.

After some time, he cleared his throat, but she maintained her stare.

'What are you thinking?' he asked.

'That I'm not sure how I can get you back to the cavern, or how I can get home.'

At his silence, she turned and found him looking over the trees.

'I have to go back at some point.'

'Do you?'

'Should I wait until the chief wants to take this healing ability from me?'

Teven pushed himself up slowly, groaning a little from the effort. 'Henda said that he can't.'

'But is she certain? No one else seems to have been right about what I am.'

'I think everyone has a very good idea of what you are. It is only you who doesn't seem to believe it or understand it.'

'I certainly don't understand it.' She reached for him, but he waved her off. He stepped slowly along the pathway, and she followed behind.

It took a long time to reach the top. Although it was still early morning, she feared it would be dark before they reached the cavern. She wondered if the dragons would help her out. If they could.

'Why are they different?'

'Who?' Teven wheezed as he reached the top of the path. She was sure he should sit down, but he kept moving, slowly making his way towards the trees with her following closely behind. She wasn't sure she could hold him up or stop him hitting the ground if he fell, one way or the other.

'The dragons,' she said, concentrating more on his weaving gait.

He stopped and looked back. 'They are the same.'

'They are leathery here, and down there...' She pointed back down towards the trees.

He shrugged and turned back to the trees.

'Do you not know, or do you not care?'

He laughed, but it was a strained, wheezing sound.

'You are not well,' she murmured, coming up beside him and wrapping her arm around him.

'I need to walk in there on my own.'

'But you can't.'

'I need to. He might not care what happens to me, but I must walk into the cavern.'

Cora nodded and continued forward. He pulled against her, but she was stronger than him. 'I will allow you to walk into that cavern as though there is nothing for anyone to notice, but until then, I'm helping.'

He sighed and continued on. It was only as they neared the entrance and she allowed him the space to walk on his own that she wondered whether people would question that they had been out of the cavern all night. If members of the Penna were to do that, everyone would be talking of it. Particularly a man and a woman. There were times when young couples tried to sneak away. If they wanted private time, they tended to use the birthing chamber when everyone else was asleep. But even then, chances were high that someone would see.

The chief would see Teven as a threat the moment he realised that

Teven was Oldra. He must have some idea of what he was, and Cora didn't know how he had managed to hide it for as long as he had. Now she wondered what other skill he might have. He might be more like Arminel, with the healing abilities she had guessed at when she'd first arrived. But then he might have some sight like her mother.

She watched him closely, wondering if he had seen her coming. Did he really think she would stay? Teven teetered a little to the side as he walked down into the cavern, and she clenched her fists to stop from reaching out for him. No one appeared to look up as they entered, but she was sure these people watched far more than she realised.

The cavern was still dimly lit. Cora looked up at the pale orbs and wondered for the first time in her life what powered them. In her world, as in the cavern she had recently left, they were clear and bright and reflected the outside light. But even in the overcast world she lived in, they shone brightly of a day.

It was one of those aspects of her life that she didn't question. She might have questioned her own abilities and her mother's motives, but for most of her life she had survived without questioning very much at all. Yet, no matter what others thought she was or hoped her to be, her life had been mapped out. She knew where she would be and what she would become.

'Cora,' Teven whispered. She focused on him as he stood by the fire. 'Did you notice the water by the door?'

She shook her head and then turned swiftly to walk back the way they had come. There were still several baskets filled with water. Teven did so much, she wondered what the clan would do if he left. She looked around, standing by the doorway and trying to see into the dark edges of the cavern to determine how many people lived within it.

Would the others take them in? It had only been for Teven's lifetime that they'd been away. Even though his uncle was not keen to take Teven in, he may be willing to take the others. She walked slowly back towards Teven. She wondered if these people really knew just how close they were to family.

'You can't say anything,' Teven whispered, as though reading her thoughts.

She nodded once. 'There is enough water,' she said.

'They will need wood soon enough.'

'Rest. We can head out later today, or even tomorrow. Would you like me to see what people need?'

'The chief won't like you talking with people.'

'It won't really change what he wants, or whether I can go home. If he were any decent sort of man, he would check on them himself.'

Teven opened his mouth to protest, but then he bowed his head and turned away instead.

Cora turned to find Merik behind her.

'Another night out of the cavern. I would think you were plotting against me—or are you simply trying to find the snow?'

'She is too far away,' Cora said. 'Would you let me go if I could find a way?'

He shook his head. 'But you appear stronger every day. Have you found your gift?'

'I can heal.'

He glanced over her shoulder towards Teven, but he said nothing more. After a moment too long studying her, he turned towards his cavern.

'Why is it so dull in here?' she asked after him.

He turned back, but said nothing.

'The orbs should be brighter during the day.' She pointed up to the ceiling above her.

'They are what they are.' He turned back and picked up his pace.

'But what are they?' Cora asked quietly as he walked away. She turned back to Teven, who appeared paler. He sat heavily by the fire. 'Do you have a fresh tunic?'

Teven nodded, but didn't move.

'I think you should turn from the people,' Cora said, moving to the wall of the cavern. She knew they were still visible to everyone, although with the dim light she hoped they weren't too clear. He moved carefully, too slowly. Cora found what she was looking for and returned with it. He waved her away, but she had already begun to worry. He needed to keep the mark a secret, and he needed her help whether he wanted it or not.

He groaned when she helped lift his ruined tunic over his head. But he nodded slowly as she held the fresh one out. He groaned again, despite biting down on his lip, and Cora found herself looking around the cavern to ensure not everyone was watching them. They might just assume Teven had been injured while they were out.

She ran her hand over his forehead, brushing his dark shaggy hair from his face. 'Rest,' she said.

Teven actually went off to sleep quite quickly, once she got him to lie down. Then she sat back by the fire and wondered just what Merik really thought he could get from her. Her hand tingled when she thought of what she had done for Teven. The burning he had felt as a new baby was so sharp in her own chest. As was his mother's pain. What she must have feared to do such a thing to her baby, just to keep him safe.

And despite what he was, he had managed to hide it from his father. Although he had never really been given the chance to think of Merik as a father, and he had managed to find his kin. Although they cared for him, they could not take him in.

It was such a different world, she struggled to get her mind around it. If such a thing had happened in the Penna, the people would have come together to help. They would not have allowed it to get to the point where a new mother could think such actions were her only choice. And if something had happened and she had died, they would have all helped with the child. A family would have taken him in, but the clan as a whole would have supported them. As they did all the Penna.

She smiled at the idea. Her mother would have made sure of it. Cora wiped quickly at the unexpected tears. She missed her mother so desperately, far more than she would have thought. Gerry would have so many ideas as to how she could work with the people of the area, how to not annoy Merik while keeping him from what he wanted. She would have understood the pain Cora felt when she put her hand on Teven's chest. And she would have found a way home.

But Cora didn't have her mother, and Merik would do what he wanted as he had always done, whether it harmed his people or not. Teven would continue to sacrifice himself for those people. Cora looked up and wiped again at her face. She didn't know these people at all, and she had been here for so long already.

She glanced over her shoulder at Teven sleeping soundly. He had been healed, but it had taken a lot from him. Rhali was nowhere to be seen, but she always did as she pleased. Cora only hoped the girl was safe. As she looked into the flames before her, she realised there was someone on the other side.

She waved them forward, and a young man moved around to stand before her. Then he smiled and sat down beside her.

'How is life here?' she asked. 'Is there anything you need?'

'We will need wood soon,' he said, glancing across at Teven. 'Is he ill?'

'A small injury while we were out. He just needs some sleep.'

The young man looked at the pile of leather than had been Teven's tunic.

'I hoped that Rhali would help me mend it,' Cora said without moving. 'Have you seen her?'

He shook his head. 'Would you go for wood?'

Cora nodded. 'I can.' She waited a moment, but he didn't move or say anything else. 'Should I ask others what they might need?'

'Wood,' he said again, standing slowly. He bowed his head to her, then disappeared around the fire.

Cora was tempted to visit with each hearth anyway, just to see who they were and what they might need. She might be able to learn so much more about them.

But she didn't. Pushing Merik would only cause more problems and make them less likely to talk to her. She didn't want to cause any more problems for Teven, who was sleeping more soundly now. She wondered if there were different rules for him because of who his father was—or was it because of his mother's death?

It couldn't be that hard to head out on her own for the wood, and she could pile it up. She noted the water was still by the door as she walked out into the fresh air. Without any real ability to keep her there, they still managed in their way to stop her going home. The beautiful green dragon could have been an option, but Cora knew she wouldn't help.

Maybe there were others who had an idea of what her future was meant to be, but they weren't sharing that with her. Or maybe her mother was the only one with such a skill. Although Wyndha had skills that Cora could have used about now. Henda had mentioned not seeing clearly, and Cora realised she hadn't had the chance to talk to the woman about what she could see.

She continued into the trees. There was no sign of Rhali or any of the smaller leathery dragons. She noticed a fallen branch and walked towards it. Maybe she should have grabbed her spear, but then she wouldn't be able to carry back wood. As she reached the branch, she heard a strange squeaky noise and stood back up. She looked around the trees but couldn't see anything, and then she heard the noise again.

She stepped over the branch and towards where she thought the noise was coming from. As she walked, the strange noise continued. And then she saw Rhali, sitting against a tree and sobbing her heart out. She made the odd squeak trying to drag in breaths.

Cora dropped down beside her and pulled the girl into her arms. She could feel the heartache radiating from Rhali, and she tried to comfort her without touching her.

'Can you heal it?' Rhali asked.

'What has happened?' Cora pushed her away to try and look her over, thinking maybe she was injured. But although she was damp from the tears, there was no blood.

Rhali scared Cora by grabbing her hand and pulling it to her chest. The burning sensation was very different from the sensation she'd gotten from Teven. It was hot, but a dull ache rather than the sharp pain.

Cora tried to pull away, but Rhali maintained a tight hold. 'Please. You are a healer; you can heal it.'

'It isn't the kind of injury that can be so easily healed.' Cora sat back and took a deep breath. 'I can't help you.'

Rhali ran the back of her hand across her nose and then sniffed. Her eyes were red and puffy and her cheeks wet, but she didn't wipe at them.

'What has happened?' Cora asked again.

Rhali shook her head.

'Is this because of the man I saw you with?'

Rhali looked up at Cora, then chewed on her lip as more tears started to fall. Her shoulders started to shake and, despite the pain Cora knew would follow, she pulled the girl into her arms.

'The chief doesn't know,' Rhali said quickly.

'He knows far more than he tells you.'

'But he doesn't know,' Rhali said more firmly.

Cora nodded slowly and allowed Rhali to lean into her shoulder.

'Can you tell me his name?' she asked. But Rhali shook her head against Cora. 'Can you tell me what has happened?'

'He said we could be together, but we can't.'

Cora gave her a moment to continue. When she didn't, Cora asked, 'Why can't you be together?'

'They won't accept anyone from our clan.'

'But you are all the same.'

Rhali gave a weak laugh and sat back. She wiped her hand over her cheeks, but her eyes were dry. 'We might have been once, but not now.'

'He came here from far away. Would he stay with you?'

'He hasn't been here very long. He was called to them, and he must stay with them.'

Cora chewed on her lip. If he had been called as her mother was, it was for good reason. She wondered if it was because of a larger fight. Again, she longed for her mother so she could ask her the question, ask her advice. She tried not to sigh. 'Where is he from?'

Rhali shook her head. 'Too far to matter.'

'How did you meet him?'

'I was looking for herbs by the cliff top.'

Cora indicated for her to go on, but she looked down at her hands. 'Please,' Cora coaxed.

'I am not allowed by the cliff. We are able to move around—I don't know why I have that freedom, but it is limited. I just walked that way one day and found so many things I hadn't found before, and I found him.' A small smile lit up her face, and then she turned to study Cora more closely. 'Your mother is from a place like his?'

Cora nodded.

'If we had children, would they look like you?'

'Maybe,' Cora admitted. 'Will you have children with this man?'

'Not when I can't be with him. Not when they won't allow me to come to them.'

'Your father would not allow it.'

'And there is that,' she said with a sigh, staring off into the distance. 'I know he will never let me leave. No one will ever have that chance. We will die buried in the dark of our little cavern with our great chief trying to be some great man. But how can he be?' she asked, turning back to Cora with questioning eyes. 'He hides in his cavern causing fear.'

'Causing fear? Why did they follow him?' Cora asked.

She shook her head and looked back to her hands. 'I don't know,' she said softly. 'My mother never spoke of it.'

'You have another brother, don't you?'

Rhali nodded, but didn't look up.

'Why are you isolated from him?'

'He is to be Chief, if he can meet the expectations of his father. He wanted to run away with…'

'The girl who died,' Cora finished for her.

She nodded in agreement. 'They were foolish, and he is lucky the chief didn't punish him further.'

'How did he punish him?'

'By allowing the girl and her son to die. I knew as soon as she came to me that she was with child and how he would react. He was so kind, so reassuring that her son would be strong. But I knew it was all lies and that he would ensure neither of them survived.'

'But she died in childbirth. My mother is amongst the most skilled healers, and there are some that even she can't save, babies and mothers alike.'

'He has different skills.'

Cora looked at her. Merik wanted Cora's skill, and she assumed he must have something, but she had yet to see what it was. What if it was something dark, something she hadn't come across before? This man managed to keep a whole clan in the dark of the cavern. They wouldn't leave him and they wouldn't save themselves, relying on a boy for food and water. Well, not exactly a boy. But he would have been. His mother had been pregnant when they left the others. What would they have done before he was old enough to go out? Who taught him to fetch water and wood and to hunt?

'What can he do?' Cora asked, almost too scared for the answer.

Rhali shook her head and climbed to her feet, brushing dust and leaves from her clothes. 'Where is Teven?' she asked, then looked around. 'Are you trying to leave us?'

Cora stood and placed a hand on her arm. The worry and concern made Cora shiver, and she decided the truth was best. 'Teven was injured, but he is well now. He is resting at your hearth.'

Rhali sighed with relief and nodded. 'So why are you here?'

'We have been gone a long time, and the supplies were getting lower in the cavern. I said I would go for wood.'

'I'll help,' Rhali said quickly, directing Cora through the trees.

Within a short amount of time, they were headed back to the cavern with their arms full of sticks and small branches.

'We are going to need more,' Cora said as she followed Rhali into the cavern where they piled the supplies by the water. Without a glance towards her own hearth, she headed straight back out. They spent the rest of the day searching out good-sized branches and dragging them towards the cavern. Some of them were too large to take inside, and she wondered how they could break them up.

Cora realised she had no idea how the men of her own clan managed to bring in the wood that they did, although their trees were slow growing and she was sure the wood took a lot longer to burn than it did here. They needed a cutting tool. That may also be why the fires didn't burn as high here. With the reduced and different resources, they had to conserve what they had.

'Teven has an axe,' Rhali said.

'Axe?'

'He chipped away at a rock with a smaller one, and it is sharp and strong. It is like a large knife that he uses for wood.' She disappeared inside the cavern, then reappeared a few minutes later almost dragging the tool behind her. It had a large, tapered blade on the end of a very long handle.

'He swings it up and then drops it down.' She tried to show Cora how she had seen him use it, but she could barely lift it.

'Let me try,' Cora said, holding out her hand. She was much stronger than Rhali. The axe was weighty, but it was no different from the long and heavy spear she had carried. Rhali made the motion with her arms of how Teven had used it, and then Cora tried. She lifted it above her head and let it drop onto the wood. It hit with a *thunk*, and the branch remained intact although she had to move the blade back and forth to release it from the wood. She tried again, but failed to hit the same mark.

She looked up at Rhali, who bit her lip. She tried again and hit the first spot, then again, and the branch broke. She smiled and rolled her shoulders. She felt like she had done very little serious exercise since she had arrived here, not that she could even remember how long that was. If she were at home, she would have been training regularly with her fellow Draga, hunting with her father, and taking care of any number of tasks for Arminel. If she had been any other woman, like Junah, she might have carried water for the warm room, but she was not like the others. Now, as she moved towards another branch, she realised she was not the same as the others here either.

Her mother might be right. No matter where Cora was, she had a different purpose. There was something specific she had to do, only she wasn't quite sure what it was yet.

Breaking up the wood was cathartic. Although she had to focus on hitting the same place as she worked the larger branches, it gave her a quiet place to think. Rhali remained with her, moving wood to a pile by the

cavern, carrying some inside and helping her lift the larger branches into positions where she could cut them.

In so many ways, Cora's life had turned out like her mother's. She had found herself far away from home, amongst people she didn't know and finding out just what skill she had. Although these people didn't embrace her like the Penna had her mother, and although Teven was Oldra, Cora doubted he would connect to her as her father had her mother. And yet she knew there was a connection.

Cora didn't want to stay here with these people in the sunshine. She might have wanted to stay with the people in the valley, with light and an Ancient. She couldn't live in the dark. And although she loved the sun on her skin, she missed the snow. She put the axe down, wiped the back of her hand across her sweaty brow and tried to transition.

'Do you want some water?' Rhali asked, drawing her from her thoughts and the threatening homesickness.

She nodded slowly.

'You go to the stream. I will carry this in and check Teven. Take your time.'

Cora nodded again and headed towards the water that ran a short distance from the cavern. It was bright in the sunlight, and she was amazed at how it moved. She stood beside it for too long, watching the water flow over the rocks, and thought for a moment that she saw movement. She took a step forward, wondering if it was the fish that Teven had tried to catch.

She looked along the waterway in the direction the water flowed. Where did it go, and why didn't it flow over the cliff? She bent down and scooped a handful into her mouth. It was cool, almost like melted snow. She smiled. Then she splashed into the stream, allowing the coolness to wash around her legs as she transitioned, enjoying the feeling. If she was to stay here, she didn't think her transition would last much longer. And it might not be very useful in the sunshine.

She headed back to the shore, feeling refreshed. Although she liked hot water to wash with, she wondered if she could find a part of the stream deep enough to submerge her whole body. The stream wasn't very deep, nor very wide. She looked back wondering where it flowed from, but then continued along its path. The sun was high in the sky, and her stomach rumbled.

She looked back towards the cavern, but she was enjoying her time alone, despite her earlier thoughts of her mother and the looming homesickness. She would have to be here until she worked out what her gift of healing could truly do. Or if there was another reason for her to be amongst the trees with leaves.

She was reminded of the dragon's warning, and she imagined her mother for a moment with all the dragons directing their dragonlight through her. She shivered. She hoped that wasn't her destiny.

The little stream twisted through the trees. At several points she had to get back into the water to follow it, for the trees were too thick around the edges. Then it opened into a large, deep pool before her. She heard rushing water and saw darkness on the other side of the pond. The whole area was closely surrounded by trees. She wondered whether they would have been able to reach it had they tried to find it from the cliff face. Teven would have struggled trying to squeeze through the tight spaces.

The ever-present sunlight managed to make it through. There were no trees hanging over the middle of the pool, and the sun lit the clear water, highlighting the golden rocky bottom. It looked very inviting. Knowing that there would be no one around, Cora peeled her already damp tunic off along with the sodden leggings.

She splashed out and found the bottom dropped away beneath her quite quickly. She stumbled a little, then found herself standing up to her neck in the cool water. Moving her arms slowly around her to try and keep her balance, she breathed slowly and tried not to panic. Her feet were still on the bottom, but if it became deeper, she wasn't sure what she could do.

A memory flashed through her mind of her mother moving through water, splashing and laughing and floating. She pushed off the bottom and tried to paddle with her arms and legs, but she didn't get very far. It was harder than it looked. She stretched out her arms before her and then dragged them to the side, moving more easily now. She smiled, sucking in water, and then found the bottom of the pond was too far below her to reach.

As she dipped beneath the surface, a hazy world appeared before her. Strangely beautiful with the smooth, golden stones lining the bottom of the pond and the light dancing above her. She kicked up, broke the surface and gulped in a lungful of air before disappearing below the surface again. It was calm and quiet, and for a moment she thought she could just stay there.

Then her mother's face appeared in the hazy water that surrounded her. She looked worried as she stared directly at Cora. 'You must find who you are.'

Cora's feet found the smooth stones and pushed off, through the vision of her mother and towards the surface. A stone wall appeared before her. She broke the surface and leaned over it. The water ran over the edge in a slow, steady stream into the darkness below. She leaned against the stone, the water lapping around her as she stared into the darkness. She was keen to get down there and see where the water went. Although she didn't know if someone or something else might be there.

She wondered suddenly if the dragons would be able to take her, or if they might even stay there. At the edge of the stone wall, where the pond met the land again, appeared to be a ledge. There might be a similar walkway down as there was down the cliff, although that travelled at a steady gradient. There wasn't the space for such an incline. She wondered if this was really a good idea.

It was only once she was standing on the shore that she remembered her clothes were at the other end of the pond. She transitioned, but it wasn't enough. She didn't think she could move back through the water. With a groan of disappointment, she made her way through the trees and back to the edge of the pond to her clothes. Dressed and damp, she was starting to chill in the shadows of the trees. She transitioned and made her way back to the hole. It was only once she was at the top that she paused, wondering briefly if these were the shadows she should be wary of, before she stepped into the darkness. Her mother was right—she had to find out who she was.

19

The pathway was narrower here than on the cliff, and Cora hugged the wall as she made her way down. Surprisingly, the gradient was similar. She spiralled around the darkness, occasionally looking up at the open sky above her, which was cut from view when the pathway led behind the water dribbling down from the stream above. Other than the water, the light above and the darkness below, there was nothing but the gently descending pathway.

When the pathway levelled out, it took Cora a moment to realise that she had found the bottom of the darkness. The water splashed into a shallow pool. Beyond the dribble of water was the warm glow of a fire. Still transitioned, she moved forward slowly. The wall gave way to an underground cavern. She wondered just how deep it might be. Then she turned and looked behind her. For a moment, she thought of the cavern at the base of the cliff. She might be closer to it than she had realised. And they hadn't been particularly keen to see her last time.

Cora took a deep breath and wondered if she would ever consider carrying her bow with her again. She had spent so much time alone that day doing just what she wanted to do; she could have taken the time to make some arrows.

When she turned back to the water, the man standing directly in front of her scared her half to death. At least she thought he was a man. With the light behind him, he had a tall, broad silhouette. Thankful she had transitioned, she braced herself for an attack, but it didn't come. When he turned away from her and walked towards the light, Cora chewed her lip and followed.

The cavern felt damp, but the further they walked, the lighter it became.

And then they could have been standing at any Penna hearth. The fire burned brightly, a metal frame straddling it and a pot hanging over the flames. A tightly woven mat was laid out before it and a square, low table sat to the side, although it was lower than those of the Penna and had no bench seats along it. Cora allowed her transition to slip.

The man sat cross legged by the fire, then pointed to the space before him. The light in the space was comforting. It was as bright as the midday Penna cavern, and the fire gave it a warm glow. He pointed to the mat again, and she bowed her head before sitting down.

He was a man not much older than Cora, with clear Penna features—or those of Teven's people, although she was still to learn who they were. He was not the human man Rhali had met. He wore leather clothing like those of Teven's people, the colour more a muted grey. She was reminded of the Penna, although there was a bright red pattern stitched around the hem of the short tunic he wore.

He was a handsome man, she thought, feeling the heat come to her face.

She wasn't quite sure how to feel or what to say. She waited for him to speak first, but although she studied him, he said nothing. She met his eyes, wondering at the green colour that flecked the deep brown, and noted that he studied her too. She could sense the muscle and strength within him and wondered if he too was a warrior.

'You are different from what you appear,' he said in a voice that rumbled through her. It was deep and familiar, like her father's.

She nodded, unsure how to place who this man was or what she should say.

'You are not of the Nerrim.'

She was confused by the name, then wondered if that was Teven's clan or the other, or both.

'I am Penna,' she said, clearing her throat.

'You are a chief.' He reached a finger towards her heart, although he couldn't see the mark.

'I will be, one day, if I can return to my people.' She put her hand over her heart.

He smiled then, and Cora felt her whole body warm. 'You are your people, little chief.'

'What?' she asked.

'How did you come to be here?'

'I climbed down from the stream,' she said, pointing up.

'How did you come to be *here*?' he asked again.

'I fell,' she murmured.

He nodded slowly.

'Do you know of Dra? Do you know if he is…?' She wasn't sure what she wanted to ask—if he was well, or alive. She wasn't sure she wanted to know if he wasn't, but then she wondered if she would know already. 'I can't feel them,' she said, looking down into her hands.

'You will.'

'How do you know this?' She pointed at the red she had noticed on his tunic. 'Are you an Ancient?'

'Do I look that old?'

'Not all Ancients are as old as they appear,' she said, wondering just how old Arminel truly was.

'Why did you come?'

'I wanted to see where the water went.'

'Teven?' he asked, although there was something in his tone she couldn't quite determine.

'He rests.'

'He is what you thought he was.'

'Oldra,' she said, nodding.

'You have great skill.'

'It appears I can heal more than I thought possible.'

He sighed and then climbed to his feet. Cora sat back, unsure what he might do, then squealed as something moved in the shadows. He turned and looked carefully where she had been looking. Then he raised his hand, and the light in the space increased. There was nothing there.

Cora sighed with relief, but her heart was pounding.

'What did you see?' he asked.

She shook her head.

He squatted down before her. 'What?'

'Merik,' she said quickly.

He growled, and she leaned back. 'He must really want what you have,' he said as he stood. With a small piece of leather, he moved the pot off the flames. The smell of the stew filled her senses, and her stomach growled.

'I don't know if he understands what I have.'

'Hmmm,' he said, putting stew in a bowl and handing it to her.

She hesitated for only a moment and then took the bowl from him. He handed her a wooden spoon, and she nodded her thanks as she started to eat.

He watched her for a moment before sitting again on the mat. 'How long since you have eaten?'

She shrugged and continued to hurriedly eat.

'Does he limit your food?'

She nodded. 'He appears to limit everyone,' she said through a full mouth.

They continued in silence. When she had finished, she looked up from the bowl and focused on his face again. 'Who are you?"

'A good question,' he said.

Cora felt her stomach drop. Here she was telling him all sorts of things, and she didn't even know who he was. Merik was a man with unknown skill, determined to take what she had. She was stupid to assume all Ancients could be trusted. But as she sucked in a breath and focused on his face, something drew her to this man. She knew she could trust him.

'You know Teven,' she said. 'You know something of me.'

'Artell.' He bowed his head. 'Ancient of the Nerrim.'

'Nerrim,' she said slowly. 'Why do you live in here?'

'I like it, and they leave me alone.'

'Do you want to be left alone?'

His gaze was intense, and she lowered her eyes again.

'I'm sorry,' she said. 'I haven't met many people since I've been here.'

'You met some of the Nerrim.'

'They tried to kill me,' she said with a sigh, 'and nearly killed Teven instead.'

'An unexpected move on his part.'

'People here don't like strangers.'

'I am sure your people are the same.'

She nodded.

'You saved him,' Artell said. 'And revealed him.'

'Why did his mother do that to him?'

'I think you already know the answer to that.'

'Then how did he hide such a gift for so long?'

'How do you know that he hid it?' Artell asked.

Teven hadn't told her who or what he was, but maybe others already knew. Perhaps his mother's attempt to protect him had been in vain. Cora felt the sharp pain again that she had felt at putting her hand over his heart, and she pushed her hand over her mark. The woman had lost so much, yet Merik knew what he was.

The soft hand on her knee startled her, and Artell withdrew it quickly. 'It does not follow that it was in vain,' he said. 'Her sacrifice removed him from his father's favour. That may have saved him, in a way.'

'I did not invite you in,' she said, her voice firmer than she intended.

'You didn't need to. I could see your thoughts clearly on your face.'

She nodded slowly. 'I'm not sure why I am here, but I think it is for a purpose.'

'Then let us explore who and what you are to see if we can determine that.'

She nodded. But as he held out his hand, she shook her head. 'I'm not comfortable with this.'

'And yet you want to know.'

'Is there another way?'

'Certainly.' Without warning, the knife reflected the firelight before he sliced it through his thigh.

He slumped back as blood gushed from the wound. She pressed her hands over it, panic filling her chest. 'What is it with you people?' she murmured as she tried desperately to slow the bleeding. The blood pumped at a steady pace, pushing against her efforts and between her fingers.

It could have been the vision Merik had flittered through her mind. She wondered just what the man had seen.

She took a deep breath, trying not to think of the life leaking far too quickly from this man she had only just met, and focused on the wound within the skin. The blade must have been sharp, for he had severed the main blood flow as well as the muscle. She focused on the blood, willing it to slow so she could see the damage. His breathing slowed with it.

Cora could feel him slipping away. Although she tried to stay calm so she could focus, she felt the desperation creeping up the back of her throat with a bitter taste.

The blood continued to slow, and then the vessel walls stitched back together, the muscles joined and the skin healed. She lifted her hands slowly.

Without hesitation, she prised the knife still held tight in his hand and cut the material away from the wound—or where the wound would have been, for the skin wasn't broken. It was starting to bruise, and she was sure it would ache for a few days, but then he deserved it after pulling a stunt like that.

She blew out a soft breath and wiped the back of her hand over her forehead. Looking at her hands, she hoped the rest of her didn't look as bad. She turned back to the doorway for a moment, wondering how long it would take her to climb all the way back up to the top and wash the blood from her skin in the deep, cool pool.

Looking back at the man before her, she sighed. Did he even realise what risk he had taken? She ran a bloody hand over his forehead. Although he felt a little clammy, there was no fever. She felt the pulse in his neck, which appeared to be back to normal. She looked at his pale features, his eyes still closed, and pulled at the ties that kept his tunic closed at the neck. They didn't move as easily as she'd hoped. She looked at the knife before thinking better of it and working on the knot with her sticky fingers.

When the knot gave way, she pulled quickly to expose his chest and the clear mark of Oldra. She leaned back and sighed. Her father came to mind with his certainties, and although she hadn't wanted to believe him, she had. Now she knew not one, but too many Oldra.

She groaned out loud. But as she made to stand up, a strong hand closed around her wrist. Opening his eyes, Artell pulled her forward, and her other hand landed on his chest. He cried out from the pressure, but as she leaned back, she kept her hand on his chest and closed her eyes.

There was a warmth, but no overwhelming heat. She had a sense of him, but not, at the same time.

'Do you fondle all your patients?'

'Only those stupid enough to risk their own lives to try and prove a point.'

'What point? And it wasn't much of a risk.'

She looked at him then. Was he that confident of her skills, even though he had no idea what they were? Then he was sitting slowly and taking her hands in his.

He studied them, turning them over, and his brow creased.

'Do you have healing skills?' she asked, trying to pull from his hold.

He looked up at her face and reached for it, but she brushed him away.

'There is a lot of blood,' he said slowly.

'I can't heal instantly. It took a moment to see what damage you had done.' She gulped down the panic trying to overwhelm her again. She didn't know if her willing the blood to slow had helped her or put him in more danger.

'I just meant to scratch the surface,' he said, looking at the ruined leggings. He ran his hand over the place and winced.

'A lot of blood means bruising. It will be sore, hopefully for some time.'

He looked at her again. 'You hope I hurt?' He sounded disappointed.

'It will remind you not to do anything stupid like that again.' She stood up and moved a few paces away. It was getting harder to breathe around him. She looked back to the opening. She should get back, check Teven, ensure the chief wasn't going to take his frustrations of her disappearance out on him or Rhali. But she was tired.

He was up then, holding her as her legs gave way, and he staggered a little. She laughed at the foolishness of it all. He helped her down onto the mat and then sat beside her. 'Are you hungry?'

She shook her head. 'Tired. You?'

'I could eat.' He made to stand again, but she put a hand on his arm.

Blowing out a long breath, she climbed to her feet. She collected the bowl she had eaten from and filled it with stew from the pot. As she handed it back to him, he nodded.

'What were you looking for behind my mark?'

'I just needed to see it. Recently I have felt other's pain in their hearts. I didn't want your pain,' she said quickly, sitting back on the mat. 'I just wanted to know if you were the same.'

'As you?'

'I don't know,' she said, trying to stifle a yawn. She had no idea how her mother did this so well and so often.

'There,' he said, pointing across at a sleeping mat just beyond the woven mat.

It was covered in furs, as in the caverns she had recently visited, and she longed for the soft woollen blankets of home.

'I haven't seen any animals yet,' she said, reaching for the furs.

'Don't,' he said quickly. She pulled back her hand in surprise. 'Let me help you wash the blood away first.'

She looked down then and realised just how covered she was. Not only her hands—it was spattered across her chest, and she was sure it probably covered her face and neck as well. She nodded once and sat where she was. He climbed awkwardly to his feet and moved to the back of the cavern, out of view, then returned with a small woven basket filled with water.

He didn't appear to have heated it, and yet when she held out her hand to him and he wiped it with the soft cloth, it was warm. There were too many questions. She sat still and allowed him to wash away his blood. He had caused this mess, she thought as she looked over her clothes.

When he was finished, he pointed towards the furs. She gladly climbed in and fell quickly into a deep sleep. But she had strange dreams. The shadows moved around her, followed her no matter where she went. Then she was watching Teven sleep, but the chief stood over him, his face twisted in hatred.

She woke with a start to find Artell standing closer to the entrance, arguing with someone. 'There isn't the space,' he was saying as she rubbed the sleep from her eyes and walked closer. Beyond him, she could see Serassa. She smiled into the dragon's deep golden eyes.

'Hello,' she said, rubbing her hand across her face and leaning into her neck. 'I thought you had disappeared.'

I thought you had made new dragon friends, Serassa said.

Despite the exhaustion she still felt, Cora laughed.

'She wanted to sleep with you,' Artell said. 'As though I have room for a dragon. If I take in one, they will all want to share my fire.'

I will return you then, Oldra.

Cora's heart fluttered, but she knew that Serassa could not take her as far as she wanted to go. She nodded once, and with her arms around the dragon's neck, Serassa started for the opening.

'You may return if you wish,' Artell called after her. 'I may be able to teach you something.'

'I may be able to teach you something,' she said quickly, and she caught the smile he tried to hide as the dragon took to the air.

20

The cavern looked just as it had when she'd left it, although the piles of wood had disappeared. She assumed they had been taken by families into their hearths. Serassa had dropped her right by the opening to the cavern. Although it had gotten dark as they travelled, she hadn't seen any animals. She wondered what these people did for food. Perhaps the chief might let her go with Teven to hunt.

Teven and Rhali sat quietly by the fire at their hearth when she arrived. They both glanced at her and then back to the fire before Rhali climbed to her feet and filled a bowl from a pot for her. She didn't want to take what little these people had, but even Artell had managed to make stew, so there had to be supplies somewhere.

'You have been gone all day,' Teven said, trying to sound light, but she could hear the concern behind his words.

'Do you feel better?' she asked.

He nodded and put a hand to his chest. 'Odd, but better.'

'Odd?' She put down the bowl, but he smiled and handed it back to her.

'Not unwell, just different.' He put a hand over his heart, where the mark was, and she smiled.

Then his face clouded. 'What happened to you?'

She shook her head.

'You are covered in blood,' he said too loudly. Rhali turned back from the fire with her finger to her lips. 'What happened?' he asked in a hoarse whisper.

'I went into the water, and then I found someone who needed help.'

'Who?' he asked more firmly.

'He said his name was Artell,' she whispered.

125

'Then he lied,' Teven continued in the firm, too-loud voice. 'Artell died years ago.'

She opened her mouth and then closed it. He'd been alive enough to nearly die with her hands covered in his blood. She clenched and unclenched her fingers. Despite her need to understand what she was, Cora just wanted to be home with her mother.

'Who is Artell?' Rhali asked.

'He was of Edgris's family...' Teven started. Then he stopped and looked at her, his face paling, and Cora turned to see Rhali's getting redder.

'You didn't know,' Cora said slowly.

'I knew they were there,' she said in a hoarse whisper. 'I didn't know how like your father you are,' she threw at Teven.

'Don't argue,' Cora pleaded, but they both glared at her.

'I am nothing like him,' Teven growled. 'He doesn't want me to be.'

A shiver crossed Cora's spine. She turned slowly to find Merik standing at the edge of the hearth.

'They don't want him,' he said, looking at Rhali and then Cora. 'No one wants him. So, it matters little if he tries to visit. I take it your last attempt did not go well,' he said, pointing at Teven's torn tunic.

Teven only looked at the ground.

'Where did you go?' Merik asked Cora, looking at her with an uncertainty she hadn't seen in him before.

'Today? I went to get wood.'

He waited, and she knew he wanted more.

She tried not to sigh. 'I went to the stream. I wanted to wash Teven's blood from me.'

'And you return covered in another's blood,' he said, stepping forward and putting a finger to her chest. She looked down at the blood beneath his finger. 'This is your blood,' he said slowly.

She opened her mouth to explain and then snapped it shut.

'Have you found your gifts yet?'

'I'm not sure what you think I will find,' she said, standing taller, but she hoped he wasn't as aware of where she had been or what she had been up to.

'Exactly what I need,' he said, then stepped back and disappeared into the shadows of the cavern.

She watched for a moment before turning back to the two studying her at the hearth.

'You control the lights,' she said to Rhali.

The girl shook her head too quickly.

'When I was in the birthing chamber, where you first took me when I fell...'

'Where we thought you would die,' Teven interrupted.

'Rhali changed the lighting. You can make the orbs brighter. So why is it so dark in here?'

'That is not my doing,' she said sternly.

'But you could fix it.'

'I can't,' she said, more subdued.

'You can.'

'Stop it,' Teven snapped. 'You have no idea how we live, or why we live the way we do.'

'Do you?' Cora asked too quickly.

'We cannot question what we have. We are here, and that is all there is to it.'

Teven's words made her angry. How could he want to live like this? How could he want the scared and worried people of the clan to live like this? A girl had died, after all, simply because she had fallen for the wrong boy and they had conceived a child.

'Who was he to mate?' Cora asked aloud, and they looked at each other. 'Your...' She stopped and took a breath. 'The boy from the hearth.' She nodded beyond the fire. 'He wouldn't allow them to be together, but this is a small group, and he needs a family of his own if he is to be Chief one day.'

'He is too young,' Teven said.

'It would not have mattered if she was to be the chosen mate.'

'This is not like your clan,' Teven said, moving closer to her and taking her arm. 'This is a very different place. Don't try to understand.'

She nodded slowly, wondering if the scar on his heart was deeper than she had imagined it to be. She could hear movement behind her, and he released her quickly. She turned to find the mother of the girl she had just been talking of. Cora felt her face grow hot and hoped the woman hadn't heard her words. She hadn't been rude about the girl, but the memory would still be raw.

'Thank you for the wood,' she said. 'Teven works so hard. It is good to see him rest.'

Cora nodded her head in return, and Teven sighed.

The woman took a careful step forward, but she was still outside the hearth boundaries. 'Is there any meat?'

Teven shook his head and, without a word, she bowed her head again and turned away.

'Where does the meat come from?' Cora asked.

'Far. Too far for you.'

'Not too far for a dragon,' she whispered. She could sense Serassa out in the trees somewhere, and it was comfortable. She had felt alone for so long. She worried for Dra, but the advice or presence of any of the dragons would be of benefit. Ariandi was always full of good advice.

'What have you done to Serassa?' he asked softly, again too close.

Cora shook her head.

'I can't hear her,' he murmured, turning away.

'We should both hear her,' she said. Teven turned back, his finger to his lips, but she shook her head. 'We are both Oldra; we can both talk to all. We should hear all. I feel Serassa but no others, not even the one we spoke to yesterday.'

'They are linked to another clan.'

A sick feeling filled Cora. She was separated from her own people, and in doing so had become separated from her dragons. She knew the dragons of the Keetar; she could talk with them when she chose, and they her, but they were not part of the collective conversation of the Penna dragons.

Was she so separated from everyone now that when a dragon chose to talk with her, they separated themselves? Despite the feeling of loss, Cora smiled. And then she started to cry.

Teven stepped forward. 'I'm sorry,' he whispered.

She shook her head.

'Having another here like me has confused things.'

'I don't think we are meant to be connected,' she said quickly, wiping at her face.

'Connected?' he said, blushing.

'Oldra and Oldra,' she whispered. 'I feel Serassa, but you don't. She has chosen me,' she said through a sob.

'That is why I don't hear the dragons of the Nerrim unless I am there?'

She nodded. 'Separate clan, separate dragon clan. How many dragons do you hear?'

He shrugged. 'I don't know. Sometimes many, sometimes only a few.'

'Who did Serassa belong to?'

'No one. She was too young, not yet fully formed, not yet connected to a group.'

Cora looked at him closely. 'I'm not connected to a group, and in many ways neither are you. But she has taken me on without pulling us into a clan.'

'This is a clan,' he whispered hoarsely, the frustration back in his voice.

'But it isn't a dragon clan. There are no dragons here. The people don't even believe they exist.'

He sighed and looked back to his sister, then straightened up. 'Rhali belongs to my people. She is family.'

'There are many of your family down in the valley, and they didn't claim you either. Rhali belongs to this clan. She heals this clan.'

He shook his head again, and Cora could sense the frustration and anger. 'I am this clan,' he snapped. Then he grabbed her arm and dragged her out into the cool evening air. The sun had disappeared, but the sky still held a hint of light. She thought he would stop and shout then, but he pulled her around and into the birthing chamber.

'I do everything I can for this clan. You said yourself they respect me as a leader.'

'I can't understand it, but the dragons are connected. I can sense Serassa. She is with me, like Dra was, like the dragons of the Penna, always in my head. And now they are not. It is like I have lost them, like I'm separated from them.'

'So, you took one of mine for your own.'

Cora stepped back from his anger, but he stepped with her, and she realised then that she was trapped in this small space. How had she felt so connected and comfortable with him? Now she was only nervous. She was scared of him, she realised. And she didn't need that, not when she had his father wanting so much from her—now the son seemed to want to take what little she had as well.

'She chose me,' she snapped. He pushed her against the wall and grabbed her hand, pressing it to his chest.

'You know me,' he whispered, the frustration replaced with something she couldn't quite place. And then he was kissing her. It took her by surprise, and although she pushed against him, it wasn't with any real effort. She was curious to see what her father had talked of.

Cora tried to hold on to the moment for too long before pushing him away. As he smiled down on her, Serassa appeared. Then the small dragon was pushing her way inside the small cavern, trying to get between them.

'This is not something to come between,' he murmured.

Cora's heart thumped. Her face was hot, and she knew. No matter what connection she thought she had with Teven, whether he was Oldra or not—he was not the man for her.

'You look disappointed,' he said, sounding it.

She nodded slowly; thankful the dragon was there. 'I expected sparks,' she said.

'Are you saying I'm not a good kisser?' he asked, grinning.

She shook her head. 'It is not what it should be,' she said, again wanting an escape. The dragon managed to put herself between them as she moved towards the door and out into the night air. The dragon pushed Cora out before she blocked the door.

'Why did you come?' Cora asked.

Because you called. Your voice is loudest now.

Cora nodded. 'Will you take me to Artell?'

He won't let me in.

Cora laughed despite the heavy feeling in her chest. 'He will let me in, I hope.'

You think he is the Oldra, she hummed, directing Cora away from the cavern.

Cora put her arms around the dragon's neck, and they lifted into the sky. They touched down near the cliff edge, far enough away from everyone. 'Are you happy with only my voice?' Cora asked.

We will grow.

Cora sighed. Maybe her place was out here, alone. Maybe they would find others. 'What if my father is wrong?' she asked. 'What if Artell isn't the one either? Oldra must be with Oldra,' she said. She had heard it so many times, and her father had smiled that special way every time he'd said it. 'Not everyone can have what they have,' she murmured.

The dragon nudged her, and she smiled.

Come.

Cora climbed back onto the small dragon and closed her eyes against the world, but it wasn't long until the feeling changed around her. Although it was dark, she knew they were somewhere darker, and then they were landing at the base of the dribbling waterfall.

'I told you there was not enough room,' Artell called.

Cora must be here with you. Oldra must be with Oldra.

Artell appeared in the opening then. The dragon took to the wing and disappeared into the inky black above her. Cora sighed.

'Is that true?' he asked.

Cora was beginning to think her father had made a terrible mistake. Artell motioned her in, and she followed him back to the fire.

'My parents are both Oldra,' she said slowly.

'Neither of mine were,' he said matter-of-factly.

'Oh,' she said, then shook her head and took a deep breath. 'My father has told me my whole life that Oldra can only be with Oldra, and that I would understand that when I met the man I was to be with.'

Artell scratched at his head and looked at her as though she was explaining something only she thought was important. 'Teven is Oldra,' he said.

She nodded.

'But you are here. How do you know that he is not the Oldra you were searching for?'

'I'm not searching,' she said, although she realised it must look like that. 'I didn't want to believe him. I had Deen.'

'Deen and Teven, lucky girl.'

Cora looked down at her hands and willed the tears that seemed so determined to fall that this was not the place, nor the time. 'You have sight,' she said.

'Do you want me to look into our future?'

'Mine,' she said. 'Just mine.'

'I don't know that it is worthwhile sharing what is to come. You may try to change it.'

'I don't think I can, no matter how I try.'

'You were running away,' he said.

'I didn't mean to run this far, but I think my mother knew where I was going.'

'She never told you?'

Cora shook her head. 'Only that I would be something great. Or that I was something great. She thinks I saved our people from the shadows before I was born.'

'Are you scared?'

'Not of the shadows,' she said, which was mostly true. Merik appeared in them too often, but Cora wasn't quite sure what she should be afraid of when it came to him. 'Is Merik an Ancient?'

'He is hard to define; but then, so are you. What does your mother think you have?'

Cora shook her head.

He held out his hand, his face serious. 'I will look for you.'

She placed her hand in his and again was surprised by the lack of emotion, the calm comforting warmth. She closed her eyes and opened her mind to him.

They stood in the shadows, which felt cloying and scary for the first time in a while. Merik's face appeared in them again, and she jumped, but the warm hand in hers kept her grounded. As the face drifted in and out of the shadows, Cora wasn't sure if she was scared or he was disappearing. Then she felt a sharp, burning sensation over her heart. She put her hand to the mark.

A choir of voices filled her mind. So many dragons, yet none she knew. Although as she listened to their call, she knew every one of them. Serassa stood out amongst them.

Then she was standing in the middle of the Penna cavern. It looked just like it always had, and yet very different. An old woman moved slowly through a nearly empty main cavern as Cora stepped forward.

'Mama?'

The woman stopped and looked Cora over, her eyes sad. Then she turned away.

'Mama, what has happened?'

The woman stopped and turned back over her shoulder. 'Don't let him take what is yours.'

'I don't have anything for him to take.'

The old woman turned and appeared as the mother Cora remembered leaving. 'He will take all he can, as he has from his own people. He cannot see you here, but he can see you. He has seen what you will become, as have I. Listen to your heart and the hearts around you.'

As she faded into the shadows, Cora blinked into the light. She released Artell's hand and stepped back. Her mother still knew so much more than she would tell. And none of it helped her. Look into her own heart—what did she think she would find there? Surely not enough to help these people, or to stop Merik from whatever it was he wanted. And it wouldn't get her home.

'She has great gifts,' Artell said softly. Cora looked up, remembering he was there. 'You too will be a great Ancient.'

Cora laughed. 'I am supposed to be Chief, according to my father, and I don't have any real skill.'

'You healed Teven, not only the wound in his chest but the scars on his heart, revealing who he was.'

She shook her head. She may have lifted some of the pain, but she wasn't sure of the man he was.

'You healed me,' Artell said, stepping forward.

'I wasn't given a choice.' Cora felt the same panic close in around her as she had when she had felt his life slipping away. 'I struggle to heal. It is not as easy as it should be, as it is for my mother.'

'I don't think it is meant to be easy. I wonder if your mother struggles more than you allow her. She is a woman like any other.'

'She is like no one else.'

'There have been Ancients before.'

Cora nodded, unsure what he was getting at.

'They have had various skills. They do things differently. You have lived long enough to know them. Are they all like your mother?'

She thought about the Ancients she knew and those she had learned of through her mother and others. 'I'm not like them. I'm not the great Oldra they all talk of.'

'Maybe not,' Artell said softly. She looked at him again.

'I'm not good at anything. I'm not good enough to be Ancient. I am simply an Oldra. I talk to dragons, all dragons.'

'How many dragons do you talk with now?'

She looked down at the ground then, feeling more overwhelmed than ever before. 'One,' she murmured.

He took her hand and led her to the mat where she watched him sit down, but she wasn't sure she should sit with him. 'You were to show me the future,' she said.

'Maybe it is not set.' He smiled up at her. 'You could look at my past.'

She sat down slowly then. 'Do you not know it?'

'It may not be as I remember.'

'I'm not sure how it happens,' Cora said as he held out his hands again. 'I haven't searched for it, it tends to find me.'

'Then let us see.'

She took his hands in hers and focused on his face. His eyes were pale, but not the same as Teven's, and she focused on the hint of green. He closed his eyes, and she felt him open up to her. She closed hers and found herself standing at a hearth in the cavern in the valley. It was open and bright, and she felt at home. A small boy wandered between the hearths, but no one paid him any attention. He was searching for something. Cora walked slowly towards him.

'You should not be here,' she said in a small boy's voice. 'You should go before they become angry.'

'Won't you help?'

'I can't. You know we can't.'

'Artell,' a woman's voice called, and the hide that led to the Ancient's cavern was pulled back.

The older woman motioned him forward with a smile, then looked at the other boy and gave him a gentle wave to go. He hung his head and headed for the door. As Artell watched him go, Cora felt the concern the boy had for the other and the disappointment that there was nothing he could do.

'Don't encourage him,' the older woman said as he entered the cavern.

'I'm not.'

'What have you worked on since we last met?' she asked, indicating the mat by the fire. He sat quickly and crossed his legs.

'I encouraged the suns to rise early.'

'An easy task,' the woman said slowly.

'No one will let me get close enough to help with anything else. I saw…' He stopped, and Cora could feel his heart pounding, the fear too real.

'What did you see?'

'Mother,' he said, the lump tight in his throat and the loss overwhelming.

'She is not gone,' the older woman said kindly, reaching forward and putting her hand on his. He pulled away quickly.

'I don't like to see what is to come. It comes without me asking for it. A touch, a thought.'

'Henda,' the older woman called, and a young woman appeared.

'Yes, Ancient?'

'Work with the boy. I fear he may let his gifts take him over.'

The woman nodded, and Cora recognised her for the woman she had met. She looked nearly the same. The older woman climbed to her feet and left them alone in the cavern.

'How do you stop it?' Artell asked.

'You cannot,' Henda said. 'But then, my gifts are not as great as yours. I can only see when I am looking. You can sense it.'

'I don't want to sense it. I see so much. There is so much pain and loss.'

'But surely there is joy as well.'

'There may be, but I see little of it.'

'What of your mother's new baby?'

He shook his head then, and Cora felt the loss and hurt. She pushed her hand over the burning mark in her chest. The woman beside him looked sad, and her face fell.

'Will the child die?' she asked.

Artell shook his head and then nodded.

'I am sorry. There is always some pain.'

'There is *only* pain,' he snapped. 'I cannot watch her die.' He climbed to his feet, wiping at the tears. 'I cannot watch them all die.'

And then he was running out through the main cavern, the people around him a blur. Someone called to him, but he continued on, his legs pumping and his heart aching. He ran through the trees, ran and ran until there was nothing left and he dropped to the ground exhausted.

You cannot run from who you are, an old voice hummed through him.

'I can try,' he murmured, climbing to his feet and continuing through the trees.

Cora opened her eyes and looked at the man sitting in front of her. His warm hands were still in hers. 'You aren't scared of my future,' she said.

'I don't know you,' he murmured, pulling from her hold and standing. When Cora looked up, he was looking beyond her.

She turned. At the sight of the red robes, she climbed quickly to her feet and bowed her head.

'I thought you might need some supplies,' Henda said, a knowing smile on her lips. 'But I see you have all you need.'

'You could take her with you,' Artell said. Cora remained where she was. She wanted to see if he was serious, and his words hurt her more than she realised they could. He was right—he didn't know her. And she certainly didn't know him.

'She is where she needs to be, as well you know.'

'I'm not sure where I should be, but Teven and Merik will be waiting,' Cora said, turning and bowing her head quickly to Artell and then moving past Henda. She stood beyond the waterfall looking up at the distant stars. Something rarely seen in her world. One of the moons inched into view, and she realised she had been standing too long looking up at the world. She sighed and made for the path out.

As her foot found the incline, she turned and pressed her back to it. Then a hand took her arm in the dark, and she sucked in a breath.

'Stay,' he said.

'They will come looking for me,' she said.

'They don't even know I exist.'

She took a step forward and closer to him. Looking up, she wondered why she had come to him in the first place. 'I mentioned your name.'

He continued his serious look. 'Did they believe you?'

'No,' she murmured. 'Why?'

'That day I ran, I didn't return.'

'We aren't far from the Nerrim clan,' Cora said.

'Henda worked out very quickly where I had gone. She sees more than she would let on. The old Ancient you saw, she would have known as well, but she wouldn't admit that I could not be what she was so sure I would become.'

'What was that?' Cora asked.

'The greatest of them all,' he said as he turned slowly and walked back through to his little cavern. 'I didn't believe it either.'

'In the same way I don't believe it of myself?'

'I guess so. I didn't want the gifts I had been given. And I didn't know how to live with them.'

'But you have worked it out.'

'I stay away from people,' he said too loudly. 'I make sure I'm not close enough to learn anything I don't want to.'

'Why do you want me to stay, then? What do you think I can do for you?'

'Why do you think I am keeping you here for my own good? It might be for yours.'

'You think Merik can take what I don't have.'

He sighed rather than asked another question, and Cora looked down at her hands. Then she looked around. Was this a good idea? To come here in the first place, let alone stay? The cavern itself was quite small; there was a fire, the mat, a work area off to the side and a single sleeping mat.

She focused on it for a moment and then looked away. 'I think I should go.'

He shook his head again and then looked down. 'I think you might be able to help me.'

'Where is Henda?'

'She returned to the cavern.'

'How?'

He indicated into the dark. 'There is a path through the cliff.'

'That might have been easier,' Cora murmured.

'But it would have been closer to the cavern, and you can't be seen.'

She nodded slowly. 'So close, and yet you don't visit the cavern?'

'At times.'

'They know you are still alive, then?'

'Yes, they do. My father accepts my ways only because I am Ancient, but then I don't always dress as one. And although he would not tell me what I should do, he would rather I helped Henda.'

'Is she Oldra?'

He nodded.

'So many,' she said. 'Should you connect with her? Our Ancients were mated…'

'She is as old as my mother,' he muttered. 'Why must an Oldra be with an Oldra?'

'It is just the way,' Cora said with a shrug.

'Do you have a sense of how they came to know that?'

She nodded, feeling her whole body burn at the thought of her parents together. Her mother had told her that she had known the moment they had kissed. But Cora also knew that she had been conceived in that fiery coming together, and she didn't want to relive that. Not that she had yet, but thinking of them, the little cavern came to mind.

She squeezed her eyes closed against the memory trying to share itself with her, and then Artell's soft, warm hand was in hers. The icy water chilled her as she stood in the lake, the water lapping around her and Pira muttering about how he didn't understand her as he pulled her from the water and into his arms.

The blanket was soft and warm, and he was too close. She could feel the electricity, and then they were kissing. The fire shot through her body, and she knew just what he was to her in that moment.

Cora pushed away from the memory and out of Artell's grasp.

He was flushed, and he blew out a long breath.

'I don't want that,' she said.

'That connection?'

'That memory.'

He nodded slowly, his brow knitted. 'I see why your father thinks there is something you will find with another Oldra.'

'Maybe I've had it, and I couldn't see it because I was looking for what he said I needed.'

'Then return to Teven and kiss him and find what you need,' Artell snapped, his harsh voice slicing through her.

She stood slowly, unsure at the strange cold feeling that covered her skin. She bowed her head and headed into the darkness. She could only hope she was headed in the right direction to find her way out and into the valley. She didn't want to return to Teven—she didn't want to risk whatever it was that Merik thought he might be able to take from her.

She needed someone who knew what she was, and Henda was her only hope. The pathway was dark and twisted. Cora was reminded of the hallway that led to the Ancient cavern, but there was no light, and then the cold air wrapped around her. She breathed a sigh of relief and then paused. She had no idea where she was, how close or far she was to the cavern, or who might be waiting for her in the darkness.

She took a deep breath, stepped away from the base of the cliff face and tripped. Just catching herself before she fell, she doubted it was a good idea to continue. When she looked back, the world around her was just as dark. She knew she wouldn't be able to find her way back unless Artell wanted her to, and he wasn't very welcoming right now.

No one wanted her there, and yet no one would allow her to leave. She moved into the darker shapes of the trees, determined to find her own way. Maybe she would find herself on the way. Everyone seemed so sure that there was something else about her that she didn't know herself.

Then strong arms closed around her, a hand covered her mouth and an unfamiliar voice whispered in her ear, 'Shh.'

21

Cora was dropped in the middle of the cavern of the Nerrim. The lighting was dimmer, but it was late at night. She sat on the floor and waited. There was a general murmur around her, but she didn't look up at the people.

'You were told to stay away,' the chief said, standing before her. She looked up slowly. His face was creased into an angry scowl. Cora was disappointed that no matter where she went, no one seemed to need or want her, other than Merik. She felt lonelier than she thought possible.

'Whose blood is that?' someone asked, and she looked down at the splattered mess she still was. If she transitioned, would she be able to hide in some way from these people? Instead she remained silent. She had to be strong. She could be strong. She was Draga, after all, and as future Chief she was representing her people.

'Cora,' Henda's soft voice asked. 'Did something happen with Artell?'

She nodded once, and a gasp rippled through the crowd.

Anger rolled off the chief. 'When?' he asked, motioning to two men behind him who were quick to disappear. The group around her crowded closer.

'This afternoon,' she said. 'He wanted to see what healing I could do, but he cut deeper than he expected.'

'He was well enough when I saw him,' Henda said.

'He will be bruised and sore, that is all,' Cora added quietly. She still wanted him to feel his stupidity. And she didn't particularly want to see him again.

'You didn't harm him?' the chief asked, his concern evident.

'I saved the idiot,' Cora muttered, voicing exactly what she did not want. The crowd murmured louder.

'That idiot is our Ancient,' the chief growled.

Cora sighed. 'Then he should behave as such.'

She wasn't sure what they wanted or what they would do, but she was tired and wrung out, and she honestly didn't care what they thought of her or where they would send her.

'Cora of the Penna,' a deep voice rumbled, but she didn't look up. Artell had either followed her or been sent for, but either way this man didn't live as separately from his people as he had claimed.

Cora was nudged from behind. She climbed slowly to her feet and then bowed her head towards him without making eye contact.

'My apologies, Chief. She has gifts I wanted to explore. She is far from home and although she stays with the others, it is not her choice.'

Cora remained waiting with her head bowed and hoped her legs would continue to hold her up.

'Did something happen to Teven?' Henda asked.

Cora shook her head, but the crowd continued to murmur. It was not a name they were happy to hear. She glanced up as several men moved closer through the crowd. Large broad men, and she missed her bow. These were the warriors of this clan. These were the men she should be comfortable with.

She almost asked if they could show her where to hunt. The people of the other cavern were hungry, and she would like to help them. But Teven knew where to hunt; he just wasn't prepared to take her. And Merik would not appreciate the help.

'What does he think you have?' Henda asked.

'I don't know,' she said.

'I may be able to find out,' Artell said.

'Will you stay?' the chief asked him, and Cora looked up at the wanting in his voice as Artell shook his head. 'Go about your business,' the chief snapped at the people. Cora was reminded of her father. 'Come,' he said, motioning her forward. Without a look at Artell, she followed him across the cavern to his hearth as the people dispersed.

There were some young people there, but he waved his hands and they too moved away. It was set up similarly to Artell's hearth. A large woven mat, and a low table with no seats in the middle of it. He indicated the mat and she sat slowly. He sat near her, and a young woman appeared with two cups, which she sat on the table beside them.

He held out his hand to the cup, and Cora picked it up. She put it to her lips and then waited. He drank from the other cup as she tipped hers up to taste the ale inside. She sat it down with a smile.

'I am Edgris of the Nerrim,' he said, patting his chest. 'You are welcome, Cora of the Penna.'

He waved, and the young woman appeared again. 'Find some clothes for our guest,' he said.

'You don't need to do that.'

'I do. Was it so bad?'

'With Merik?'

'Artell. How was he an idiot?'

Cora sighed and looked back to the cup. 'He cut far deeper than he intended. He wanted to test my healing skills and very nearly killed himself in the process.'

The chief gave a gruff kind of laugh. 'I am sure he knew just what he did.'

Cora looked down at her hands and rubbed her fingers over her palms. 'I felt his life slipping away,' she whispered. The panic she had felt returned and it burned at her chest, just as her father's injury had her mother's. Although she had lived that moment as her mother had, so many times before, she had a better understanding of it now. The hot tear falling on the back of her hand surprised her. She wiped quickly at her face and then gulped down the ale.

The woman reappeared with a bundle of clothes and looked at the chief, unsure what to do with them. 'They are not as you would wear,' she said apologetically.

'Nothing here is as I would wear,' Cora said, climbing to her feet to take the clothing. The tunic was much longer than she expected, and she held it out. It was a soft yellow, similar in colour to the tunics worn by the Penna women. She was reminded again of how she didn't quite fit. But she nodded her thanks.

'What is it?' the chief asked, his voice kind, and she turned to him.

'I am not a woman,' she said.

He laughed, and the young woman before her flushed.

'Then what are you?' he asked.

Cora wasn't quite sure. 'I am Draga, Oldra, daughter of chiefs, but I'm not a woman.'

'You can be a woman and all of those things too,' Henda said, appearing at the hearth. As the chief bowed his head in acknowledgement, she stepped forward. 'Your mother is a woman. She is mother, healer, seer, Ancient, Oldra, chief and friend. You do not have to be only one.'

Cora nodded, and Henda took the clothes from her arms. 'Come and dress. Then you can rest.'

Cora turned back to the chief, who nodded. 'We will talk more tomorrow.'

She bowed her head and followed Henda towards the cavern of the Ancients. She noticed Artell walking towards the chief's hearth on the way, but she looked away before he could make eye contact. Why had his words about Teven hurt her?

They entered the cavern, and Henda motioned to a space by the back wall. There was a basket of water and a soft cloth.

'Wash and change. Then we can talk.'

Cora did just that, keen to get the clothing off. She had never been so covered in blood, and the bitter scent of it was starting to seep into her pores. She didn't think she wanted to be around it ever again. For the first time, she wondered at the emotional weight such an ability might have on others.

When she was dressed, Henda called her back to the mat and motioned for her to sit down. Then she sat behind Cora and untied her hair. With her time in the water and everything else she had been up to, she was sure her hair was a mess. Henda ran her fingers through it, snagging occasionally as she pulled it free.

As she ran a brush through it, she asked, 'Why do you think Artell lied to you?'

Cora tried not to sigh. She hadn't voiced the concern, and yet she felt it. He had given her the idea he had lived alone all those years, away from people so as not to sense their future. 'He may not have lied. He may have only told me part of his truth.'

Henda laughed and pulled at a snag in her hair. 'That is very generous of you. He visits with us; he will even stay here.' She pointed past Cora at one of the sleeping mats. 'But he feels more than he likes, and he spends much of his time alone.'

'What if he is needed here? What if they need a healer?'

'I am the healer. He has different gifts.'

Cora pulled away and turned to look at Henda. 'What am I?' she asked.

'Only you can find it. You can heal. You are a strong healer.'

'It took me a long time to find that ability.'

'You can see the past of others.'

'Not everyone,' Cora said.

'Have you really looked?'

'I'm not sure I want to. Most of it is painful, or...' She flushed at the thought of her parents.

Henda laughed again. 'We rarely get what we want as gifts, but what we need.'

'Essara is wise,' Cora said, but she wasn't sure she believed it in that moment. Did the snow really understand what she had given her, and would it matter now that she was so far away?

'Sleep now,' Henda said.

'I'm not sure I want to. I don't know what dreams I might have.'

'Let Essara guide you,' Henda whispered, putting her arms around Cora and pulling her close. 'Now go,' she said, pointing to one of the sleeping mats.

Cora slipped in between the furs and curled up. She was far more exhausted than she had admitted, and for the first time she felt as though she was in a safe place. She drifted to sleep quickly.

She woke to a dark room, realising that she had not dreamt at all. What had woken her? There was a whispered conversation by the fire. She tried to move to hear better, but without making a sound so as not to alert them she was awake.

'What were you trying to prove?' Henda asked sternly.

'It was an accident. I thought if I could get her distracted with using her healing, I might be able to get a better look at what she is.'

'And how did that work?'

'It didn't,' he murmured. 'That blade you gave me was sharper than I realised.'

'What did you see of her?'

'Not her future. Her mother called to her. There is a strong connection between them. She wanted to know that Cora was safe, and I think she knows what is to come.'

'You saw nothing of her future here?'

'Maybe she does return. Maybe she isn't the way to push Merik from the shadows.'

'Hmm,' Henda murmured. 'And what did she show you of your past?'

'Only what I wanted her to see, my move to the cavern. She doesn't trust that now. I saw her parents...'

'She showed you their past?' Henda asked excitedly.

'Her father is sure she must connect to another Oldra. I saw them come together. The connection was overwhelming. I don't know that I want that.'

Cora felt her mark burn sharply at the comment, but she wasn't sure what it was a reaction to. Was she disappointed? Was her father wrong? Was it only something her parents shared? She squeezed her eyes closed. They wanted her here for a reason. They wanted her here to do what they could not.

Artell had described Merik as difficult to define, but did he have the strength to get what he wanted? And what was that? Cora had found her healing, but there was more. It was like they were looking for more, but she couldn't identify it.

She tried to think of Wyndha and the gifts she had. They were all different. But what made Cora the great Oldra her mother was so sure she was? None of it made any sense.

In her mind, Wyndha walked through the cavern of the Penna. Her white tunic matched those of the other Draga. She was a warrior first, Cora thought as the woman walked fluidly past a hearth and smiled at her. Another memory of her mother's.

Arminel came to mind, taking her hand in his and reaching for her with his mind. *One of my own*, she thought. So often she dreamt of others—rarely did she dream her own past. Maybe because she held her memories so close. Or was it because she was focused on everyone else?

Cora focused on the conversation that had stopped by the fire. Henda was so like her mother, yet so different. Her mother had been prepared to sacrifice herself for her people; these people wanted to sacrifice Cora to save themselves.

Was Henda Oldra? Artell had indicated that she was, as was every Ancient she knew of. Cora focused on the idea of the woman as she lay still, her eyes closed. She imagined the red tunic. Her dark hair bobbed as she raced through the cavern. The older woman from her memory of Artell appeared just as old, although the Henda she saw was almost as young as Artell when he ran away.

'What do you hear?' the older woman asked. But instead of listening for the answer, Cora focused on the woman. She didn't know her name. No one had mentioned it, yet she should have sensed it from the memories as though they were her own.

'Silphi,' Cora whispered. The old woman turned to her with a smile and bowed her head. 'Do you know what I am?' she asked.

'I am not the one to ask,' Silphi said, turning her attention back to Henda. Cora watched as Henda continued to run, then dropped to the mat beside Silphi.

'We flew so high,' she said, still breathless from the running and, Cora was sure, from the excitement of the dragon flight. She remembered her own excitement at that first time, and she still felt it when she flickered. Her mind leapt to Serassa, wondering if she could flicker with her, and the dragon came to her mind.

Do you want to leave them?

I'm not sure. I think I can learn from them, but I'm scared, Cora thought in return.

I will do as you wish.

'Thank you,' Cora whispered.

'Cora?' Artell asked, his voice barely audible above the gentle crackle of the fire.

She sat up then.

'Are you awake? Who do you thank?'

She shook her head. 'I'm not sure what… I might have been dreaming,' she murmured. 'Can I have a cup of water?'

'Do you always dream?' he asked as he handed her a cup.

She shook her head.

'Have you ever dreamt of something that wasn't your past or someone else's?'

She was almost tempted to admit that no one in her dreams had talked back to her before tonight, but then she hadn't stopped and asked them questions before tonight. Maybe she had more access to the Ancients than she'd realised. 'Only once,' she said.

Both of them watched her too closely.

'Before I came here, not long before, I dreamt of Teven. I was standing at a hearth with him. Although it wasn't the hearth of the cavern where he lives.'

'Do you know where it was?'

She shook her head. 'Merik was in the shadows.'

'Always watching,' Artell murmured.

'So it seems, although he doesn't see it all.'

Artell shook his head and looked at Henda. When he turned back to Cora, he smiled. 'You need your rest,' he said, indicating that she lay back. 'We would like you to stay with us.'

'If your chief agrees, I will stay.'

Artell looked at her quizzically for a moment and then nodded. 'I will check with him, but we are the Ancients.'

'Ancient or not, he is Chief. It is his cavern and his people at risk in having me here. It must be his decision.'

Artell sighed, but he nodded. Then he sat back down by the fire. As Cora waited, Henda rose to her feet and headed out of the cavern.

'Would it not be best if you asked?'

'It matters not,' Artell said, and Cora lay down.

Mama would know what to do, she thought as she closed her eyes and found a comfortable place within the furs.

22

Cora opened her eyes to find herself in the Ancient cavern of the Penna. Arminel clapped like a child, and her mother smiled. Cora threw herself into her mother's arms and held her tight.

'I knew you were special,' her mother whispered, and Cora leaned back.

'I'm not here. Is this another dream?'

'You have travelled far,' Arminel said, the grin wide across his old face.

'Can I visit Re-Mah too?'

'Who have you visited?' he asked.

'Only those I am with, mainly their pasts. But when I went back to when one was a child, I was able to interact with the Ancient of her past. Silphi.'

'You hadn't met her?'

Cora shook her head. 'I didn't even know her name until I was in the memory.'

'Anyone else?'

Cora took a deep breath. 'I may have met Wyndha. But,' she added quickly at the look of both wonder and sadness on Arminel's face, 'it may have been a memory of when Mother first came to the Penna.'

'When I first saw her, I thought she was the most amazing woman in the world,' her mother mused.

Cora nodded. 'It was your memory.'

'Any other memories you have discovered?' Arminel asked.

Cora opened her mouth and then closed it.

Her mother looked at her questioningly, then blushed.

'It didn't get that far,' Cora blurted. 'I pulled myself from it. But I saw your first kiss.'

Her mother smiled, and the love she felt for her mate radiated across the

145

distance between them.

'He doesn't want that,' she said, feeling the threatening tears prickle at the back of her eyes.

'Who doesn't?' her mother asked, gently placing a hand on Cora's knee. 'The Ancient I saw with you last time?'

Cora nodded, but she wasn't sure what she wanted herself. She had thought there was a connection to Teven, yet now she was certain it wasn't there. She had only just met this man, and there were no sparks—no trust, she reminded herself.

'It may not be as you expect.'

'I'm not sure what to expect,' she admitted. 'Dra,' she cried. 'Did he return home?'

Arminel nodded, but he looked sad.

'Is he hurt?'

'Only his heart,' Arminel murmured. 'He misses you. They all miss you.'

Cora's lip trembled. She missed them all so very much. 'I have found a new dragon. I think she is young, as she looks very different. She has chosen me,' Cora said, wondering why it was so hard to admit it. 'But there are only the two of us. Her choice has given me a greater understanding of the dragons and how they connect to us. The people here have dragons, green dragons like the trees, but although they will talk with me—well, one has—it isn't the same as Serassa.'

Gerry nodded slowly, and her smile was sad.

'I'm not going to make it back, am I?' Cora asked, but she already knew the answer. It was a painful ache in her chest.

They looked at each other, and then Arminel held out a hand for hers, which she gladly took.

'I want to come home,' she said. 'I want to come home now.'

Her mother took her other hand and smiled as though she understood far more than Cora. 'I think you have far more choices than you realise. You may be able to return. You may not want to.'

'Did you see this?' Cora asked hurriedly.

'I have seen so much it is hard to determine what belongs to whom.'

'I miss you,' Cora whispered. 'But you still annoy me.'

Her mother laughed. 'You will find what you are meant to be and where that is. You may cross the world to return to us and then go back, you may return and stay, or you may not. I have not seen what you will choose. I only know that you will do what is right by your people, as any chief would.'

'What if I'm not destined to be Chief?'

'Your father would have much to say on that,' she said.

'I miss him too. I have met two chiefs, one very much like father, the other...'

'Be careful,' her mother said. 'He may be stronger than he looks.'

'Cora,' a distant voice called, and all three of them turned to look behind her.

'I love you,' Cora said to her mother, then kissed Arminel's cheek before the world around her disappeared and she blinked into the dim light of the Ancient cavern of the Nerrim.

Artell sat beside her, his hands clenched in his lap. She tried not to sigh. Despite the distance and the conversation, she felt rested. She only wished she had really been there and could stay.

'Will you come with me?' he asked. 'I want to test some of your skills.'

'No, thank you,' she said, sitting up. Confusion flittered across his face. 'You might succeed in dying this time. And I might not want to save you.'

She stretched her arms above her head and climbed from the warm furs. Padding across to the fire, she found a pot over the flames. As she pulled it towards her, the water boiling rapidly, she realised he was still sitting in the same place.

'What did you dream?'

'Nothing of your past,' she murmured.

'Why would you dream of my past?'

'I've had your blood on my hands. It seems to follow that whoever I heal gets into my head and I learn more of them.'

'What did you learn of Teven?'

'We have talked of this,' Cora said, looking around for a cup. Then Artell was too close, a cup in his hand. 'Thank you,' she said, holding out her hand.

'What did you dream?' he asked again. 'There is something different.'

'I heard you talking,' she said, taking the cup and pouring the water into it. 'I know you plan to use me, only I'm not sure what for.'

He looked at her as though trying to work out what to say to placate her. She sat down, the hot cup in her hand.

'Will you use me as bait to draw him out?'

He continued to stare.

'And then what will you do? Will you let him take me? How do you think you can stop him? Or do you not even intend to try?'

He let out the breath he had been holding.

'I have seen the shadows of my mother's past. I have seen the man that used them. He didn't travel with them—he *was* the shadows.'

Artell leaned forward, and she leaned away from him. 'We can do this together,' he said.

She shook her head. 'Give me time to learn what I can do, and then I may be able to help you, but that is all there is.'

'I thought you wanted more.'

She shook her head too quickly. 'I think you are right; my father was mistaken.'

'He seemed very certain,' Artell said, almost disappointed.

'My parents are not like others. And although I am to follow them, I cannot expect the same.' She blew across the top of the cup and sipped at the water.

'What have you learnt?'

'You see what I am to be. You tell me what I should be learning.'

'I want to help,' he said. 'Is this new hostility because of what you heard last night? I don't think you heard the full story.'

'I heard enough,' she murmured, then turned towards the doorway at the ruckus in the main cavern.

Artell indicated that she stay where she was, but she was on her feet and through the hide curtain. Teven stood in the middle of the cavern, several men around him and a bow over his shoulder. It looked out of place, and then she recognised it as her own. It was so new, and yet she hadn't had the chance to use it.

'You have to give her back,' Teven shouted into the men around him.

'We haven't taken her,' the chief said. 'She walked through our doors.'

Not quite, Cora thought, but she was glad she was here. In some ways, she had more space to breathe.

The group opened up for her as she walked towards him.

'What have they done to you?' he asked.

She shook her head and held out her hand. He reached his hand out towards hers. 'My bow,' she said.

His hand dropped. Then he took the bow from over his shoulder and handed it to her. She bowed her head in thanks.

'You need to return with me.'

'No,' she said softy. 'I have been welcomed here,' she said, glancing towards the chief. It wasn't quite right, but his subtle nod indicated that she could stay. 'I don't want to return to Merik.'

'You can't call him that,' Teven whined like a child. 'He is Chief.'

'He is not my chief. And if I am to learn what he is so sure I can learn, I must stay here.'

'Must you?' Teven asked.

'Yes. You are well enough now to do as you must for your clan. I need to do what I can for mine.'

'Your clan?' he asked.

'If I am to return home,' she said.

'Is that what you want? You don't want to stay with me?' He sounded far more wanting than Cora thought he could be. What did he think there was between them? He had hardly spoken to her, just done his father's bidding and forced a kiss on her that had only proven to her that her father had been wrong all this time.

'It is not where I am meant to be,' she said softly.

'Who are you to be with?' he asked, pushing through the crowd and across the cavern. She watched him go, wondering what he would think when he found the boy he thought dead sitting in the cavern. But he stopped in the doorway, and Cora could see Henda standing before him.

'She is strong,' she said. 'She will train with me.'

Teven bowed his head and turned back. His face a mixture of sadness and anger, he stomped out of the cavern. Several men made to follow, but Edgris called them back. Then he looked across at Cora. 'I hope you know what you do,' he said.

'So do I,' she murmured, then headed back to the Ancients' cavern and Henda.

23

Cora sat silently on the mat of the Ancient's cavern and watched the woman fuss over a pot on the flames. Artell had disappeared, and she wasn't sure if he was hiding from her or Teven.

'Who is the human boy?' Cora asked.

'I think he would consider himself a man,' Henda said without looking around. 'He was called by a dragon.'

'Why?'

'Sometimes they do what they do, and we know nothing of it.'

'He was called for a purpose.'

'How can you be sure?' Henda asked, turning from the flames.

'Why call someone if there is no reason? My mother was human; she was called for a great purpose. Darring was called because they needed Draga.'

'Two?' she asked.

Cora nodded.

'Would they fight for you?'

'Is there a need?'

'You sound too calm, too measured. Where is the nervous girl of yesterday?' Henda asked, waving the spoon. The porridge flicked across the mat, and Cora raised her eyebrows. Henda dropped the spoon altogether. 'You found it,' she said, lowering to her knees before Cora.

Cora shook her head. 'I need to be here to find it. I understand that. I also understand that you intend to use me in some way to defeat Merik, although you don't know what he is.'

Henda sat back. 'He talks too much.'

'As do you,' Cora said. 'I heard you last night.'

150

Henda looked down at the mat. 'I am sorry,' she murmured. 'But he is stronger than he appears.'

Cora waited.

Henda sighed, then glanced at the doorway before continuing. 'He can travel in his dreams, enter those of others, watching and learning.'

'I have seen him in the shadows of my dreams.'

'He is looking for something great, although I'm not sure what it is. He will take that power for himself; then he can do as he pleases.'

'But he is with his own people, whom he neglects while he searches for this unknown gift. He could be more powerful than he is. How will he take this gift when he finds it?'

'He can take strength from others.'

'Then he could have taken my mother's, for she is much stronger than I am.'

'He might have seen what you would become from her, and so left her as she was.'

'Rhali said he caused the girl's death.'

'He may have taken her will to live, strengthening his own. It is not a gift I understand.'

'Can you see what he will do?'

'He will suck the life from all the people and live long after we are gone.'

Cora stared at the woman opposite her. 'Has he lived longer because of what he has taken already?'

'He was very ill as a boy, and he should have died.'

'Should have?' Cora asked.

'It was something we could not heal.'

'He healed himself,' Cora said. 'I have done such a thing.'

'Another child, a sister of his, was helping with his treatment. She cared for him, wished him well, and he grew better, although no one knew how. The sister withered away to nothing.'

'How is that possible?' Cora asked.

'It scared a lot of people, and it isolated him somewhat as he grew. The other children were wary of him.'

'What did the Ancient say was the cause?'

'She did not know, but his mother was sure that Essara herself had saved him. She didn't seem to wonder why the daughter had died as she had. There were some strange occurrences that I have heard of as he grew, before he reached the decision to leave.'

'What sort of occurrences?' Cora asked.

Henda shook her head. 'It is all long ago. Whether he has a gift or not, I have seen what he will become.'

'Does he visit your dreams?'

Henda shook her head. 'I am not as strong as he is. I'm not much use at all, other than some healing.'

'You are Ancient.'

'Sometimes that is not enough. I know Artell is much stronger than I, a better Ancient than I could ever be, yet he chooses not to be here. He struggles being close to the people. Namings are painful, and the few he has performed worried the families of the child more than he wanted. He can feel the joy,' she said, 'but he focuses on the pain.'

'Why?'

'It may be his mother's death; he was too young to feel such a thing.'

Cora was reminded of the vision she'd had of him running away, and although it was a terrible thing for a child to live through, she also knew he had chosen to show her that memory. There were other memories that might have better explained who he was. 'Why does Teven think Artell is dead?' she asked.

'He would come to visit Artell. They were close, in a way. When Artell ran away, although he would visit, it was thought best to tell Teven he was gone, trying to keep him away.'

'That seems cruel,' Cora said. 'He was just a boy with no one to care for him.'

'Some of our hunters would allow him to tag along, learn how to hunt and fish and collect wood.'

'And yet you would not take him in, leaving him with that man.'

'He wanted to stay for his sister. She didn't hold enough gifts for Merik to be interested. When her mother died, she would have followed if Teven hadn't cared for her.'

Cora nodded slowly and ran her fingers through her hair, remembering the long braid he had tied for her.

'You have gifts,' Cora said. 'You must have something, or you would not be Ancient. You may be a better healer than you allow, but you have deferred to Artell.'

'He does not heal.'

'Rhali can heal with herbs, but she doesn't have the gifts to heal as you would.' Cora looked over the woman before her. 'You hesitated with Teven, yet that wasn't because you couldn't heal him; you didn't think you should.'

She shook her head quickly, but Cora was sure she was right. 'I must do what I can for my people.'

'Even if that means people will die?' a measured voice asked behind her.

The chief stood in the doorway, and Cora sighed. She wasn't sure that she wanted to stay with these people. She might be able to hide herself away as Artell had and learn what she was from the other Ancients. She wondered if she needed to know them by name or learn about them from others before she could talk to them in her dreams.

'What is it?' the chief asked, stepping forward.

'I may know what he wants from me,' she whispered. 'I don't think I should stay.'

'He is strong, but we can protect you here.'

She shook her head. 'He can still find me.'

'Not at my cavern. He can't see you there,' Artell said, entering the cavern behind the chief.

Cora stepped back, shaking her head again. She didn't want to put herself close to him again. He might be the similar to Merik in many respects. He might not want her gifts to stop Merik. She was only sure he wanted to use her.

'We will keep you safe,' the chief said again.

'Then I will stay here,' she said, looking at Henda. 'But I would like the chance to make my own arrows. I am a Draga without weapons.'

The chief nodded and waved a man forward. 'Tilwin will go with you. He knows the woods well and where you can find what you need.'

'Thank you,' Cora said.

'I could help,' Artell said, but she shook her head, and the man indicated the doorway.

She followed him out through the cavern, where some people looked up from their hearths and more dragons seemed to fill the space. They nodded towards her, but she couldn't hear them. Her heart ached, and a lone voice called out.

'Where is your dragon?' Tilwin asked when they were outside the cavern.

'Keeping her distance for now,' Cora said.

'You came by dragon,' he said. 'Where is that animal now?'

'He returned home,' she said with sigh. 'I can't reach him.'

'Is it lonely without him?'

She looked at Tilwin, taking in his serious face. The chief must have talked with the clan about what he had learnt from her, as her father would do if a stranger were to appear in their midst. He was older than she was, but not by much.

'I just thought that if my dragon disappeared, it would be as bad as losing my mate.'

She nodded. 'We have been bonded my whole life,' she said.

'Truly?'

'He chose me early on. There were times that I resented not being able to find my own dragon, but I think it is always their choice.'

'And now?'

'She chose me too. And it changed everything.'

Tilwin stopped then and looked her over. 'What happened to your arrows?'

'I lost them when I fell, or they were taken from me. I'm not sure which.

Either way, I need more.'

'Do you have arrow heads?'

She shook her head. 'I'll sharpen the points like our practice arrows. It will be effective enough.'

'What are you hunting?' he asked as they headed off.

'Where do you hunt?'

He stopped and pointed into the trees. 'Further down the valley, there are a variety of animals.'

'There are none near the other cavern.'

'I don't think it was a consideration when they left.'

'Did you know them?' she asked.

He shook his head and continued walking. Before long, they were amongst some younger trees with branches strewn around the ground. Tilwin produced a sharp knife. He cut a number of branches from the tree and handed them to Cora as he went. Once she had an armful, he looked at them and then those on the ground.

'They take some aging, but they will be suitable.' He collected an armful of branches from the ground and indicated that she spread what she had in her arms across the ground in their place.

Cora was surprised at the ease with which Tilwin accepted her and talked with her. They spoke of her life with the Penna and how she had come to be where she was. The conversation continued when they returned to the cavern, and she was invited to sit at his hearth. She accepted a cup of ale from his mate, a friendly, smiling woman. Cora wondered why they were so accepting now, when they had been too eager to kill her not long ago.

They sat in silence by the fire and scraped over the branches they had collected, smoothing out the already narrow lengths. Tilwin had a bowl of arrow heads, and he showed her how they attached them. It was a little different from what she knew, but it didn't take long to adapt. She ran her hand over the fine blade, then looked at it closely.

'Is it different?' he asked.

She nodded. 'Do they break off before they imbed into the flesh?'

'Are you thinking of a man or an animal?'

Cora looked up and noticed that Tilwin's mate had frozen mid-activity by the fire.

'The animals have different fur where I'm from. The cold means they have a thick wool. And not so long ago, we fought men on dragonback. The arrows are larger, heavier and sharper.'

Tilwin laughed, and his mate turned a nervous smile Cora's way.

'What else do you hope to learn while you are with us?' the woman asked. Cora noticed she was with child, but she said nothing. She wondered if the women of this clan sought the advice and gifts of the Ancients. Artell wouldn't want to see what might lie ahead for them, and Cora didn't have the ability. But she wondered if she could ask others for help.

'You look well,' she said to the woman.

'She has not been herself,' Tilwin said.

'It can be a change,' Cora said.

He looked at her with confusion, and the woman shook her head. He looked between them and then stood quickly, making her stand back. Was she worried what he might say? Was the child of another man?

'Perhaps I should return to Henda,' Cora said, climbing to her feet.

'Take the arrows,' Tilwin said, squatting to pick them up. She nodded her thanks and hurried across the cavern.

<h1 style="text-align:center">24</h1>

'Why does she not tell him?' Cora asked with little introduction when she pushed the curtain back and found the chief sitting with the two Ancients. 'Forgive me,' she said, turning away.

'Come in.' Edgris waved her forward.

'Who do you speak of?' Henda said.

Cora sucked in a deep breath before answering. 'Tilwin's mate.'

'She is worried. She has lost babies before.'

Cora nodded. 'Has she asked for help? Has she asked you to see how the child grows?'

'Not anymore,' Artell whispered.

'She looks well, but Tilwin said she has not been herself.'

'She tries to hide it,' Henda said, looking at the chief.

'I know of her condition,' he said. 'I have children of my own; I have seen others. There is a hope there, or at least there was.' He looked at Cora closely. 'Can you help her?'

'I can't see what might come,' she said. 'Only what has been.'

'Are you willing to tell me what you think Merik wants?' the chief asked.

She shook her head. She only hoped they hadn't worked it out. She might have had the chance to talk to Ancients far away or already with Essara, but she wasn't sure if she could talk to all previous Ancients as she hoped. And if she could, it would mean she could access their knowledge and skills.

'You healed Teven's heart,' Henda said.

'I'm not sure that is the best description. He hasn't appeared healed the last few times I have seen him.' She shivered.

'He scares you,' the chief said, leaning forward.

Cora shook her head, but in some ways he was right. She had been scared by what he might do when he had kissed her. And his anger had worried her when he'd appeared in the cavern.

'Will you look at my heart?' the chief asked softly.

She looked at him closely. 'Are you unwell?'

He smiled kindly. 'I wonder what you will see.'

Cora wasn't sure she wanted to see anyone else's past, or pain, but she bowed her head as he motioned her closer. Trying not to bite into her lip, she raised her hand. He pulled at the material to reveal the mark of Oldra, and she placed her hand directly over it.

She closed her eyes, trying to calm her breathing and focus on what she could feel. There were no sharp burning pains, but there was an ache. She looked deeper. It was for all those he had lost, for the family taken away that he could not free, the mate and child he had lost. It was because he cared for his people. She smiled, despite the ache. He had the heart of a leader, of a true chief. There was more love than pain, more care and understanding. She saw him as an old man, still strong, still guiding the clan.

She pulled her hand back and bowed her head to him.

'I don't feel any different,' he murmured, rubbing his hand over the mark before tying his tunic. It was still loose around the neck. Although they were so different, this man reminded Cora of her father again.

'What did you hope for?' she asked.

He shrugged then.

'There was nothing to heal. The pain you have is for the losses you have experienced with your people. You need to have them to appreciate the joys and wonders.'

'You sound like an Ancient,' he said, smiling kindly.

'I am not what you hope I am.'

'Even more,' he said with a grin. 'You have worked with an Ancient.'

She nodded. She would like the chance to work with more.

'Would you see what I am?' Artell asked, but she shook her head. She was sure there was far more pain inside this man than he had let her know, and she wasn't sure she wanted to get anywhere near it.

'Have you sensed something in him?' the chief asked.

Cora tried not to sigh. She needed some space, but she wasn't going to get it no matter where she went in this world. 'He feels the pain of others,' she said.

'Do you think you will feel that too?'

'I may,' she said carefully. 'I could feel Teven's pain, and his mother's.'

'Truly?' Edgris asked. 'You felt her pain?'

Cora nodded, and a shiver ran down her spine.

'Could you feel Merik? Could you change him, do you think?'

'I didn't change Teven,' she murmured. 'And I couldn't get that close to

Merik. I don't know what he can do.'

'Try Artell,' the chief said. She could sense his excitement, as though he was keen to see just what she could do, but she shook her head again. And clenched her fists in her lap. 'We are here with you,' he pressed.

'But will you be here in the night when I dream his nightmares?'

'Will you dream mine?' the chief asked seriously.

'More of your past might come to me now. This is new; I'm not sure.'

'Will they come for you?' he asked. As she tried to understand his meaning, he added, 'Your people.'

She shook her head. 'I am where I am meant to be. I will return when it is right to do so.'

'Again, sounding like an Ancient,' the chief said with a grin. He climbed to his feet, glancing only quickly at Artell. 'I shall leave it to you to determine what you should do.'

She bowed her head to him, and he left the cavern. She could feel the eyes of the other two on her, trying to sense just what she was. And how they could use that.

'I would like to rest,' she murmured. 'It is harder than I would like to admit to see so much.'

Artell nodded with a sigh. Cora climbed into the sleeping mat and closed her eyes. She wasn't sure she wanted to dream of the chief, or anyone else for that matter. When she next became aware of her surroundings, it was dark, the cavern lights dim, and Merik stood over her. She jumped up and stepped back, nearly tripping over someone. She turned to find Artell slumped across the ground. She looked around in the dim light and realised she was still in the Ancients' cavern.

Henda was lying by the entrance. 'What have you done?' Cora asked, struggling to keep her voice level.

'You must return to me and bring your gifts.'

'I don't know that I have what you want. I'm still searching.'

'You have found them,' he said.

'Who?'

'The Ancients, all of them. I have many names for you to call. I can take this from you, I can take it from them, and I will be the most powerful of them all.'

'How?' Cora asked. 'How can you do this?'

He reached for her heart, and a sharp pain sliced through her chest.

'Stop!' she cried out, sitting up. She pressed her hand to her heart, it ached and she wasn't sure if that was due to the dream. Had he really reached her through the shadows?

What if he could take from her without being there? She looked around then, the light brighter than she expected. Henda sat by the fire, watching her closely. Cora looked around for Artell. He appeared beside her with a cup, and she jumped.

'Thank you,' she murmured, and her hand shook as she took it from him. He closed his hand around hers for a moment to steady her and directed the cup to her lips. The water was cool. Cora transitioned to protect herself from anything else that might try to get at her. But Artell's hands were warm and comforting and still wrapped around hers, and the transition failed.

'Ice,' he murmured.

'I wanted to teach Teven, but he couldn't.'

'Does it melt?' Artell asked.

Cora nodded and tried not sigh, instead sipping from the cup again. He was too close, but she didn't want to continue to push him away.

He waited.

'Dragonlight will melt it, and it is hard to maintain if I am overwhelmed.'

'Dragonlight?' he asked. 'When would a dragon be aiming their light at you?'

'In battle,' she said. 'Although it has been some time, and I haven't seen any myself…' She trailed off as he studied her. 'My people were at war with another,' she said. 'It ended just before my birth.'

'Your mother took on dragonlight?'

She nodded. Had she told him of what her mother had done, how she had risked them both? Although her mother might say it was because of Cora that she could do as she did.

'Now tell me of the dream,' he whispered.

She looked up into his too-close face and shook her head.

'Can all of your people turn to ice?' Henda asked, drawing his attention.

'Yes,' she said. 'You cannot?'

'Ice would not do well in the sun,' Artell said. 'We haven't the need.'

'Living in the snow, we do. It keeps us warm as well as protected from swords and arrows.'

'Can you show me?'

She nodded once and took his outstretched hand, trying to keep her mind from his as she had when she was younger and didn't want Arminel to reach her. Then she transitioned. He grinned, and then his hand turned to ice. 'It is easy when you see how,' he said, turning back to Henda. He closed his eyes for a moment, and Cora could feel him searching, but it wasn't her mind he searched.

His transition of ice slipped, and then his hand in hers hardened, only it wasn't ice—it was stone. Henda cried out. Cora looked him over. It wasn't as though he had changed; she could sense a shell protecting him as the ice did, and he moved as easily as he had before. But instead of shimmering ice, he was matte grey stone. He grinned at her and squeezed her hand, and she realised that she still held him. She closed her eyes and concentrated on what he was, and then her own transition changed to stone.

'Oh my,' Henda exclaimed. 'What did you do to him?'

'What did he do to me?' Cora asked.

'You changed that yourself,' he said with a grin.

'Yes,' she said, releasing her hold on him and standing up. She moved around the room, stretching and bending her limbs. She felt just the same as she did when she transitioned to ice, just as protected. 'Hit me,' she said, turning back to him.

He picked up one of the arrows, and she nodded. But as he lifted it up, Henda stepped between them.

'I can withstand an arrow when I transition; this should be no different.'

She moved slowly and, with surprising force, Artell stabbed at her shoulder with the arrow, snapping the shaft and bending the fine point. Cora let it go and then transitioned again instantly.

As Artell dropped the arrow, she let it slip again and then rubbed at her shoulder.

'Did it hurt?' he asked, rushing forward, his own stone transition slipping.

She shook her head but continued to rub. 'You used some force. I felt it push against me, but it didn't break the skin.'

'I am sorry,' he said, the excitement of his new skill disappearing as quickly as the transition itself did.

'My mother talked of feeling a sword push against her,' she said, watching him. 'It didn't break the skin, but she said it was still unsettling.'

'I can imagine,' he murmured, looking at the ground.

'How did you do that?' she asked.

He looked up as she transitioned and then back again in an instant. 'Where did the stone come from?'

'I thought ice would be impractical, and that if you were going to protect yourself it would be better to be hard like stone. And then I was.'

She smiled.

'Will you look now?' he asked, stepping closer.

'What if I find something you don't want me to see? Will you let me look for myself, or hide what you think I don't need to know?'

'What will he take from you?' Artell asked instead, stepping closer again, but although he was too close, she held her ground.

'Let me look first and see if I can trust you with this, or whether you would take it for yourself.'

Artell nodded once. She lifted her hand to his chest and placed it across the leather tunic. She could sense the mark beneath the fabric, and she wondered for a moment if she could only do this for those with the mark, if it was a way to see between the marks. She might have to test it on another.

She realised then just how close they were. She leaned against Artell's body, his arm around her lower back holding her up and against him. 'I want you to see,' he whispered.

'I might see more than your heart,' she said.

'I will take the risk.'

She closed her eyes to concentrate on the quickening thud, but the warm hand on her back and the hard body she was pressed against pulled at her senses. She blew out a long breath and refocused on the mark. She felt Serassa almost as strongly as when she spoke to her, and she wondered if the dragon had pulled Cora back into a larger group.

Then the hurt of his mother's death was dull and hot and took her breath away. It wasn't sharp, not still tormenting him as Teven's mother did him. But she hadn't died in the same way, in the same sacrifice that only made his life harder. The pain of the clan was there, as it was with the chief, only it was sharper, burning into her hand and her chest. She tried not to wince and move away. His hand still rested on her back, but it didn't hold her locked against him. She could run if she wanted. But then there was a little joy, like hope in the sea of burning pain.

Babies came and went from her vision. They may have offered hope before he learnt of their ends. Some had bright and long lives. She wondered why he didn't just look at the first few years and stop. Maybe it all came at once and he had no control.

In the darkness of his shadows, she thought she saw Merik, but it wasn't him; it was Edgris. Not because he was dark, but because he stood beside it.

And then it was as though she stood in his small cavern. It was a calm, secure world. The pain and panic she had felt were gone; only contentment remained. Then that little spark of joy again, and she saw the dragon curled by the hearth and the woman leaning against it.

She wasn't sure she wanted to see who it was. Another Oldra, another one with the gift of dragons. But as she drew closer, the long, wavy, dark blond hair hid the woman's face. Cora pressed her hand harder against his chest, and his arm closed around her tighter. Then the woman looked up, and Cora saw herself.

She opened her eyes, confused as to how she had found her way into his heart when he was sure it was not what he wanted. Then he closed both arms around her, his lips pressed against hers, and she was lost. The overwhelming contentment she had felt in his heart surrounded her and held her tight. The joy and happiness of knowing him and being with him took her breath away, and yet it filled her with all the nourishment she needed. She didn't want to let him go. She wanted to hold him close for as long as she could.

Her arms had twisted around his neck, and she pulled herself close as his arms pulled even tighter around her. It was as though she couldn't get close enough to him. Couldn't close the gap she could feel between them.

Then someone was coughing, and Cora reluctantly released her tight grip on the man before her to look around at Henda, her face almost as red as the robes she wore, and the chief, who looked somewhat confused.

25

Cora stood by the fire in the little cavern Artell called home, his hand still tight in hers. She wondered at her reluctance to release him. It wasn't so long ago she felt he was too close to her, untrustworthy, and now she knew in her heart that she could trust no one like she could him.

They had been ushered from the cavern by the stammering Ancient and the wary chief. 'Talk out what you must,' he said, 'but...' He hadn't finished as Artell had dragged her from the cavern, through the cool darkening woods and into the cliff face.

'Will he visit?'

'Who?' Artell asked, his face creasing.

'Your father,' she said.

He smiled. 'How did you guess?'

'You have his features. And the way he speaks to you—even though you are Ancient, he is still your father.'

'No one knows how to enter except Henda, and that is only because of her gifts.'

'Will I learn?'

He nodded slowly and then stepped closer again, dropping her hand. He cupped her face and drew it closer. 'You will stay,' he whispered.

It took more will than she thought she had to pull away from him. 'I cannot stay,' she said.

'Your father was right. We are connected. There is no one else for either of us.'

'I understand that,' she said, putting her hand to her heart. The burning sensation she felt in her parents wasn't there, and she wasn't sure if it would ever come or they were yet to trigger it. As much as she wanted to stay, as much as she was sure she needed Artell more than she needed the air around her, she had an obligation to the Penna. And Merik was dangerous.

'You are to be Chief,' Artell said, his arms slipping down to his sides.

'My father might not be right about everything,' Cora said. 'There is more to consider than the two of us.'

'My people, your people, Teven.'

'Merik,' she said.

He sighed. 'What does he want?'

Cora sucked in a deep breath, but she knew she could tell him. 'I can talk to the Ancients.'

He laughed then, and she stared him down. 'You *are* talking to one.'

'Dead ones,' she said, watching his face change. 'Ancients far away.'

'Your mother?'

'And Arminel. Silphi, and with effort I am sure I could meet with Wyndha.'

'You talked with Silphi?'

She nodded.

'How?'

'I dreamt of Henda as a girl, and Silphi and I talked as she ran around.'

Artell's mouth worked, but no words came out. He shook his head as he paced back and forth across the cavern. 'You could learn so much,' he finally said.

Cora watched him, unsure what she could say. She too had thought of what she could learn, how the Ancients could help her help the people. But she worried more for what it might mean in the hands of someone else. 'Can he take this from me?'

'I don't know.'

'Maybe I should go, before he has the chance…'

Artell grabbed her then, a desperation she had seen before glinting in his green-brown eyes. 'You could use this to stop him.'

'How?'

'I don't know,' he snapped, releasing her. He stalked again across the cavern.

'This is hardly helpful,' she said, and he slowed his pace. 'I don't even understand what he is. He could not see the past, yet he could slip into the dreams of others. He could not see the future, only glimpses, and they made no sense.'

'What did he show you?'

She remembered the fear as his life slipped away beneath her hands, blood and desperation the same as in the vision. She wondered then if Merik knew who the man was beneath her hold. She had thought it was Teven, but her glance of the future had been Artell.

He was standing before her, his arms wrapped around her shoulders, and he rested his cheek on the top of her head.

The panic she felt dissipated in his arms. Despite her uncertainty, she smiled. She understood her father so much better now.

'I told you there was no room,' he said quickly. Cora looked up at him, sensing Serassa by the opening of the cavern.

'She is not the dragon I saw in your heart,' Cora murmured. She turned then to look at the dark face and bright eyes in the shadows. 'Is there another?'

In the silence from the two of them, she stepped back and looked at Artell again. 'What is it?'

'I can't find them,' he whispered, the pain evident. She understood the loss. 'There is only one.'

Cora sighed. Her little clan of two had become three, but what did that mean for Artell? 'Did you do this?' she asked Serassa.

You did this. In choosing him, he has become one of us.

'One of you?' Artell asked. 'Who are you?'

'It was just the two of us,' Cora murmured, feeling his disappointment. 'I became separated from my people, and my dragons. Serassa chose me, but in doing so she separated herself from the other dragons.'

'You talk with all dragons,' he said.

'But I am connected at all times with only those dragons of my clan.'

He took her shoulders and pulled her close again. 'You mean you no longer have a clan?'

'I do. It is just a lot smaller.'

'Who else is in it?' he asked, and she could hear the uncertainty. 'Teven?'

'You,' she said. 'It appears we are a clan of three.'

'I have a clan,' Artell said hurriedly. 'You could join us.'

'It isn't up to me. Serassa has chosen, and in connecting with me, you have been chosen too.'

'Then you are Chief and I am Ancient.' He pulled her closer and kissed her, taking her breath away. 'We should start producing children so as to have a clan to support.'

She laughed as she pushed him away. 'That is not how it works.'

'How will it work?'

'I don't know.'

Although she was starting to feel even more overwhelmed, Artell smiled. 'What?' she asked him.

'You could ask Silphi,' he said. 'Merik left to start his own clan, but she said it wasn't right, that he wasn't gifted to do such a thing.'

'And yet he is gifted enough that he worries you.'

'I was too young when he left. Henda remembers more.'

'She would be easier to ask,' Cora said, turning for the doorway.

He gripped her arm and stopped her. The dragon continued to watch from the shadows. 'You know,' she said, 'that space there looks comfortable enough for a dragon.'

'You are Chief of this cavern already, I see,' he said with a laugh.

Thank you, Oldra, Serassa hummed, but the dragon was gone when she looked back towards the door.

Cora looked at the space by the fire and remembered the vision of herself. 'You saw me coming.'

'In a way,' he said, and she turned back to him. 'I didn't fully understand what you were—what we were.'

She nodded. 'I didn't really believe my father. I knew they had a connection. But I didn't fully understand it. I thought they had simply loved each other all along. But it was more than that.' She put her hand to the mark, remembering the sharp burning that had overwhelmed her mother when they had kissed. Cora, on the other hand, had felt something very different, but she knew it meant the same. 'Just before I left, she told me he was disappointed when she first arrived, and I didn't know that. They needed a warrior and expected a strong man, like Darring, to be called by the snow. When he found my mother, she was something else.'

Cora had sensed her mother's life and past so many times, she might have confused it with her own. But she had not seen her father's. She wondered if she could, if she truly wanted to see everyone's past. She had seen the girl's life, before she died.

'Would you like to try?' Artell asked, and she realised he was holding her hand.

She nodded. They sat on the mat by the fire, cross legged and facing each other. He held her hands, and she focused for a moment on the heat of the flames before thinking of her father. She knew what he looked like as a younger man, she had seen him in her mother's memories so many times. There was a moment after Gerry had healed him when she had brushed the hair from his face and she focused on that image of him.

'So far from the cavern,' Pira murmured, trudging through the snow, his transition keeping him warm. 'What was she thinking?' Then he stopped. Ahead of him, shivering in the snow, was the girl he had seen at the house. Her long hair was damp about her face, and she looked terrified. He wanted to wrap her in his arms and stop the violent shivering. Instead he made some quip about her clothing, and she turned her amber eyes on him, and the world around him ceased to exist.

He slipped the coat from around his shoulders and pulled her close. They had to move quickly, or he wouldn't get her there alive. Cora watched every moment of their journey back to the cavern. In trying to maintain his calm, he came across as distant and difficult. He was sure she would cry, and he didn't want to be the cause of that.

'You were not what we expected,' he murmured, looking over the clothes she wore, the tight leggings and fitted tunic as she stood by the fire at his hearth.

'I look like a man,' she had said.

She looked anything but.

Cora opened her eyes to a grinning Artell, but she felt hot and uncomfortable in the memories of her father. 'He loved her from the beginning, and he knew exactly what she was when she arrived.'

'It appears so. Although didn't you say they needed a warrior?'

'She's one of the best,' Cora said.

'What is that?' Artell asked, squeezing her hand. 'Jealousy?'

'My mother is the best at everything. When she first arrived, they didn't know what skills she had, but it didn't take long before she learnt to transition and showed skill as a strong healer, a great seer...'

'Says the girl who can talk to all Ancients.'

Cora laughed then, and he surprised her by springing forward and kissing her. She pulled away well before she wanted to.

'I have to go back,' she said.

'No, you stay with me and Serassa. I've seen it.' He leaned in for another kiss.

'I'm not sure I want that.'

He sat back then.

'I thought you didn't want this,' she said.

He raised his eyebrows. 'I wasn't sure I could...'

Cora waited, unsure if she wanted to hear what he had thought of her.

'I didn't know that I could care for you as intensely as your parents felt. But it is not what I thought. It is somehow calming to be connected, like it takes the fear away.'

'I find it calming too,' Cora said, reaching out for his hand. 'You don't fear the possible pain to come?'

'No,' he said. 'No, I don't.'

'Then what do we do next?'

'Merik,' he said. 'We know he wants your gifts, all of them, we need to determine how he thinks he will get them.'

26

It was only as the shadows were closing in around the small cavern that Cora blinked back the tiredness. She wasn't sure what she wanted, yet when she looked at Artell by the fire, she knew there were some things she was very sure of—and yet she wasn't.

Would she be able to stay here with him, isolated from the others and not at the same time? She felt both complete and as though there was a gap in her heart.

'I need to talk to my mother,' she whispered.

Artell turned, concern etching his features.

'I'm not going anywhere,' she said. 'At least not yet. And you still need to tell me what Merik is.'

He shook his head.

'You thought I was a way to stop him, but what are we stopping? That he has taken part of your clan and moved away, keeping them isolated and scared? Or is there more to this?'

'He wants what you have.'

'Tell me why he left.'

Artell sighed and sat beside her on the mat, where she stretched and tried not to yawn.

'I think you should sleep first,' he murmured, indicating the sleeping mat.

'I think you want me in the furs for a different reason,' Cora said, then looked up into his blushing face.

'You don't want this,' he said.

'I don't want to leave you. There is more to this than just the two of us.'

'Three of us,' he added with a grin.

She tried not to sigh.

'Can you see his past?'

'Only parts of it. Maybe Silphi is the best Ancient to ask. She was there, so she would understand who and what he is.'

Artell nodded and indicated the furs again. Cora climbed in and closed her eyes, too aware of him sitting beside her. She wasn't sure if she would need to sleep or just think of the woman to reach her as she lay still in the warm furs. Then Cora was standing in the Ancient cavern of the Nerrim.

'Welcome, child,' Silphi said. She appeared younger than she had the last time Cora had seen her, although not by much. She waited, but no children came running through the cavern. 'What would you ask of me?'

'I would like to know about Merik,' Cora said. 'To you now, he is just a boy, but I would like to know what gifts he has.'

'And what he will become?'

Cora nodded.

'You have come alone,' Silphi said, looking around her. 'Artell has the gift of the future; he sees so much. He has seen you, I'm sure. Would you like him here?'

'I am scared of the connection,' Cora said.

The older woman smiled. 'Life should not be feared. Bring him.'

Cora reached out and took Artell by the hand, and he appeared beside her. His mouth dropped open, and the woman smiled. 'You grew to be a fine man,' she said, reaching out for his face.

'Do you know me?' he asked, and Cora turned to him in surprise.

'Isn't she the Ancient who trained you?'

'But she did not know me in this time,' he said in a loud whisper.

Silphi laughed. 'I have always known you,' she said. 'As I have known all our people.' Her voice was sadder.

'Can you tell us of Merik?' Cora prompted gently.

'He wishes to be an Ancient,' Silphi said, looking towards the door. 'He believes he is stronger than any that have come before.'

'Is he?' Cora asked. 'I have seen some skill, but he only sees fragments of the future.'

'He is not what he thinks he is, and yet he will find what he needs to make him so.'

Cora's hand went to her mark automatically. 'He will take from me.'

'He will try. He has searched a long time for someone with your gifts. He does not have the skills he wants, and he thinks he can take them from the Ancients who have gone before.'

'If he can do that, will it change what you are, your history?'

'I'm not really here, child,' Silphi said with a grin. 'You are but a dream.'

'Dreams can be scary,' Cora murmured.

'As your mother discovered, pulled and tormented with the death of those she loved. He was not what a father should be.'

A sadness for her mother tugged at Cora's heart. She had never told Cora who he was. She had seen him so many times herself in her dreams, and yet she had never made the connection. Now she understood why her mother talked of it so little.

'Merik hides in the shadows,' Cora said. 'He appears in my dreams, watching. He knows what we are, who we are.'

'I think he guesses at what you are. But his guess is accurate. You are much stronger than you will allow yourself to be.'

'Everyone says that.'

Silphi reached forward and took her hand. 'You know what you are. You may have fought against following your mother, but you knew. Look deep within yourself.' She touched Cora's heart as Arminel would have, with a steady finger. 'You found the skill to heal. You always had it, but you would not allow it. You have discovered me, and there will be others. Allow us in.'

'But if I do that, he may be able to reach you.'

'We may not be so easily taken,' Silphi said.

'What can he do?' Cora asked.

'He can talk you into willingly giving him what he wants. He will try to take what is most important. He will show you the world, but not as it is.'

'The people of his cavern don't believe in dragons,' Cora said.

The Ancient before her smiled. 'And why is that? Many of those people were born in this very cavern, surrounded by green scales.'

'How is that possible?'

'How can any of us do what we do?'

'Is there a way to end this?'

'You will find it, and then you will grow.'

'Grow?'

'You are three,' she said, looking at Artell. 'You will be more.'

Then Cora was blinking into the dim light of the cavern, her heart thumping. She felt she had learnt so much, yet she still felt as though she didn't quite understand the world. It was how she often felt when she spent time with Arminel. As though she understood what he said, but that the words meant something very different.

'How will we grow?' Artell asked, and she realised that he still sat beside her with his hand in hers.

'I don't know,' Cora said.

'Sleep.' He tucked her hand into the furs and stood. Stretching his arms above his head, he walked to the fire.

'Artell,' she said, sitting up. 'This is your sleeping mat; I should stay by the fire.'

'We could share,' he said hopefully.

She smiled at the green light in his eyes and waved him back. He almost leapt onto her. 'Sleep,' she said.

He nestled in beside her, and she rested her head on his shoulder, then rolled into him and put her hand on his heart. She could feel the warm glow of it. She moved her hand down across his waist and closed her eyes. She remembered him then from the woods, and her dream of Teven and the dragons.

Cora woke feeling hot and sticky beneath the furs. She nudged at Artell, but he didn't move. The light slowly increased in the small cavern, and she saw the thick, dark liquid covering her. Artell stared up at her, unseeing. Panic closed her throat as she realised he was gone. The blood, his blood, covering not only his body but hers as well.

She looked about wildly, trying to determine what had happened, who had come to them. Then Merik's face appeared in the shadows beyond the fire. Her heart stopped.

'What have you done?' she screamed.

He looked at her as though she was a child with no understanding of the world. 'What have you done?' he asked, his voice too calm.

She looked down then, standing over Artell, a blade in her hand, his eyes still staring at her. Had she done this? Why would she do this? She had just found him.

'Connected to him, you can't return to the Penna.'

'He could have come with me.'

'You are part of his world now. You would have been trapped here with the Nerrim.'

'I...' She stopped and focused on his face, too close but still shrouded in shadow. 'You aren't here,' she said. 'This is not real.'

'Of course it is real,' he whispered. The panic and horror washed over her again, and she stabbed towards him with the sticky blade in her hand.

'Hey,' Artell moaned. She sat up, her body still feeling as sticky as it had covered in his blood. She felt about, hoping that she hadn't actually stabbed him during the dream. 'Will you stop poking me?' he said, and the lights rose as though it were daytime. 'What has happened?' he asked, full of concern. Then he pulled her close.

'Merik,' she murmured into his chest. 'I killed you. He...'

'I am not dead,' Artell said, squeezing her closer. 'I'm fine.'

'I was so sure I was covered in your blood.'

'Why would you think that?'

She chewed on her lip rather than answer, burying herself deeper into his hold.

'You don't want to stay,' he whispered over the top of her head.

'I'm not sure what I want.'

'Really?' he asked, looking at her. 'What might you need to help you decide?'

She shook her head.

'I'm hoping you don't want to see me dead,' he murmured, and she burst into tears. 'That is not what I wanted you to do.'

'Maybe it would be easier if I weren't here.'

'But you are meant to be. Serassa says so.'

Can I come in yet? the dragon hummed through them both. Cora laughed through her tears, wiping at her face.

'Yes,' she called as Artell groaned.

The small dragon appeared in the opening, and Cora pushed her way out of Artell's arms to race at her. She threw her arms around the dragon's neck and pushed close against her.

It is so nice to have a home, Serassa hummed.

'At least you are small,' Artell said. 'This cavern isn't exactly large enough for one.'

'We can fit you wherever we are,' Cora said. 'We are three.'

We are going to need a bigger cavern.

'When we grow,' Artell said, sounding very much like Silphi, which he must have realised because he smiled at Cora.

'Why are you different?' she asked, looking at Serassa.

Different from what?

'Other dragons,' Cora whispered as she moved around the dragon, looking over her leathery body. 'You look the same, only different.'

You keep saying different.

'The dragons I grew with and those of the Nerrim are very like you, only larger, and they have scales rather than leathery skin.'

I have scales, Serassa grumbled defensively.

Cora looked her over carefully.

They have not grown yet.

Cora smiled and ran a hand over her side. 'Then Teven was correct, and you are just the same.'

Only I am your dragon. I belong to your clan.

Cora looked back towards Artell. 'Is that the Penna or the Nerrim?'

'I am starting to wonder if we are somewhere between. Perhaps we have the chance to start our own traditions,' he said.

'I am just understanding those I should already know. I want to see some of this world,' Cora suddenly said, throwing her arm around the dragon. She worried that she was too heavy for the smaller dragon, and then she felt bad that she hadn't considered it before.

When you are ready, I am ready.

'Now you sound like the oldest dragon of a clan. And I am ready to see the world.'

'It is dark, and you haven't taken the chance to rest yet,' Artell said. He looked more nervous than Cora had seen him.

'You aren't planning something stupid to keep me here?' she asked.

He shook his head. 'I don't think I could keep you even if I wanted to.'

She wants to be here, but she wants to be there. It is difficult.

'Thank you,' Cora said, moving out of the way as Serassa pushed into the cavern and curled by the fire. It was almost where she had seen the dragon of her vision. Cora was tempted to sit down beside her and sleep, listening to her gurgling insides as she had with Dra as a child.

Artell had climbed back into the furs when she looked over. She didn't want to cause him any pain. Serassa was right. She wanted to be here with him, and yet she wanted to go home as well. If they were the beginning of something new, she wondered where it would be. Would they need to remain close to the Nerrim, as Merik had done? Had that been necessary, just the way it happened? Or had he wanted to punish them for not being what he needed them to be?

She slipped into the furs beside Artell. With his back to her, she wrapped her arms around him and breathed in the scent of him. She felt at home when she was with him. As though wherever he was, that was where she was meant to be. But something else pulled at her.

She woke with a jolt the next morning. Merik had been watching her again from the shadows of her dreams. Only she had dreamed of the chief and their relationship as brothers when they were children. Merik had been cruel, but Edgris was strong. He knew that Merik only did as he did to look powerful. But he was relieved to see his brother leave. Edgris hadn't believed Silphi that Merik might actually become powerful, although he wondered how he had talked that young woman into carrying his child when she had appeared so scared of him. They all did, but sometimes to save the cavern, you had to sacrifice a few.

'I don't want to have to make those decisions,' Cora murmured as Artell sat up with her. He tried to coax her to lie back down, but she wanted to see the world. When she pushed the furs back, Serassa was looking at her with wide eyes, and she was sure the dragon was smiling.

Serassa lifted her out of the cavern into the clear, crisp morning. She transitioned to help keep herself warm against the morning chill, then changed the ice to the stone Artell had shown her. It had the same effect, protecting her from the chill, and she could still feel the morning sunshine trying to warm her.

She grinned into the wind as they flew over the trees. She glanced towards the cavern of Merik and Teven, but they went in the other direction, leaving both caverns and their people behind. As well as Artell.

'They are so close,' she said.

They would not have survived if they had travelled further away.

'I wonder why he left them at all if he could not support his own people.'

Where will you put your people?

Cora wasn't sure it should be her choice. She watched the green landscape blur beneath her. It was so comforting to be on dragonback, and she was relieved to breathe in the fresh air. 'Can you flicker?'

Not yet, but we are already far from the three caverns.

There were three, and although Artell had still been a part of the Nerrim, he had isolated himself as well.

The trees were thick, like those around the Penna cavern and yet so different. The green leaves not only softened the world below but hid the ground from her. She wanted to leap from the dragon and roll in the leaves, yet she knew from experience that the ground was a lot harder than it appeared.

She allowed Serassa to guide her, but it felt to Cora as though she had a plan in place and was taking Cora to somewhere particular.

My favourite place.

'I am happy to be taken wherever you would carry me. I'm not too heavy, am I?'

A soft purring rumble moved through the dragon, and Cora accepted it for contentment. It was some time before Serassa slowly descended, flying around the trees. Then Cora saw a large clearing, which they landed in the middle of.

A stream ran though it and, at one point just before the tree line, it widened into a pond almost like the one she had been in beside Artell's cavern. 'It is beautiful. I have never in all my life seen so much green.'

The grass grew in short, soft, narrow stalks, similar to what grew over Teven's cavern. She wondered then if they called themselves something different. Or if Merik did, for she didn't believe that the people had much choice in anything. As she turned and took in the beauty, she noticed a hill just tucked within the trees, almost as well hidden as that of the Nerrim.

'What is here?' Cora asked, walking towards it.

The dragon jumped between her and the hill, playful in her stance, but Cora wondered what else might be behind it.

Mine, she hummed in Cora's mind. Cora felt a sense of worry, or fear.

'I just wanted to look. And if it is yours, is it not mine as well? We are three.'

No, just mine.

Cora waited, but the dragon offered no further explanation. Could this be where she hid from the others, or were other young dragons hiding in these woods? As she turned away, she noticed the dark gap within the green and knew in her heart that this was a cavern. Had this dragon belonged to someone else? What would they think of her being here?

Instead of exploring as she so desperately wanted to, Cora followed the dragon towards the stream, where they both leaned into the clear water and drank. And then Serassa curled in the sun.

'You have only just woken. We have much to see. What else can you show me of the land? How far are we from the snow?'

A single golden eye blinked at her, but the dragon remained silent. Cora tried not to sigh as she sat down on the cool, damp grass and leaned into the Serassa. It was beautiful. As much as she missed the snow, she could sit out here in the sunshine and watch the trees sway in the breeze all day long. They made a different sound from the trees she knew. Rather than the clacking sound of dry branches smacking against each other, it was a lulling rustling sound that she could have drifted asleep to.

But she thought of Merik and what he might get in her dreams, and she sat forward.

Would you listen to my heart? Serassa asked.

'Listen to it? I hear your insides making all sorts of noises all the time,' Cora said with a laugh.

I want to know what you can see.

Cora stood slowly and ran her hand down the long face of the dragon. Then she moved around and ran her hand over the dragon's side. She indicated that Serassa stand, and the dragon raised herself from the ground. Cora ran her hand down the long neck and across the chest between her forelimbs. Then she waited. It was as though she could feel the dragon mark—as though the whole dragon before her was a single mark. She felt a tingle in her own mark, but not the burning sensation she had expected.

She was starting to wonder if her parents' sensation had been singular to them. But she remembered Arminel talking of a similar sensation. She sighed. She knew she was meant to be with Artell, and yet all the signs were very different. There were different things that had made her mark twinge with fire. Teven had been one of those things, and Cora wondered what her connection to him was. Although he wasn't likely to want to talk to her about that now.

The dragon pushed against her, and Cora focused on her heart rather than all the thoughts racing through her own. She could feel a strength within Serassa. But she didn't quite see what she might be or where she had been, as she had with Artell.

She sighed and looked closer. Serassa was young and finding her place in the world. Yet there was something about her, like Ariandi, strong and wise. Something shifted, and Cora saw the dragon in her mind as a large graceful beast, very much like Ariandi and pale. She was the green of the dragons Cora had seen here, only she might be mistaken for white from a distance.

Cora longed for the snow again, and then she was sitting on her backside in the grass as the dragon had knocked her down. 'Hey,' she cried as she looked up, then scuttled back. Before her stood the dragon of her vision. Large and white, although the scales had a green tinge when she looked more closely.

She stretched out her wings as Cora climbed to her feet.

Thank you, Great Oldra, the dragon hummed through her body. Cora could feel the happiness ebb from her.

'Serassa!' Cora cried, throwing her arms around the dragon's neck. 'Look at you.'

I told you I had scales.

'Did you know…' But her question was cut short as Serassa looked up behind her, and she knew another dragon moved closer.

Now is not the time to meet, Serassa said, her voice firm. Cora wasn't sure if the words were meant for her or the dragon behind her. As she turned, Serassa wrapped around her. She had grown more than scales. She was as large as the dragons Cora had grown with, and her first thought was that Artell was not going to fit her in the cavern.

You have taken her for yourself, a male voice rippled through her.

Cora tried to push out of the dragons' hold.

You would leave me. He sounded so sad, and Cora stopped pushing. Serassa let her go and moved towards the other dragon, touching her nose to his. A leathery nose.

'You live here,' Cora said.

The dragon looked at her with the same golden eyes and stepped forward.

The dragon appeared just as Serassa had not very long ago. And although Serassa tried to get between them again, Cora pushed at her to move. She sat down with a huff. The male dragon bowed his head to her, then rubbed his nose along her cheek.

I see why she chose you, he hummed. *You are very strong. I have no clan and would be honoured to be a part of yours. He is also strong.*

Cora could feel him searching through her and the connection to Artell. Perhaps he should be here for this.

Perhaps they all should, the dragon hummed.

'All?' she asked.

'Your clan. All of them should come.'

'We are only three,' Cora said slowly, wondering what this dragon knew that she didn't, or Serassa for that matter. She reached out and ran her hand across his face, then down his neck. As she moved along his side, she could feel his heartbeat resonate through her.

She put her hand to where his heart was closest to the skin and took a deep breath. A whole world filled her senses as the mark on her chest burned hotter than it had before. His name, *Meyza,* formed in her mind as she stood inside the large cavern with people moving around, the hearths set out like those of the Penna and Nerrim. The light was bright. Children squealed with delight and dragons filled the spaces between hearths.

But as Cora looked around the people, they weren't clear; she couldn't quite focus on any one face. Then a man strode towards her, strong and confident. People bowed their heads as he passed them, and she could feel the respect they had for him. As he got closer, Teven smiled at her and put a hand on her shoulder.

She stepped back, overwhelmed by what she had seen and somewhat confused. She wasn't meant to be with Teven—it was Artell. And yet she had never really believed that she would remain here, so far from the snow.

You do not need the snow. You need your people around you, and you will be content.

'These are not the people I expected to be around me,' she said. 'Where do you fit into this world, Meyza?'

You can see.

Cora wasn't sure what she could see, but she stepped back and placed her hand over the heart of the dragon, trying to steady the uncertainty she felt.

Breathe.

She took a deep breath, closed her eyes and focused on a dark green dragon sitting almost where they were now, shimmering in the sun. Then Teven was walking forward and leaping up onto his back, his smile wide as he patted the neck of the dragon and they lifted into the trees.

It felt as though it should be. But a nervousness pulled at her. She searched the shadows of the trees around her for Merik, but she couldn't see him. Teven was dragged again into a future she wasn't sure of.

When she opened her eyes, the small leathery dragon she had talked with glistened dark green before her. 'Have you told him?' she asked, thinking of Teven and what that would mean for her and Artell.

The time is not right.

Cora ran her fingers through her hair and tried not to sigh. Again, she had no idea where she was meant to be or where she fit. 'Can I see inside?' she asked Meyza.

He bowed his head, and she looked back at Serassa standing in silence beyond him. Cora waved her forward and, without a word, Serassa followed her into the cavern.

Dim lights lit up a wide tunnel that led into a much larger space. Cora stopped, and Serassa nudged her from behind. The cavern was larger than that of the Penna or the Nerrim. The smooth, domed walls were made of well-packed earth. Small globes of light appeared dotted over the ceiling, but the light was low.

You will need another to bring them to what they should be.

Rhali, Cora thought. She had the gift of light, but then so did Artell. She moved further into the space. 'Did you do this?' she asked.

We have been waiting.

'For me or for Teven?'

Instead of answering, the dragon nudged her from behind. She was overwhelmed at the sheer size of the space before her. She could nearly fit the Penna and the Keetar in this one cavern. A wave of homesickness washed over her, and she knew that this was not meant for them. But how would the two of them—maybe four—and two dragons survive as a clan of their own?

You will see, Serassa hummed.

Cora shook her head. 'Just like an Ancient,' she murmured. Glancing to the side, she was surprised by Serassa's colour and size.

Serassa nudged her again, and she saw the gap in the wall. 'Has someone lived here before?'

Only dragons.

Cora moved through the gap and was surprised to find a smaller cavern. She was reminded of the birthing chambers, only this one had something dark in the corner. As she edged closer, she thought they were rocks, but as she squatted down, she saw they were egg shells. Large egg shells.

'You were hatched here,' Cora said, turning back to the opening where Serassa stood silently. It was hard to tell from the fragments how many eggs had hatched here and whether it was only one clutch or several over years. The room was warmer than the main cavern. Cora wondered if it was closer to the edge of the hill they were buried within and so it warmed from the sun. It would be perfect for human or dragon.

Come. There is more.

Cora nodded and stood slowly, following the dragon across the cavern to another gap in the wall. This opened into another large cavern. Larger than Artell's, yet similar in size. It was narrow but long, and in the distance, something shimmered in the dim light.

'Another dragon?' she asked.

Serassa curled in the middle of the space and Cora, tucking her hair behind her ears, walked slowly towards the back. It was calm and warm and quiet. She turned back to look at Serassa. She felt instantly comfortable in the space, as though it was where she was meant to be. Closing her eyes, she could imagine a fire and woven mats, perhaps cushions in coloured wool like those of Arminel's. People visiting would only need enter the front of the space.

She could set up an area to work with herbs near where she stood. And beyond, in the darker corners, she could set up sleeping mats. The space was large enough that she could set up more in case she needed to treat anyone.

Cora shook her head. She was starting to think of this as her own space, as though she was to be an Ancient. She nearly laughed at the idea. Artell was the Ancient. She was to be Chief.

She looked back at the dragon briefly. But if Teven was to be Chief, what would that mean? Cora imagined curling up with Artell in the far dark corner of the cavern. And then something glistened in the dim light.

'Essara,' she breathed, moving forward. Dark crystals pushed their way through the wall. She ran her hand over them, feeling a shiver through her mark as she did. 'This is the place of Ancients,' she whispered. 'It is not for me.'

You are the greatest Oldra of all. Are you not to be an Ancient?

'I didn't think so,' she said.

As the doubt washed over her, Merik appeared in the shadows. He grinned at her, and she looked away. She rushed out of the cavern and into the main space again. It was huge, and she stopped to close her eyes, imagining it as she had seen it in the other dragon's heart. She could see the people. Some she thought she recognised; others she didn't. Deen's sister Junah smiled at her, and her heart leapt. From amongst the crowd, she saw Merik watching the world.

But amongst all the faces, she couldn't see Artell. When she looked for him, she saw Teven again. He nodded her way. She looked down to see her hands were covered in blood. And she knew in her heart that it was Artell's. He was gone, and she was left to do what he should have. The blood matched the long red robes she wore. She wiped madly at her hands, running through the cavern and the people and out into the sunshine.

She sucked in a deep breath and then focused on the emptiness around her.

'Cora,' Artell called, his voice as loud and clear as though he stood behind her. She swung around, searching for him.

She blinked into the bright light, and Serassa was there. Cora leapt up onto the dragon's strong shoulders. Her scales were smooth and bright beneath Cora's hands, which no longer appeared covered in blood. Then they were in the air.

Do not panic.

'I can't help it. Something is wrong. He is calling for me.'

They flew faster towards the cavern, and then Serassa flickered. The world was as it had been when she had flickered with Dra, only very different. She sensed rather than saw that the world around them slowed, yet she knew the dragon travelled fast. Then they were landing at the base of the waterfall, and Cora was running.

27

Merik grinned at her from the shadows. She tried to work out if he was really there, or whether this was another hideous dream. Artell sat facing the fire, and Cora slowed as she approached, too scared of what she would find.

He turned and looked at her, his face bruised, and she threw herself down to him, cupping his face in her hands. 'What happened?' She looked around, but Merik was gone.

'I thought I should check on where you might be, only I found someone else.'

'Merik,' she breathed.

'Worse. Teven.'

'And he hit you?'

'He strongly believes that I should give you back.'

'As though you stole me? They were the ones keeping me against my will.'

'Really?' he asked.

'I thought I needed to be there to learn what I was, but if I could have gone home, I would have.'

'And now you are here.'

'I want to be here, with you.'

'You don't quite sound like you believe that,' Artell murmured.

Cora sat back on the woven mat and rubbed her hands together, sure that she could still feel his blood on them. 'I don't want to lose you. I don't want to be the reason we aren't together.'

'What did you see?' he asked.

She shook her head. She wasn't quite sure of anything, and Merik was too close. Always close. She jumped as he grabbed her arm.

'What did you see?' he asked again.

'Merik,' she blurted. 'No matter where I go, he is watching me.' She shivered. Artell pulled her close then, and it didn't seem so frightening when she was wrapped in his arms. She nestled against his chest. His heart thumped against her ear.

She looked then again into his heart, wondering if what she had seen of herself and the dragon at his hearth was here or at the other cavern, but she couldn't tell.

'I'm scared,' she said. 'Just when I think I have it worked out, the world tears it apart.'

'What else did the little dragon show you?'

'Too much,' she murmured, 'and she is not so little anymore.'

Artell turned and groaned. 'Really, you were too big before,' he said to the dragon.

A soft chuckle filled her, and then she felt something else from Artell. Fear, perhaps. 'What is it?' she asked.

'She is white.'

'I thought she was green.'

He smiled, but it was sad, and she could feel the pain that he focused on when he saw into the lives of others. He pushed her gently from his arms. 'I should visit with Henda,' he said.

Cora felt the divide opening between them. She pressed her hand to her mark as it hurt, a sharp pain travelling deep inside her. Was this how it ended? Had she only imagined the connection?

Hold on to it, Serassa urged.

'He is safer away from me,' Cora groaned as the pain sliced deeper. She gasped, unsure what she had done or whether it was something or someone else. She tried to see into the shadows, assuming Merik was close again. He had already found her there once before.

'Why?' Artell whispered. He sounded so distant, so far away.

Cora wanted to curl into a ball and hide away, but she couldn't catch her breath.

'Breathe, trust who you are and what you know to be true,' her mother's voice whispered at the back of her mind.

She sucked in a deep breath, but she wasn't sure of anything. She could not keep him safe. As Merik continued to show her, she would be the end of him. She didn't want that. She couldn't allow that to happen. Was this the pain he felt at the loss of others? Was this why he lived as he did?

'Cora?' Artell asked cautiously. 'Cora?' he asked again, kneeling before her. 'What is wrong?'

She shook her head, tears suddenly flowing. She couldn't form any words that would help him understand this.

He took her in his arms, and the feeling dissipated somewhat. The calm of his hold did something she had never experienced before she had found him. It was like she was home. She clung to his tunic. 'Don't leave me,' she murmured.

'Do you think I would give you back to Teven?'

'Teven is there in my future.'

'Since when do you see what is to come?' Artell asked, his voice jovial.

'The dragons have shown me.'

'Dragons?'

'We have more, but…'

'You didn't see me in this vision,' he answered for her.

'Only your blood on my hands, again.'

'It is Merik, not the truth. I have seen you in my future; therefore, it must be so.'

'Truly?' she asked, looking up at him.

He grinned and then pressed his lips to hers. The sharp pain in her chest continued to lessen, and she pulled herself closer to him. Desperate for the calm she had in his arms. Desperate to close the gap that had opened between them. She heard the distant flap of wings, and there was only the two of them.

He winced as she ran her hand over his face. She sat back, placing her hand carefully over the large bruise, and closed her eyes. The cold seeped between them, and he sighed.

'Better?' she asked. He nodded and leaned forward.

Wrapping his arms tighter around her, he pulled her closer and she kissed him again. His fingers worked their way under her tunic, and she gasped. The fire danced across her skin. Then his hand was fiery and flat against her back, pulling her closer still.

She wanted to see his mark, needed to feel his skin against hers. As she pulled at the base of his tunic, he yelped and leaned back. Then he grinned and pulled his tunic over his head. She placed her hand flat over the mark on his chest, and they were engulfed by the flames.

Cora woke wrapped in his arms, her body still burning and the furs thrown back. Despite the hot, sharp pain in her chest and across her skin, she felt content and calm. The panic of the previous day had disappeared, and although she still searched for Merik in the shadows, she couldn't see him.

She had, however, dreamt of Teven. Talking with him at a hearth, laughing with him over something… She was surprised that it was not the past she had lived, nor did she think it was the past he had lived.

Was the dragon showing her more of a possible future, or was she so connected to Artell now that they shared his skill? She sat up and looked over his sleeping form. 'Teven,' he murmured, and rolled towards her.

'What was that?' he murmured, then put his hand to his heart and moaned. 'I am burning.'

'It seems that there are sparks after all,' she said, trying not to smile, but she couldn't keep it from her face.

He traced a finger over her mark as she leaned over him, and she flinched away. 'How long will it last?'

'You should ask your mother,' he murmured.

'Do you want to come with me?'

'I should dress first.'

She laughed, bent down and kissed him again. The heat flared in her heart as she lay down against him. 'Let's not go anywhere,' she murmured.

'Teven,' he said, and she sat back up. 'I dreamt of him.'

'I saw,' she said.

'Really?'

She nodded. 'At the hearth.' She sighed then. 'That means it is your future, your discussions with him. You are there.'

'Are you still worried that I wouldn't be?'

She nodded. 'Did you see where it was?'

'I thought it was the cavern of the Nerrim, but I'm not sure.' He looked at her closely for a moment. 'What have you discovered?'

'I think I have found the cavern we will take our clan to. But I don't know that we are ready yet, and I'm not sure who will be with us.'

'Teven,' he said again. 'But what does he do?'

'I think he is Chief.'

'I thought you were to be Chief.'

She shrugged. 'I can't see it clearly.'

'What did you see?'

'Too much of your blood, but I think that was Merik. And I wore red, but that could be Merik as well,' she added quickly.

'Ask your mother,' he said again, then lay back and closed his eyes.

Cora slipped her tunic over her head before she lay back beside Artell and closed her eyes. Her mother appeared quickly before her, looking frustrated, and Cora paused.

'Your brother is not the man he thinks he is,' she sighed. 'I wish you were here to help keep him in.'

'He is older than I was when I headed out to hunt alone on dragonback.'

Her mother nodded quickly. 'You were a very different child.'

'And he is a man. Maybe he needs the space to learn just what he is.'

Her mother sighed and then smiled. 'You have become the Ancient I knew you would be.'

Cora opened her mouth to disagree, but as she looked down, she realised she wore the red robes Arminel had worn her whole life. She sighed. 'Perhaps like Wyndha, I have joined with an Ancient and so I am one.'

'You were always one,' her mother said, closing her arms around her. Cora was grateful she had been able to find the gift to reach her.

'I fear that Merik may try to take it from me.'

'I do not think he has the means.'

'He twists the mind.'

'Only if you allow it.'

'It isn't that easy,' Cora said. 'I see Artell's blood on my hands. I can't lose him, and I can't lose him that way.'

'You have had his blood on your hands,' her mother whispered, taking Cora's hands.

Cora leaned back from her and took a breath. 'He tried to test me, but the blade was sharper than he thought it was. I felt him slipping away.'

'That is the feeling Merik clings to. But you saved him. You didn't let him die, and now he burns within you.'

Cora blushed. 'How long will it burn?'

'Days,' her mother said. 'But you can draw on it if you need to. I was able to. But then I had you,' she said, running her fingers through Cora's long loose hair, 'burning away inside me.'

'You didn't know?'

'Not until after it was all over.'

'What if…' Cora stopped. The Ancients she knew didn't have any children. It wasn't the way of the world. She felt a sudden moment of loss.

'Do not think it yet. Your future is not set.'

'Are you sure?'

Her mother smiled. 'I always knew you would leave, that there were others who needed you more than we did. It may be difficult, but I know you will embrace it.'

'Others will join me,' Cora said, knowing it with a certainty she hadn't felt before.

Her mother nodded once.

'When was the last cavern established?'

'The Keetar moved.'

'They moved. They were already a people.'

'It is not a question I can answer. You can look back where I look forward. You will find those who can guide you.'

Cora pulled her mother into a tight embrace. 'I found a place. As much as I want to return, I know I am where I am meant to be.'

'Come and visit with your father when you can.'

Cora nodded, then realised she was already back in the little cavern she shared with Artell. This was her home, until they could pull their people together at the new cavern. She glanced around. There was still no sign of Merik, and yet she knew he was close.

28

Cora was surprised that she wasn't wearing red when she focused on the room around her. Artell was by the fire, stirring the contents of a pot with the two dragons curled in close by. It was comforting to have them all near, but the already small cavern appeared much smaller.

Henda stood in the doorway, looking over the scene before her. She wore red, and although they looked very similar to Arminel's robes, they were different. Cora wondered whether the Penna would give her cloth if she visited.

'You seem to have increased the number you are happy to have in your little world,' Henda said to Artell, and he nodded without turning from the fire.

'Would you like to stay?' Cora asked, then glanced at Artell, who continued stirring.

'Teven is looking for you,' Henda said instead.

Artell froze mid-task.

'We have not told him the truth, but we must at some point. How will you explain not giving her back?' Henda asked.

Cora looked at her seriously. 'You offered me sanctuary,' she said. 'It is too late now to return.'

Henda gave Cora a disapproving look. Then her face fell in disbelief before she sucked in a deep breath and glared at her. 'I had thought you might stay with me, but I did not expect this. Now that you have bonded, you too are Ancient.'

Cora nodded once.

'What will Merik think?' Henda asked.

'He may already know. He sees so much from the shadows.'

'You are stronger together. What will that mean for me?' Henda asked suddenly. 'We should talk with Edgris. Two Ancients is enough; three is something else.'

'We won't stay,' Artell said, turning from the fire. 'We were never meant to stay.'

Henda rushed forward and threw her arms around him. 'What will your father say?'

'He will understand, and we will not be too far.'

'But far enough,' Henda said, looking back at Cora as though it were all her fault.

'Essara directs us as she sees fit. It is not for us to question,' Cora said.

'How can I be sure you follow Essara and are not working for Merik?'

'Henda!' Artell chastised.

'I don't know her.'

'I do,' he said. 'I know her as I know myself.'

'You have only known her a few days.'

'We are bonded, and I trust her.'

'Enough that you let not one but two unknown dragons into the cavern?'

'They are our dragons,' Artell said. 'They have chosen to be with us.'

'An Ancient with a dragon! Who has heard of such a thing?'

'He is not mine. He belongs to…' Artell stopped and looked at Cora.

'Is he still out there?' Cora asked.

Henda nodded, but didn't look at her.

Cora straightened out the tunic, the one Teven had given her that had belonged to his mother. She ran her hand over the deep green dragon as she moved past him. Artell sighed as he pushed the spoon into the stew and followed.

'I hope you know what you will tell him,' Henda said, striding ahead.

'No,' she said. 'I don't.'

Henda was still mumbling when they emerged in the trees. Then she led the way to where Teven was waiting on a fallen log. He stood quickly as they approached, and Cora sucked in a deep breath.

'There is still something different about you,' he muttered.

'I have found where I need to be,' she said.

'Not with an Oldra then,' he continued in the same tone.

She tried not to sigh. How were they going to work with him in the future when he behaved like this? He had been a man who did as he was required whether he wanted to or not, but he too had changed.

'How is your father?' Cora asked.

'He doesn't like that title.' When Cora opened her mouth, Teven held up his hand. 'Nor you calling him by his name.'

'I don't think it really matters what name I use; he will still try to take what he wants.'

'He is stronger than he looks,' Teven murmured.

'So am I,' Cora said.

'You are not staying with the Nerrim,' he said.

She shook her head.

'She stays with her new mate,' Henda said quickly.

It was not the way she wanted to tell him, and his face fell.

Cora heard the footsteps behind her as Artell emerged from the trees. Teven glared at him, then stood slowly. He looked at Artell and then back to Cora.

'Teven,' Artell said, stepping forward.

Teven groaned aloud and then nodded slowly. 'You did more than meet then.'

'It was meant to be,' Artell said as Cora tried to form the words.

'So she was telling *me*,' he said, his grin too similar to his father's. Cora stepped back beside Artell. Teven sighed and nodded once. 'It is what it is. You will not return to us?'

'There is someone you should meet,' Cora said quickly, and Artell groaned.

'It is a small space,' he whispered hoarsely.

'It is important.'

Artell sighed, then motioned for Teven to follow. They were only just within the trees when the large dragon appeared between them. Teven initially took a step back, but then he stepped forward and ran his hand down the dragon's face.

'I can hear them both,' he said, looking to Cora beside him. 'Will there be more?'

They both nodded.

'Why can't I hear them?' Henda asked, suddenly confused.

'You are not part of this clan.'

'How does any of this stop Merik?' Henda asked, the frustration clear in her voice.

'I think this is something very separate from Merik,' Cora said.

'You can't call him that,' Teven said, remaining close to the dragon, although the whine was no longer present in his voice as he said it.

'You are needed with us,' Artell said. 'There is a purpose to our little clan.'

'He will destroy you,' Teven said softly.

'I don't think he can reach me now that I understand what he is,' Cora said.

'Are you sure?'

She wasn't certain, but she nodded to reassure the man before her.

'Where is Serassa?' Teven asked. As though called, she appeared from the trees. He stepped forward and looked over her. 'You have grown.'

She bowed her head to him and then nudged him with her head, pushing him.

'Yet just the same. We are a clan of three, with two dragons. What happens now?'

'I don't...' Cora started, then looked around for Henda. 'Where did she go?'

'Back to the cavern?' Teven suggested.

Artell shook his head and raced back through the trees. Cora and Teven ran behind him. They found Henda sitting on the ground, staring into the distance, large tears tracking down her cheeks. Cora dropped in front of her and put her hands on her knees.

'Henda?' she whispered.

'I can't save her,' the woman murmured, looking at the ground beyond Cora and then up at the cliff face. Cora turned and followed where she looked.

'No one could have saved her,' Cora said, taking her shaking hands and holding them still.

'How could she have done such a thing?' Henda asked, her voice faint.

'It was a long time ago,' Cora whispered.

Henda glared at Cora and pushed her back as she stood. She pointed to a space on the ground, but there was nothing there. The tears flowing faster down her cheeks as she sniffed. 'How can you be so heartless? I have lost my sister.'

'Sister?' Teven asked, stepping forward.

'You didn't know?' Artell asked him.

'I don't know anything!' Teven said too loudly. 'He hasn't allowed it. Your people allowed her to die and did nothing to assist me. I don't even know her name,' he added quietly.

'He is in your head,' Cora said to Henda. 'He is making her relive it,' she said, turning to Artell.

Artell nodded, but stayed where he was. 'I don't know how to stop it.'

'Henda,' Cora said softly, climbing to her feet and reaching out for her. The woman pushed her away. 'Henda, why did she leave with him?'

'The baby,' she said. 'He told her the baby would die if she did not go with him.'

'How could she have allowed herself to come to be with child? She knew what he was, or what he was rumoured to be.'

'He showed her something different. A different world from the one she lived in, the one we all lived in. When she realised what he was and what he had done, it was too late. Our father didn't want to let her go, but he had no choice.'

'How did he get the others to follow?'

Henda shook her head, her breathing calmer. The panic at reliving her sister's death appeared to have passed.

'Did he train with you? With Silphi?'

Henda looked up and focused on Cora. 'He didn't have the skill. There was something, but not enough to work with for the good of the people. Silphi would not take him on.'

'Did he resent that?'

She shook her head. 'He said he didn't need her.'

'Did he find someone else?'

'I spent my time with Silphi, not with him. He went hunting with others.'

Cora turned back to Artell. 'We need to talk to your father,' she said.

'There is not much he will tell us.'

'Merik grew stronger and learnt what he could do. I need to know if he learnt that from someone else.'

'There is no one else.'

'How does he get into my dreams? How has he seen me for so long? How does he have the power he does to convince you something is real when it is not?'

'He is just a man.'

'If that were true, someone would have stopped him by now. He rarely comes out of the cavern, yet those who don't want to be there remain.'

You need to see within him. Only you can see what he was and how he came to be that man, Serassa pressed into her mind.

'But I can't get close enough. As I look into him, he may do the same to me, and I don't know if he can do what he has threatened to do.'

'You haven't dreamed of his history?' Artell asked.

'Only when he left the Nerrim, but he is in my dreams.'

'There may be a way for you to use that knowledge of him.'

'But how? You had no idea of what he really was, and yet you feared him. He would have left the cavern around the time I was born.' Cora looked at Teven. 'We must be close in age, or you might even be older. He was already powerful when he left the cavern, and he knew what he needed to become more powerful.' She shook her head. 'I have no idea what to do.'

She looked at those standing around her and then stepped back. In the shadows of the trees ahead of her was Merik, watching closely and grinning broadly. It wasn't an image of him—he was there.

'He uses the shadows,' Cora whispered as the group turned, and he disappeared. 'He has found something in the darkness.'

She looked back to the group, and then Artell's eyes went wide. Before she could guess at what he might have seen, strong arms pulled her away from the others and shadows closed around her.

29

Cora stood in the darkness, aware only of the man behind her and unsure of where she was or how she got there.

'You can't shine so bright without your mother's gifts,' he whispered hoarsely in her ear, and she shivered from the feel of his hot breath on her neck. 'You don't have the dragons. And...' His hand slipped down and across her midsection. 'You have not created a child in the fire who would save you.'

Despite her fears, Cora transitioned to the strong stone Artell had discovered.

'That cannot protect you from me,' Merik said. His hand slithered over her body and pressed on her chest, over the mark of Oldra.

Cora closed her eyes against the darkness and concentrated on the man behind her. He was just a man. An older man. Not an Ancient—not like Arminel. She thought of him wise, old and far stronger than he appeared. There were days she thought he would live forever. Even though he had lost the woman he loved. There were not many male Ancients Cora was aware of. Artell was only the second, yet she was sure there were more. The hand over her heart pressed harder, pushing against the stone wall she had built. Merik's heart beat loud in her ears, pushing through all her senses.

She reached out for his heart, hoping that Serassa was right and she needed to reach him. She had thought she might feel pain as she pushed out her senses, but there was nothing there. The shadows moved in, pushing on her as she tried to see inside the space. It contained only darkness.

A man with long white hair, a kind yet crinkled face and faded red robes appeared before her. The man behind her tried to find his way into her heart as he held her tight. Cora twisted to look back at him, but he didn't appear to have noticed the man before them.

Then another appeared, not as old as the first, his hair darker and peppered with grey, cut short and messy like the men of her clan.

'We are chosen by Essara as often as women,' the elder of the two said. 'You have not lived long enough to experience all that an Ancient can.'

'Why have you come?' Cora asked, and Merik stopped.

'You wondered at male Ancients. We thought we could help you,' the second said.

'Merik is not an Ancient,' she said.

Both Ancients before her nodded.

'What do you think you can do?' the man behind her said. 'I may not be Ancient, but I have more power than any of them.'

'Where did you get it from?' Cora asked.

'I was born with it. With a gift of visions.'

'A seer?'

Both men before her scowled.

'*I* gift the visions,' Merik said with a cackle, and she felt the heat of his breath through the transition.

'Then how did you get into my dreams?'

'I was searching for you. I can put myself inside your head, as well as anything else I want.'

Cora had a thought of Artell, dead by the hearth of their cavern, her hands sticky with his blood. But she blinked through it, knowing it wasn't true. She looked towards the two men standing before her. As she blinked again, it was as though she was standing over Artell again and Merik was there in the shadows, watching her.

'You are so strong,' he said. 'I reached out for someone with greater gifts than mine, to bring them here.'

'Why would you think I would give them up?'

'Everyone gives up something when they think it will save others. Not me, of course, but I can.'

'Teven's mother wasn't tricked into giving anything up.'

'She gave up her child,' Merik murmured.

'But it didn't benefit you. He was scarred, and you couldn't use him. He was always stronger than you realised.'

'He gave up his freedoms for his sister. And where would he go? They wouldn't take him in.'

'But he might have pushed you out.'

Merik laughed then, a strange cackle, his spittle showering her neck. 'He knows what I would have done to the others. He would have had nothing to be little chief of.'

'And so you stayed as the little chief,' she said. He swung her around then, the movement fast, and she almost fell as her feet tangled. There was solid ground beneath her, yet in the continued darkness she was sure they were somewhere within the shadows. She felt a little more scared now that she was alone with him. She wanted to search out the Ancients. As she thought of them, they appeared behind Merik, and she sucked in a deep breath.

'You don't know what skill I have,' she said.

'You hid your skills away, even from yourself, for so long. You are another living in the shadows. We could be strong together,' Merik said, stepping forward. Cora tried to step back, but she couldn't move.

'He would not know how to use such a gift,' the eldest of the Ancients said.

Cora placed her hand quickly on Merik's chest, searching his heart for who he truly was, but there was still nothing there.

'Share it,' Wyndha said, her grey braids bobbing as she bowed her head and smiled at Cora.

Cora blinked back her surprise, unsure why Wyndha would say what she did or what it might mean. She had spent so long fearing what he would take, and now she was being told to hand it over willingly.

Silphi appeared beside Wyndha. 'Give him what he wants,' she suggested.

The two Ancients who had been with her nodded. And then others began appearing around her, until she was surrounded by red robes. She nodded once and then pushed the ability to talk with the Ancients into the gap that was his heart.

She wasn't sure how she managed to do it. She felt the strength in him, the skill and the confidence she had given him. He was exactly what he wanted to be. She stepped back and watched as he looked over his hands and then at those around them. Cora was confused that she could still see them, now that she had given the gift away.

'I have it all,' he murmured. 'The ability to heal, the ability to see the past and a clearer future. All the gifts of all the Ancients are mine.'

'Not quite,' Cora said. 'My gift is to talk with them. They can't give me what they have.'

'But they can,' he said. 'You just have to take it.'

'I thought it had to be given?'

'We shall give you what you want,' said the Ancient man she had first seen. 'I will give you all the pain and heartache that goes with it.'

'I don't care about the pain,' Merik sneered.

The old man bowed his head and held out his hand. Every other Ancient raised their hand in the same way, and Cora felt the push of the gifts of Essara as they flowed around her. She put her hand back on Merik's chest and directed the gifts into the darkness.

He grinned, turning his face upward and his arms out, and then his face fell. As Cora stepped back, he clutched at his chest and then ripped at his tunic. The mark of Oldra on his chest burned bright before it flickered and faded and then disappeared.

'No,' he murmured as the Ancients around them disappeared. Then the shadows lifted, and Cora blinked into the green light that filtered amongst the trees.

Merik dropped to his knees, still clutching at his chest, his face pale. Artell ran through the trees towards Cora, and Merik disappeared into a shadow.

Cora tried to focus on the man running towards her, but he was lost in the sea of Ancients who again surrounded her. 'Will you take it back?' she asked.

'No,' the whisper came, but she wasn't sure who it came from. Then a woman in white stepped out from the sea of red.

Cora focused on the woman before her and then dropped to her knees. The woman caught Cora by the hands and pulled her upright.

'You don't need to kneel before me,' she said. 'We have come all this way to find you.'

'All of you?' Cora asked.

She bowed her head. 'Bring your mate,' she said.

The crowd around her disappeared, and Cora focused on Artell standing before her looking unsure. She held out her hand, and he stepped forward and took it. And then the Ancients of old reappeared. He gasped and bowed his head to Essara.

'It is rare that we need to start anew,' Essara said. 'You have your chief,' Artell looked at Cora, but she looked towards Teven, standing off in the trees with Henda. Essara smiled. 'And together you shall grow strong.'

'I miss the snow,' Cora said quickly.

'You have found your cavern; you have found your place in the world. It may be that the sun disappears at times and you are able to enjoy the snow once more.'

Cora smiled. She would like that.

Then they were standing outside of the cavern. Artell gasped and turned slowly.

'Welcome home, Tarranah,' Essara said. 'Before you settle, return to your previous clans. Talk to the people. Others will join you.'

Artell bowed his head again.

'Go and visit with your father,' Essara said to Cora. Then she faded from view along with all the other Ancients. Wyndha was the last to go, and she smiled warmly and then winked at Cora before she too faded from existence once more.

30

Cora hesitated at the cavern opening for the first time in her life. Serassa waited in the snow, and she was surprised by the silence that surrounded her. She was encased in her ice transition, Artell in his stone one, but it appeared to have the same effect. Her heart beat too fast in her chest. How long had she been gone? How would they respond?

She sucked in a breath as Serassa took to the sky. *Would you like to come in?* Cora called after her.

Not this time. You have others who would see you first.

Artell took her hand in his and pulled her through the opening. 'We have visited all the others. Your parents will wonder why you didn't return to them first.'

'I think my mother will understand better than you think.'

'I like her. She's sensible.'

Cora looked at him for a moment. He grinned at her and then stopped. The wooden door stood closed, and Cora moved forward to run her hand over the scorch mark of the dragon that covered it. 'Wait until you see the other side,' she whispered as it creaked open.

Silence greeted them on the other side, and for a moment she wondered if this was a dream. Then she focused on the people—so many people standing and looking at her—and she squeezed Artell's hand tighter. No one moved as she stepped forward, except Artell stepping with her. They seemed to watch as though doubting she was really there. She wondered if she should have dressed more like the Penna, rather than in her long red leather tunic.

Someone moved through the crowd that seemed to inch closer to them. Cora's father broke the silent edge of the group and threw his arms around her, pulling her tight against his chest. He felt bigger than life, and yet not as large as she remembered him. She sobbed against him.

Then the noise started around the cavern. He held her out, grinned at her and then pulled her close again.

'I told you,' he whispered.

'You told me I would be Chief,' she said, her voice echoing in the cavern.

He brushed her aside along with her words and looked over Artell, who seemed like he might run as her father dropped heavy hands onto his shoulders.

'The man who would connect to my favourite daughter,' he said, his loud voice carrying through the cavern.

'I'm your only daughter,' Cora said, and a soft laugh broke out amongst the watching people.

'You look young to be Ancient,' he said.

'Artell is…'

'Don't interrupt,' her father murmured, still studying the man before him. He leaned forward, and Cora felt the need to push herself between them. 'Does it still burn?' he asked, grinning broadly. Cora felt her face burn.

'Leave them alone,' Arminel said, shuffling forward. 'You should have more respect for your Ancients.'

'Is he mine?' Pira asked. 'Or is your mother correct?'

'She is always correct,' Cora said as her mother appeared in the crowd behind her father, and then she was holding her close.

'It was not long ago that you held me in your dreams,' she whispered.

Artell bowed his head. Cora's mother stepped forward and took his hands in hers, and as she closed her eyes, the gentle murmuring of the crowd died away. He glanced at Cora, but she nodded once.

'I just needed to be sure,' Gerry whispered.

'I am sorry that I could not return her,' Artell said, and the crowd murmured again. 'It is not what we are meant for.'

Gerry nodded. Cora stepped back and took Artell's hand. 'Have you told them?' she asked.

Her mother shook her head. 'It is for you to ask. Essara chose you.'

'For what?' her father asked.

'We are to start a new cavern.'

'You mean you have started a new cavern.'

Cora bowed her head in agreement, and the cavern erupted. She stepped closer to Artell, and then Wyn was wrapped around her. He seemed even younger than he had appeared before she left, and yet she had told her mother to let him go. He smiled up at her, and she knew the advice was right.

'I'm not coming with you,' he said quickly. 'I just wanted to say thanks.'

She smiled down at him as he let her go and disappeared into the crowd. She looked up at the people moving in and locked eyes with Deen.

'Can we ask to come?' Junah asked. 'Or do you choose?'

'It is for you to decide if you want to come with us.' Artell looked through the people, and the noise died down, but didn't stop. 'But I must warn you from the outset—there is no snow.'

Cora laughed despite the tension.

'Where is your bow?' Tarn asked, accusation in his voice.

'Teven has it,' Cora said quickly.

'Teven?' her father asked.

'He is our chief. I am afraid that I have not had the chance to use it.'

'I hope you haven't given it away.'

She shook her head, and Larek pushed through the crowd. 'Your mother is difficult,' he grumbled. 'But then I'm sure you could be equally so. If you can bear an old man, I would like to see a world with no snow.'

Artell took his arm and bowed his head. 'You are welcome to the Tarranah.'

The old man smiled like Cora had never seen before, and she noted her mother wiped a small tear from the corner of her eye.

'We have others who have joined us from the Nerrim cavern, and those of Teven's people.'

'Were you not going to come to us?' a woman called out, and Cora turned to Re-Mah as she made her way into the cavern through the carved doors. 'You look good in red,' she noted as she pulled Cora into a tight hug. 'You were gone too long. Visit more.'

'I will,' Cora promised, holding the woman just as tightly.

'We have two who would go with you.' She looked over the man beside Cora and then nodded. 'He will do.'

Artell coughed.

'He is just what she needs,' her mother said.

In all, there were the two Keetar and five Penna ready for the new cavern. Her mother spent too long with her arms around Larek, and Cora knew that she would never see him again. They were quite some distance from each other. Although it was possible to visit, it was further than any of them had travelled before.

'If there is no snow,' her father asked, 'what does it mean for your transition?'

Cora looked at Artell with a grin and then transitioned. Her father's eyes widened, and she grinned as she threw her arms around him. 'Come and visit us in the sun.'

'One day,' he murmured, holding her close.

The crowd moved as one outside the cavern. Cora smiled at the snow, feeling Essara in it. As Serassa landed, the people stepped forward.

'She's green,' someone murmured.

Then Dra and Ariandi landed beside her. Cora threw her arms around Dra and held tight, allowing her tears to flow. 'I was so worried,' she murmured.

As was I. But I see you are where you need to be and with one who chose to be with you.

'As you did,' Cora said.

His soft laughter rolled through her, and she stepped back, running her hand down his face. Then she moved to Ariandi and did the same.

You are stronger together, Ariandi purred through Cora.

'All of us, it seems.'

The goddess has always looked for you.

'Looked for me?'

The dragon pushed her head against Cora and then stepped back. Her mother threw her arms around her one more time, then helped them onto the dragon. The others who had dragons climbed up and carried those who didn't. They waved goodbye to the family and friends watching them go, hoping they would see each other again. Cora could visit with her mother and Arminel, even Re-Mah, but her father and brothers and the others were a longer journey away.

As they landed in the green clearing by the cavern, those who had travelled with her were in awe of the world without snow. Cora wondered if they would get some snow as Essara had promised. In all, the Tarranah were about thirty, with one chief and two Ancients.

Artell took Cora's hand, and they led the way into the cavern. Teven had already started work on building hearths. As they arrived, he directed people to different tasks. Leaving him to it, Cora and Artell continued into the cavern of the Ancients.

In the place Cora had thought would be perfect for their sleeping mats, she spread out a white blanket.

'Where did that come from?'

'My mother gave it to me.'

Artell squatted down and ran a hand over it. 'I hope we can have another. That seems nicer than the furs.'

'Perhaps I can make some,' Cora said. 'If the snow brings the right animals.'

'I am sure Essara will provide,' Artell said, taking her in his arms.

Despite all the work to be done, they headed out into the main cavern to watch their people mark out hearths. Junah marked out a space around Larek, who pointed where he thought it should go. Cora smiled as she watched over them, her arm through Artell's.

She sighed with contentment. She was right where she was meant to be. She was who she was meant to be.

ACKNOWLEDGMENTS

Special thanks to the team at Deranged Doctor Designs (DDD) for facilitating absolutely brilliant cover design work and all the marketing extras. Thank you for your support and beautiful covers.

TWG members: Melissa, Matthew J Morrison, John Hargreaves, Sue Larsen, Nicholas Jansen and Chantelle Griffith for listening and support in all things writing related. Special thanks to Yasmin for taking the time to read and comment on my stories.

Allison E Wright for wonderful editing work. She smooths out my words and manages to keep my voice.

My parents, Francine and Ken Smith. Amazing, supportive people who I don't thank often enough. Thanks for keeping me grounded and being the best parents and grandparents ever.

As always, Temwa for being my biggest supporter.

ABOUT THE AUTHOR

Georgina Makalani survives life as a servant of the public by hiding in her office at lunch time with dragons, witches, a laptop and a little bit of magic.

She lives with her daughter and two crazy cats, in beautiful southern Tasmania with a writing desk that overlooks the water.

For more about Georgina and her books visit her website: www.theflowofink.com